W9-BWE-096

I'd Rather Be With You

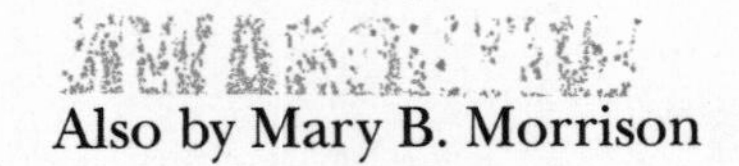

Also by Mary B. Morrison

If I Can't Have You Series

If I Can't Have You

I'd Rather Be With You

Soulmates Dissipate Series

Soulmates Dissipate

Never Again Once More

He's Just a Friend

Somebody's Gotta Be on Top

Nothing Has Ever Felt Like This

When Somebody Loves You Back

Darius Jones

The Honey Diaries

Sweeter Than Honey

Who's Loving You

Unconditionally Single

Darius Jones

She Ain't the One (coauthored with Carl Weber)

Maneater (anthology with Noire)

The Eternal Engagement

Justice Just Us Just Me

Who's Making Love

Mary B. Morrison, writing as HoneyB

Sexcapades

Single Husbands

Married on Mondays

The Rich Girls Club

Presented by Mary B. Morrison

Diverse Stories: From the Imaginations of Sixth Graders

(an anthology of fiction written by thirty-three 6th graders)

I'd Rather Be With You

MARY B. MORRISON

KENSINGTON PUBLISHING CORP.
http://www.kensingtonbooks.com

DAFINA BOOKS are published by

Kensington Publishing Corp.
119 West 40th Street
New York, NY 10018

Library of Congress Card Catalogue Number: 2013936490

ISBN-13: 978-0-7582-7302-4
ISBN-10: 0-7582-7302-9
First Kensington Hardcover Edition: August 2013

eISBN-13: 978-0-7582-7309-3
eISBN-10: 0-7582-7309-6
First Kensington Electronic Edition: August 2013

10 9 8 7 6 5 4 3

Printed in the United States of America

In loving memory of
Elester Noel, my mother,
Joseph Henry Morrison, my father.

Acknowledgments

The list of individuals to acknowledge continues to grow as I've met some of the most amazing people. First and foremost, I thank God for blessing me with the gift to write, the courage to pen what's in my heart, the continued growth in my career, and I thank Him for you.

My son, Jesse Bernard Byrd Jr., is absolutely amazing. I often say, "God gave me the right child." Not because Jesse has written his first novel, not because he owns his clothing business (*www.OiseauChateau.com*), or that he has a degree from UC Santa Barbara, but God gave me a child who is respectful and considerate of others. Jesse is passionate about his life, hardworking, and he's fearless in the pursuit of his dreams.

I'm happy my son has an awesome girlfriend, Emaan Abbass. The two of them are great together. They often plan surprise dates for one another. I've heard my son say, "If it's going to bother Emaan, I won't do it." Most selfish things that couples do, in the end, isn't worth it. An ounce of prevention can save a whole lot of heartaches. I'm glad my son and his girlfriend get it.

Jason Grisby, you are the man! I'm proud of you. Thanks for sending me an autographed pair of Adidas tennis shoes. I love them! I've put them on the shelf so I can tell people, "I know JG."

While doing research for this novel, I stayed thirty-one days at La Maison, an urban bed-and-breakfast in Midtown, Houston, Texas. The owners, Sharon Owens and Genora Boykins, definitely made me feel at home. The chef, Sergio, prepared breakfast for me every day, and Tommi tidied my room every day. Thanks, everyone!

Preparing for the theatrical release of the movie *Soulmates Dissipate,* I decided to give my website a new look. Richard C. Montgomery, Fransis Young, Kim Mason, worked with Kensington's experts, Lesleigh Irish-Underwood and Michele Santelices, to create the new *www.MaryMorrison.com.* I sincerely appreciate what each of you contributed.

Raynard Richardson and Donald Hogan, thanks for taking me to lunch while I was in Houston. Sharing memories of the days I worked with you guys at the U.S. Department of Housing and Urban Development was so much fun. Ray, that hookup with Harold V. Dutton, Jr. *might* work out. If not, I guess you'll have to find me another Houston hubby. Good luck! Don't introduce me to one of those "women are seen and not heard" kinda dudes. Not my type.

Clemetric Thomas-Frazier, my Facebook friend who's now like family, you're a true jewel. I'm waiting for you to finish your book, chick. Stop procrastinating!

"Someone old, someone new, someone borrowed, and no one blue" best describes the guys I connected with while in Houston. All shall remain nameless, but you know who you are. What can I say? I love a man in a suit and cowboy boots!

To the Honorable Vanessa Gilmore, your assistance is greatly appreciated. You truly are a diva judge. I wish you and your son, Sean, the best.

I spent countless "happy hours" at Pappadeaux, Pappasito's, and Carrabba's penning lots of pages. Thanks to all the bartenders who served me well. Andrew "Drew" Coleman at Eddie V's, I wish you the best, man, and look forward to your modeling and acting career being a huge success.

My friend since third grade, Vanessa Ibanitoru, I love you, sis. Brenda Jackson, Kenneth Todd, Bill Voget, Felicia Polk, Vyllorya A. Evens, Marilyn Edge, Carmen Polk, Malissa Tafere-Walton, Celeste Surrell, and Eve Lynne Robinson, your friendship is priceless.

Marissa Monteilh, aka Pynk, Lisa Renee Johnson, Kimberla Lawson Roby, Victor McGlothin, you're some of the most talented authors, and it's truly my honor to know you.

I often wonder what it would've been like to know my mother, Elester Noel, and my father, Joseph Henry Morrison. Well, those are opportunities that will never be on earth. I look forward to our union in the afterlife when that time comes.

My great aunt Ella Beatrice Turner and my great uncle Willie Frinkle reared me, and for that I am eternally grateful. Honestly, I'm not sure if I could do for others what these two did for me, but I'd like to believe that every day I would raise, educate, clothe, and feed four children who weren't my own. God bless those who do. A special thanks to my earthly mother, Barbara H. Cooper.

Wayne, Andrea, Derrick, and Regina Morrison, Margie Rickerson, and Debra Noel are my siblings. Thanks, guys, for always believing in me. More important, I pray you guys understand that I am eternally evolving. Artists are birthed from the womb, but I swear we come from the moon.

I genuinely appreciate all of my Facebook family, friends, and fans, my Twitter followers, and my McDonogh 35 Senior High alumni. I don't know many graduates that love their high school as much as we Roneagles do. I'm forever indebted to all of the teachers in my hometown of New Orleans at F. P. Ricard, McDonogh 36, Carter G. Woodson, and McDonogh 35. Many of you encouraged me to believe in myself, and that has made the difference in my life today.

Thanks to my editor and friend, Selena James at Kensington Publishing Corporation. You're the best. Appreciation to Steven Zacharius, Adam Zacharius, Laurie Parkin, Karen Auerbach, Adeola Saul, Lesleigh Irish-Underwood, and everyone else at Kensington for growing my literary career.

Well, what's an author without brilliant agents? I'm fortunate to have two of the best agents in the literary business, Andrew Stuart and Claudia Menza. You are appreciated. Kenneth Norwick, looking forward to it!

I thank everyone that is making the *Soulmates Dissipate* film series possible—Leslie Small, director/producer, Jeff Clanagan, CEO of Codeblack Entertainment and producer, Dawn C. Mallory, Jesse Byrd Jr., and all of you at Lionsgate. It's Hollywood, baby!

Wishing peace and prosperity in abundance for each of my readers. Dream with your eyes wide open.

Visit me online at *www.MaryMorrison.com,* sign up for my Honey-Buzz newsletter. Join my fan page on Facebook at Mary-Honey-B-Morrison, and follow me on Twitter, @marybmorrison.

I can't thank my fans enough, but it's Granville time, y'all! That dude is still crazy, as we say in N'awlins (bay-bay)!

This is novel #2 in the *If I Can't Have You* Series

PROLOGUE

Madison

If there were a hell on earth, my wedding day would've been there. A month ago, we were at one of Houston's five-star hotels near the intersection of Main and Ewing. The one man who wanted me more than my husband did show up at our wedding reception. The luxurious poolside was lined with guests dressed in the finest attire. Budding lights garnishing the walls and columns dazzled. The white lilies, roses, and gardenias surrounding us smelled heavenly. The blue water below the high arch where my bridal party stood sparkled like someone had tossed a handful of diamonds on top.

My brilliant smile vanished and the flowers couldn't keep a wilted spirit from consuming me. When I saw his face, I thought I'd die. He frightened me more than the gun he'd pointed at my head from across the room. Out of anger, not concern for my safety, my newly married husband pushed me away. My heels slipped off the arched stairway above the swimming pool and I fell into the water below.

Fear ordered my next steps. I swam along the bottom to the opposite end, climbed out of the pool, and escaped along with my guests. I couldn't blame my husband for being upset. I'd denied having sex with any man during our engagement.

Men lied all the time. For me, it was once.

The loser who showed up at the hotel during the toast wasn't a man I'd ordinarily open my legs for. If I could've changed one thing about that night, I wouldn't have recorded a video to prove to my girlfriend I'd won her stupid bet. I'd gone all the way with her ex.

We both knew the guy was mentally unstable. But neither of us thought he'd do the unimaginable. Intercourse with her ex turned violent, sending me to the emergency room. He stole the tape, downloaded it, and sent a link to my fiancé. When my fiancé came to my house, showed me the footage, and asked me to explain, I did what any respectable Southern girl would do. I said, "He's someone I dated before we met."

My man loved and believed me, until Granville Washington showed up at our reception and shot my husband three times.

CHAPTER 1

Madison

Have you ever loved someone so much you could kill him?

My signature was a heartbeat away from doing that. I'd signed the authorization to take my husband off life support. He was a good man. But there were times when being a good person wasn't enough. Some would say he did all the right things in our relationship, but he did them for the wrong woman. I'd disagree. Unlike most women, I knew my self-worth. The brilliant diamond wedding ring on my finger was there because I'd earned it.

"Mrs. DuBois," the doctor softly said. "I still have the paper in my hand. It's not too late to have a change of heart." He stood in front of me as though my time was up.

In a small private space, there was a desk, two chairs, a computer, the doctor, and me. The door with a large square windowpane was closed.

The room suddenly got colder as though someone had locked me in a morgue, alone, with the Grim Reaper. The chill penetrated me so deep I froze from the inside out. Reminded me of a trip I'd taken to New York City to celebrate New Year's Eve. I was in the midst of tens of thousands of people bundled in coats. Their faces were wrapped with scarves. My feet were stuffed in fur-lined boots. My hands were inside cashmere-coated gloves and I was in Times Square, freezing.

Tapered to my body, the sleeveless black dress I'd chosen to put on this morning was midthigh. The back of my legs stuck to the hard plastic chair. I hugged myself, then slid my hands up and down the chill bumps covering my arms. I wiggled my fingers; they were stiff. I pressed them together; then I rubbed them back and forth. I wanted to cry for my husband, for myself, but this was not the time to break down. There were too many what-ifs in my mind competing for attention; it felt like my head was going to explode. My unchanging heart was heavy and numb. I'd heard the doctor, but I didn't respond.

I sat staring at the beige tile beneath my four-inch black platform stilettos. What if my husband died before I made it to the hospital's exit? What if all of his football fans blamed me for his death? What if I hadn't had sex with that idiot, Granville? What if the baby growing inside me was the result of my infidelity? What if the tape Granville stole from my house of us having sex ended up online for millions to see? What if I continued to delay having surgery for my breast cancer? What if something went wrong with my operation and I ended up on life support? Would I want someone to take me off?

Gazing into the doctor's eyes, I told him, "My decision is final."

He remained quiet for several minutes, then said, "Okay. I'm pretty sure you don't want to be in the room when he's disconnected from the machine, but I have to—"

"Ask?" I paused, then continued, "No, you don't."

Already dressed for the possibility of becoming a grieving widow, I stood, with one foot in front of him, and opened my mouth. I wanted to ask how long did he think it would be before I received the call saying my husband was dead.

Don't do that, Madison. The doctor will think you're insensitive.

The truth was, I did care for Roosevelt. Hopefully, his transition would happen within twenty-four hours. Just in case he lingered more than a day, I'd already approved comfort care for him. The staff could insert an IV and administer morphine as often as needed to eliminate the pain I had caused.

In the end I'd done what was best for my husband. Now it was time to start focusing on my health. My father had made arrangements for my mother and me to leave the country. At his request I'd given my dad full power of attorney to handle my business. Papa didn't want me being constantly threatened by strangers, and Mama didn't want me to be in a foreign place all by myself.

How hundreds of thousands of my husband's fans could hate me, when they didn't know me, meant Papa had done the right thing. I wished people would tend to their own situations and leave me the hell alone.

Mama and I would stay gone for almost a year, until I had my baby and recovered from surgery. Southerners were accustomed to sending pregnant teens away, letting them give birth, putting the baby up for adoption, then allowing them to return home as if nothing had happened.

My circumstances were different. I was a grown woman. Regardless who the father was, I was bringing my child back to America. By the time we returned, Papa believed things would've calmed down and someone else would be media worthy of inexplicable hatred.

A woman's love for a dying man could make him want to live. Out of respect I should have wanted to say my last good-byes but I didn't want to encourage Roosevelt to live longer. Tears burned my eyes. Was my husband scared? Was he tired of holding on and ready to let go? Without me by his side, my husband would soon exhale for the last time.

"Mrs. DuBois. Roosevelt is an icon in our community. Look, he's the youngest GM in football. He's on the league's ethics committee. He's brought our team back. He could possibly take us to the championship. More than just you love him. Are you absolutely sure you want to do this?" the doctor asked. His eyes watered with sadness. "It's not too late to rip this up," he said, waving the paper in my direction.

The doctor probably sensed I was torn, but it was my decision to make my life—make that *our* lives—easier. My husband wasn't strong enough to survive on his own, and I didn't want to spend our future taking care of him. I mean, what if I had to push him around in a wheelchair? Or hire someone to bathe and feed him? I was a beautiful, vibrant, sexy, thirty-five-years-young woman ready to share the spotlight of being an executive vice president/general manager's wife. I didn't sign a license to be his caretaker.

Oh, well. I'm convinced. A blissful marriage is never going to happen. At least not with Roosevelt "Chicago" DuBois. His professional administrative football career is over.

Letting Roosevelt go was easier than telling my husband the three-month-old baby inside me might not be his. There was a chance I could give birth to a child who would remind me every day that I'd cheated. Why? Because of the bet I'd made with my girlfriend.

Four weeks ago on my wedding day, I was the envy of all women—single and married—in Houston, including my so-called best friend, Loretta. Should've left her ass alone years ago. She was a real jealous bitch. If she wasn't trying so hard to impress my husband, she might have one of her own.

Sadly I said, "Please leave."

Soon as the doctor left the room, I cried out loud, "Dear God, what's the lesson here? I know I'm not perfect, but what did I do to deserve—" I stopped. I threw my hands up, then added, "Don't answer that." I touched my stomach. My only prayer was "Let Roosevelt be the father."

That way, I'd still have a piece of him to love. Our child needed a father, but not one who might be brain damaged. Roosevelt wasn't the first man who proposed to me. He was the ninth. But he was the first one who loved me enough for me to marry him. When he died, I would become a lonely woman, but not for long. I'd scatter his ashes over the Gulf of Mexico, then celebrate the great memories we shared. We didn't have a prenuptial, so legally I'd inherit his millions. Eventually another man would fall in love with me and help me raise my child.

Many would call me a bitch. Roosevelt's mother, Helen DuBois, would be first in line. His only brother, Chaz, would stand beside her.

What they didn't know was, I was not responsible for Roosevelt getting shot. My so-called Christian girlfriend was. She was the one who'd insisted that I not hire security, and she'd shown up at my wedding reception with a gun in her purse. That's what I'd heard from our friend Tisha.

In hindsight I realized Loretta could have pulled the trigger herself. •

CHAPTER 2

Granville

"Man, I keep telling y'all I was framed."

I wasn't completely innocent. They knew that. I did too. It wasn't 100 percent my fault, but the way it went down made me look like the bad guy. Now the government got my mama thinking I'm a freeloader.

The Feds putting a roof over my head and food in my stomach at the downtown detention center was okay for a lil while, since I'd paid into the system, after all. But Mama said since space was limited, they could give my bed to someone who deserved it.

No one could make Moms believe that her darling, adorable, precious son shot a man. No, siree. Mama was so sure I didn't do it, she'd convinced me.

During her visit last week, Mama told the guard, "I've fed my two boys all their lives till they was old enough to buy me tons of seafood. I like seafood. You like seafood? I'ma bring you some next time I come. Anyway, my sons ain't never needed no welfare of any kind, and they ain't never been in trouble with the law. You and nobody else gon' make me a liar. I know my boy didn't shoot nobody 'cause I raised him better than that."

Mama was right, but complaining to the guard wasn't going to free me. I was ready to have my day in court, get out of here, and go back to a construction job so I could resume paying taxes, like the law-abiding citizen that I was.

"Dude, you still hanging on to that not guilty plea. You been in here for four weeks," No Chainz said. "Be lucky they haven't found the gun, or your ass would be in the Texas state pen, sleeping with both eyes open just to keep your asshole shut."

Before the cops arrived, all the guests were running around like chickens with their heads cut off, so I kicked my gun into the swimming pool, hoping the chlorine would wash away my fingerprints. The fact that no one had found the gun, I guess that was luck.

They housed all kinds of criminals in this joint. Murderers. Thieves. Drunk drivers. The Latinos doing time were usually in for doing something illegal to feed their family. The brahs, they were different. Most were back for violating probation. *Duh!* Didn't they watch *Parole Diaries*? To me, coming back for doing some shit you know you're not supposed to do didn't make any sense.

Regardless of how I got a break and ended up at this location, I was happy to be downtown. This way, my brother didn't have to travel all the way to state (wherever that was). Heard it was hours away. Being in Houston, Beaux could easily see me once a week.

Precious, the broad I met before getting locked up, came to see me every week too. I thought about taking her off my visitors' list, but she'd promised to slip me a cell phone on her next visit. I needed that phone so I could call Madison and apologize for losing my temper and embarrassing her.

I sat at the table, adjusting my dick. "You see how big my shit is," I said; then I spoke louder. "If any man tries to rape me, he gon' regret it 'cause after I whup his ass, he's gonna get all of this dick down his throat, then up his butt."

Our one openly gay guy stood, snapped his fingers, then said, "Granville, don't tease me. You promise?"

Jacking off had become my thing. Kissing or having sex with a man wasn't. If I got life, I might have to change my mind on some things. I'd only been in for a month.

No Chainz, my cellmate at the federal detention center, said, "Damn, dude. I keep telling you that thing ain't natural. My females in Brazil would love your ass."

He called himself "No Chainz" after his favorite rapper, 2 Chainz. No Chainz believed no matter how long a man was behind bars, his mind was always free. He was up for parole in six months and would have to register as a sex offender.

My Madison had the same number of months before our baby was due. If Madison hadn't had my baby by the time my boy was out, and if I was still locked up, No Chainz said he'd stand in for me in the delivery room. Wasn't sure I wanted his freaky behind seeing what was between my woman's legs. A man doing time wanted to stick his dick deep in a pussy soon as he saw one. Didn't matter who she was. If shit went right, I'd be out before him.

When I first got to FDC, I remembered No Chainz telling me, "Why wait for some fucked-up dream to creep into your head, G, when you can fantasize at any time?" That boy had the wildest stories of traveling the world and sexing the most beautiful women in Rio, especially the girls from Ipanema. His shit about sexy, big-breasted women, with small waists and ridiculous humongous booties, flossing real shoestring bikinis, was so vivid it would make my dick hard as a rock. Sometimes it felt like I had sand in my mouth from going down on them females while they was laying with their legs open on the beach.

No Chainz had served two and a half of his three years for rape. Said the girl was sixteen; he'd just turned eighteen. She's white. He's black. She told her old man and the jury that they were dating and their sex was consensual. That girl had begged her father not to make her press charges and pleaded with the jury not to find No Chainz guilty. But her old man was one of those rifle-toting rednecks who was outraged that his little Lucy had been spoiled by one of us. Her daddy had claimed either the system was going to give him justice or he was going to shoot No Chainz dead. Sometimes prisons saved lives.

I boldly said, "Correction. I've been in here three weeks and five days."

"Shy forty-eight hours? Round up, nigga."

My dad, rest his soul, had told me and my brother, "Y'all too big and too black to be careless." If we wanted to go with a white woman, our daddy told us, "Go to the West."

People in California didn't so much mind that interracial dating thing. Same-sex thing. I heard they sat in trees to keep 'em from being chopped down. In the South, they might not lynch cha nowadays, but they sure won't hesitate to lock you up. I managed to stay a free man for forty-five years. Guess it was just my turn.

"Okay, so explain your position again, Granville, because every day your alibi changes." No Chainz turned sideways on his stool and faced me.

A new guy I hadn't seen before sat between us at our lunch table. He leaned over his tray and started eating slop. We got quiet. He didn't seem like he belonged in prison, so I didn't bother raising him up and making him move. That, and I didn't have anything to prove to any of these guys.

My wrestling skills from back in my high-school days came in handy when I had to pin a fool to the floor for challenging me. I only hammered the ones who refused to surrender. Act too big of a fool and off you go to unit seven, on the seventh floor, to be housed with the worst criminals in here. That was where solitary was too. I wasn't trying to be in a small room twenty-three hours a day by myself. I liked to talk too much.

"What you in for?" I asked the new guy.

He swallowed his soupy mashed potatoes. Kept staring at his tray. "Life, maybe. Nothing, maybe. Depends on how the jury view my situation."

The new guy spoke slowly, like Ving Rhames did in the movie *Baby Boy*. Some said I favored the way that dude looked. Wish I had his fame. That way, Madison would be chasing me.

This new guy had a smooth New Yorkish swag that I liked, but he was white. I frowned as I listened.

"Depends on whether or not I represent myself."

Whoa. Represent himself? That's it! Why hadn't I consider that?

"Dude, what makes you think you can present your own case? The jury won't take you serious. Isn't that like admitting you're guilty?" I asked, more curious than anything.

Some guys in my unit had done that, but they'd all lost. But we couldn't all lose. Somebody had to be smart enough to beat the law.

"It's my right. Yours too. That, and I'm an attorney."

Slapping the table, I accidentally made his potatoes shoot in the air, then plop on his plate. I laughed. He didn't.

No Chainz said, "Stop playing with dude's food."

"Well, obviously he's not a good one. Or he wouldn't be breaking bread with us," I said, clearing my scratchy throat.

Raising his brows, he rubbed his hand over his blond hair, staring at me with his dark brown eyes, which sank far behind his forehead. He said, "Well, I can tell you're not a lawyer. You're the type that's accustomed to using your hands and not your head. A real Mandingo, dick-slinging African American who thinks his johnson defines him, huh, Shrek?"

No Chainz laughed. I didn't.

No, that Herman Munster-looking dude didn't call me "Shrek."

"You don't have to respond. I can tell you're not in here because you're a criminal. You're in here because you're ignorant."

My mouth curved down. Above, my lip started sweating. I slid the back of my hand over my skinny mustache, then dried it on my pants. I should've wiped it on him. I didn't know whether to be flattered, pissed off, or beat his ass.

He was about five feet ten inches, and weighed around the same as No Chainz, 190, definitely under two hundred. Even behind bars a white man had more rights than me. I'd show him that I was smart. I focused on the part where he said he might represent himself. It was kind of hard, damn near impossible for him to insult me. My mom loved and sang my praises all the time. Women, they cursed me out almost every day.

Mama had said, "Honey, that's a woman's way of saying she cares about you. Worry when she doesn't curse you out."

I was overdue for a brawl. New dude was a fist away from getting beat like a bitch.

What was messed up was Madison had refused to be put on my list to accept my calls. She hadn't written or come to see me since I'd been in here, but Precious hadn't missed a visit. I didn't care about Precious, but her coming to see me made me feel good. All inmates, no matter what the crime, wanted a human connection to the outside world.

My getting a phone soon made me happy. I wouldn't need Madison's permission. But if Precious got me caught, I'd be transported to state and she'd be arrested. That was a chance I'd take. I had to find out where Madison was.

"I didn't mean no disrespect. But can you teach me how to represent myself?"

"What you in for?" he asked, shoving another forkful of mashed potatoes into his mouth. They stuck together a little better, since they were cold. He hadn't touched his green beans or chicken.

"They say I shot a man, but truth is I aimed at air and water. Wouldn't have done that if I hadn't been provoked."

No Chainz interrupted me. "Man, stop trying to use big words to impress dude and get on with the real details. Aimed at? Air and water? That shit's new."

I stared at No Chainz, narrowed my eyes, and then explained. "I had a good construction job, making almost a hundred thou a year."

"Here we go," No Chainz said, leaning back.

I should've reached around dude and pushed my cellmate to the floor.

So what if I exaggerated my salary a little this time? Ninety thou was close. I had to account for inflation. I kept talking like I didn't hear my friend. "I met this fake beauty queen named Loretta Lovelace. She stole my heart, then broke it. At first, I tried everything to keep her.

"Loretta had that silky, gingersnap-colored skin that made me want to dip her in milk, then devour her. And she always wore that raspberry gloss I loved to lick off. She was tall, with long legs, especially when she wore heels. Those nice curves were in all the right places." I outlined the shape of an hourglass to give them an idea of what was in my head. "I missed the way she sucked my big, thick dick."

"We don't give a damn, man, about what your dick felt like, G. Tell the part how that shit happened in three weeks."

"Shut up, No Chainz. This my story. Everything didn't happen in no three weeks. I dated her for three weeks. Then one day on my way to take her to Port Arthur to meet—"

The new guy laughed so hard that potatoes flew from his mouth and splattered onto the guy's tray across the table. The guy was so interested in my story, he didn't look down at his meal. He kept eating while staring at me.

"That explains it. Say no more. Granville, dude, everybody knows all you guys from PA are fucked up in the head from inhaling all of those refinery fumes and making babies with your first cousins. Man,

I already know. You have no boundaries." The new guy insisted, "Whatever it is your ass is guilty of, plead the Fifth."

"How I'ma do that and represent myself?"

The new guy shook his head.

"What's your name?" I asked him.

"In here. It doesn't matter. Call me what you'd like."

"You got kids?"

He nodded.

I wanted to know more. "Where you from?"

"Here" was all he said.

No Chainz said, "You the real deal. We gon' call you *G*-double-*A* 'cause you *got all the answers.* Get it? This is a long story, dude. Now let my man finish so we can get a workout in before four o'clock count."

Count was like roll call in grade school. Grown folks answering, "Here," like we were children. We had to return from our common areas, go to our cells, and wait for a head count to make sure no one had escaped. They interrupted us to do that shit five times a day, like their asses couldn't keep track.

"Thanks, bro. Like I was saying. On my way to take Loretta to PA to meet Moms, she confessed that her girlfriend liked me. Turned out she was talking about my boss. You think Loretta is fine. Man, oh, man," I said, then stuffed my knuckles into my mouth and barked like a dog. "Madison makes Loretta's gingersnap skin look like liver cheese."

Madison had that soft, light, creamy, melt-in-my-mouth, praline-tasting skin. Her hair was cut short, tapered next to her scalp, and colored like a platinum blonde's. Big, tight titties, with an itty-bitty waist, and a juicy booty I got to hold on to the first time we had sex. Actually, it was the only time, but I was in love; and I'd bet none of those Brazilian booties No Chainz dreamt about were better than hers. Madison was all woman, and she was all mine.

"Yep, you country, all right," the new guy said, interrupting my thoughts.

No Chainz said, "G-double-A, we ain't got all day. Don't let him call you 'country,' Granville. Wipe under your nose and tell this dude something."

Yeah! No Chainz was right. I swiped my upper lip, dried the back of my hand on my pants. "Bet you can't beat my six-six, two-eighty-five country ass," I said, pushing back to the edge of the immovable steel stool.

Sweat rolled from my bald head, behind my ears, and down into the folds along the back of my neck. G-double-A reminded me of how I used to pound on my brother Beaux with my Wreck-It Ralph gigantic fists. Made me want to do the same thing to his ass right now.

G-double-A nodded.

"I haven't lost a fight since I've been in this joint." That was the truth, because I'd come close but hadn't had a real shanking kind of one. G-double-A didn't know that. I lied, "A few tried to run up on and in me. I whupped all of their asses. Tell 'im, No Chainz."

No Chainz squinted, then hunched his shoulders.

"I believe you, man. I already told you anyone can see your biggest muscle is not your brain. You keep them off my ass and I'll help you prepare your case," G-double-A said.

My eyes widened. "No shit?"

I paused. Why was he so quick to offer? He wasn't one of those free spirited dudes from California, and nothing in prison was free.

"Man, finish the damn story," No Chainz said. "So I can add to the journal I'm keeping on your lying ass."

"So now you a journalist?"

G-double-A asked, "Mind if I see it?"

"Naw, I don't mind if you see it. If you shut the hell up and listen *and* help me represent myself too." No Chainz nodded upward at dude.

Inmates were always trying to take advantage of another man's shit. No matter the relationship, a man behind bars had to wash his own ass and watch his own back.

"Where was I?"

No Chainz said, "Liver cheese."

"Yeah, that's right. Madison is the kind of woman who makes a man want to give her everything he's got. She invited me to her house. Cooked for me. Let me eat her creamy, sweet pussy. Yum. Yum." I snapped my teeth. "Then she got on top and rode me better than Loretta."

I thought about when Madison came down on my big dick and it went all the way straight up her ass. I thought she was screaming for pleasure; then I saw the blood. I didn't want to share that part. It was an accident. I didn't mean to rip the insides of her ass so bad she had to go to the emergency room. But had I been charged with rape, my asshole might be wide open. I shouldn't have sent the link of the video to her at-that-time fiancé, but I did it, hoping he'd call off the wedding. He couldn't have watched it, because what man would marry another man's woman?

Continuing, I said, "Then when I brought flowers to her office the next day, she told me she was engaged and showed me this big-ass diamond. I was so pissed at the dude she was marrying that I showed up at their reception and fired five times. Like I said, two in the air. Three in the water. Now he's in the hospital, on a breathing machine, claiming I was the one who shot him. When the cops arrived, the few bystanders left pointed at me. Yeah, arrest the big black guy. If this dude dies, I could get life."

G-double-A stood, stared down at me, then said, "Please tell me you're not telling me you're the fool who shot Chicago. Please, nigga, please."

I needed his help. He didn't need mine.

I paused, then told him, "I plead the Fifth."

CHAPTER 3

Loretta

The shooting was my fault, but I'd never admit I was guilty. Why should I?

True. I knew I shouldn't have dated Granville, but he constantly called me when no other man was asking me out. He ended up being someone to do something with, as opposed to sitting home alone.

Yes. I was wrong to have challenged Madison to that stupid bet. I dared her to go all the way with Granville. If I won—and I thought I would, but I didn't—Madison had to call off her engagement to Chicago. If she'd won . . . initially, well, she didn't say what I had to give her, but now she wanted the title to my house!

All the men she'd fucked and screwed over treated her like a queen. If she was honest with herself, she'd know her bad luck was karma. I wanted to but couldn't walk away from the damages I'd caused, but I wasn't sure what to do with the feelings I'd developed for Chicago. The dare started out with my not wanting Madison to ruin another great guy and ended with my falling in love with her man. I'd become a victim of my own circumstances. Naturally, I was the only one who saw myself as the culprit. How do you end it with someone when you never want it to end?

Tap. Tap. Tap.

Chicago's eyes were closed. We were the only ones in his hospital room, but his family would be back soon. I liked keeping the door closed to give us privacy when we were alone. Wish I could've locked it, but at least the person outside knocked first.

I called out, "Just a minute," then kissed his forehead.

It might be the doctor or the nurse. Chicago's brother, Chaz, would be upset if he saw me putting my lips on Chicago in a romantic way. I'd heard the relationship term "it's complicated." Never thought it would apply to me. A few months ago I wasn't dating and would've said, "When people are honest and considerate, staying together is easy."

Wiping my lip gloss off Chicago, I exhaled, then opened the door.

"Loretta, you've got to stop obsessing over Chicago," Tisha said. Her arms were folded under her breasts. "You've been up here every day for four weeks. I came to take you home. Get your purse and let's go."

She pulled me into the hallway. I closed the door to Chicago's room.

Tisha was the darkest of my friends and the most beautiful. Her black Afro was spiked at the edges, letting people know she was strong. Every time she smiled, her sparkling white teeth showed she was friendly. Everything about Tisha was authentic. She was my best friend. Madison's too. Since we were five years old, Madison, Tisha, and I didn't always agree, but once upon a time we valued what was most important to one another.

Standing outside of Chicago's room, I was glad Tisha had come, but I wasn't going anywhere. I gave her a hug, but this time she could've kept her opinion to herself and been there for me. I hadn't told her how Madison and I felt she needed to divorce Darryl.

He got back with Tisha. Kicked her front door until she let him in. Proposed so he wouldn't have to move out. All he'd done since my girlfriend married him was spend her money and stay out all night, every night. Darryl wasn't much of a stepfather to the three- and four-year-old boys Tisha had with her rich ex-husband. Now deadbeat Darryl was begging my girl to have a child for him, when he'd barely been her husband for nine months. Probably so he could boast about having his first kid. Or was Darryl aiming for income security? If Tisha had his baby and then decided to leave, she'd have to pay him and the baby child support.

Tisha was strong; but when it came to dealing with a man, she was weak. I was too. Madison was the only woman I'd never seen let a man get or break her down.

"You don't choose love, Tisha. Love chooses you." It took me a while to figure this out. How else could I explain my devotion to Chicago?

"How many times have you fallen for someone, like your millionaire ex-husband, and no matter how hard you tried to hold your marriage together, you couldn't. Who were we to tell you what was in your heart? It failed because God didn't put the two of you together. You married Darryl because . . . what?" I planted seeds, hoping to draw Tisha's attention away from my situation.

"Don't bring God into this. This is not the same thing, Loretta, and you know it. Chicago," she said, pointing at the door, "has his family to look after him. And no matter how you feel, Chicago is Madison's husband, not yours."

"Well, God sent him *for* me. He should've been mine." There. I'd finally said it.

Slap! Tisha's hand landed on my cheek.

"God did no such thing. I will not stand by and let you live this lie, Loretta," she scolded. "You wait until you're thirty-five to turn into the worst kind of whore? You're fucking Chicago's brother *and* you're standing here, claiming Chicago should've married you. You're asking for trouble, and you're so busy over here you're about to lose custody of your daughter. Raynard is seriously trying to take Raynell from you. Is that what you want?"

Covering the sting, I stared at her. Was her hitting me supposed to change my feelings for Chicago? The only reason I didn't slap her back was I couldn't risk getting thrown out of the hospital if we had a fight. A lot had happened to me during Madison's engagement to Chicago. I had thoughts that contradicted my holy character.

Some of it I understood. When Chicago introduced me to Chaz, my daughter's father didn't want me to have a man. As long as I was alone, Raynard was happy with visitation. What was his real motivation for coming to Madison's wedding, hiding behind the bar during the shoot-out at Madison's reception, and filing for custody when he knew I was a fit parent? Was his marriage to Gloria about to end and he wanted me back? Or did he regret marrying Gloria and now realized he should've done the right thing and married me? I shouldn't assume his threat for custody was his idea. Women influenced men to do irrational things. Maybe Gloria wanted my daughter in order to hold on to her husband.

"I'll get your purse," Tisha said, moving closer to the door.

I stood in front of her.

A lot of my situations were incomprehensible. It started when the police officer advised me to get a protective order against Granville. I did. That should've been a reason not to challenge Madison to tame Granville. Her agreeing to rope him like a bull wasn't enough. I had to throw sex in the bet, daring her to sleep with him. I wanted to see at least one man knock "little Miss Perfect" to her knees. Granville's obsession to make me exclusively his woman the moment I allowed him to penetrate me drove me crazy. The only way I could get him to stop harassing me was to pass the torch to her. I imagined Madison falling at my feet, burying her face in her hands, and declaring me the winner.

Exhaling in her face, I was getting tired of the standoff with Tisha.

Why couldn't I have won the bet? Madison would've had to give Chicago back that brilliant solitaire diamond, which was still on her finger. In a matter of months, I would've convinced him to give to me the biggest engagement ring I'd ever seen.

There was nothing to say to Tisha. I turned away, entered Chicago's room, and closed the door in her face. He was lying on his back, with his eyes open, looking at the ceiling.

"Who was that?" he asked.

"No one that mattered." Glad we were alone, I reassured Chicago. "You're going to have a full recovery. Try to breathe a little deeper. You may have to do this on your own today. Madison may have abandoned you, but I'm not leaving your bedside until we walk out of here together."

A tear streamed down his face. Not caring if the tear was for Madison or me, I kissed it dry.

"Don't stop. You can do this. Take another deep breath, baby."

I watched him struggle each time he filled his lungs to capacity. The third time he stopped midway, then shook his head. "Giving up is not an option. You hear me?" If I could get him up to a solid breath every five seconds, he had a chance to live another day, another week, years.

I held his hand. "Breathe with me," I told him. "When I inhale, you inhale."

Our eyes met. I wanted to exhale forever. Instead, I kissed him softly on his lips, then wiped away the shine from my gloss.

Slowly he shook his head. Another tear fell. Was he signaling for me not to do that? Maybe he couldn't believe I was there for him. It didn't matter.

His lips moved. Nothing came out as I read, "Thank you." The tip of his tongue touched behind his teeth. He tried to move it down, but he couldn't. Now I was the one shaking my head.

"Stay focused. Breathe with me," I said, then whispered, "I got you."

There were lots of signs that Chicago was my soul mate. We were honest, loving, God-worshiping people. Madison didn't pray and hardly went to church, unless there was a purpose like the day she'd gotten married. Unlike Madison, we were considerate of others. Madison talked down to Tisha, she was always degrading me, and she didn't deserve Chicago.

So why did God bless her more?

Madison snagged the most desirable bachelors. She always got the engagement ring, the expensive gifts, the all-expense-paid trips abroad, and she had her way with men in general. If Madison dropped something, men—and sometimes women—raced to pick it up. Whenever we went out, her hand seldom touched a door.

I'd seen children control their parents. Was manipulation something Madison learned on her own? Was she taught by her conniving father? Or was she born that way? My parents were good people. They'd raised me to study hard, get excellent grades, and get a good job. I'd done all of that. When it came to men and marriage, I had to figure out on my own what to do.

I covered Chicago's hand with mine, stood closer to his side. His breathing had slightly improved. I smiled at him.

After Madison and Chicago announced their engagement and pregnancy on television, people catered to Madison as though she were the "first lady of Houston." Restaurants wouldn't let her pay.

Football fans of all ages begged for her autograph as if she was a celebrity. Undoubtedly, she looked the part. Maybe I needed a professional makeover to get Chicago's attention.

Thank God, all of that attention toward Madison had changed. I didn't want the people who loved her to hate her. But now they did. And even though that was my fault too, the one thing I knew for sure was Madison was a survivor. If she walked into this room right now, Chicago would choose her.

My cell phone lit up. Raynard had texted me. I didn't respond. I knew him well. His reason for texting was to acquire evidence to show the judge that I was irresponsible and he was the more suitable parent. He wasn't. My not responding to his text meant I didn't have to choose between Raynell and Chicago.

My daughter was in a safe place while I was caring for my friend. Couples should be friends first.

The door to Chicago's room opened. Quickly I stepped back, then turned around. It was the doctor.

"Please tell me she did the right thing," I said.

"If you can step into the hallway, Ms. Lovelace, I'd like to speak to everyone outside," the doctor said.

Before leaving his side, I told Chicago, "Keep breathing. I'll be right back."

Chicago's brother, Chaz, who was also my boyfriend, their mother, Helen, their father, Martin, and I stood together. Chicago's grandfather Wally hadn't come to the hospital. The last time I'd seen him, he'd said, "Children are supposed to outlive their parents and definitely grandparents. I can't handle seeing my grandson like this. Thanks, Loretta, for taking good care of Chicago."

If Madison had signed those papers, I knew for sure that she wanted Chicago to die. Regardless of her decision, I'd try to convince Chicago's grandfather to see if he could reverse the $10 million he'd given Chicago right before the wedding. If Chicago took his last breath today, Madison would go straight to the bank and transfer everything into her name. I had to find a way to stop her from getting his money.

Everyone was silent. We stood in the hallway. I reached for Chaz's hand; then I interlocked my fingers with Helen's.

I prayed, "Lord, Father God, you have the power to sustain life. We pray that Madison has made the right decision, Father, to leave Chicago on life support. If she did not make that decision, Father God, we ask that you become his life support. This man does not deserve to die."

Silently I continued, *I do.*

The doctor said, "Mrs. DuBois signed the authorization. It's firm. Would any of you like to be in the room with Roosevelt DuBois when we disconnect the respirator?"

Helen fell into her husband's arms. Chaz hugged his mother and father. No one consoled me. After all the time I'd spent by Chicago's side, and the prayers I'd just sent up to heaven, I stood alone. Chaz was my man. Although he hadn't said it, I understood that my being Madison's friend caused him to distrust me too. We, as a family, would get through this together.

"I'd like to be in the room," I said. "Because I know, Chicago is not going to die."

Jesus, please let me be right.

I entered the room, stood beside Chicago, and started rubbing his hand. Chaz stood in front of me with his back to me. Refusing to let go, I held Chicago's hand tighter. Helen and Martin were united on the opposite side of the bed. Chicago's father touched his forehead.

Seconds before the doctor pulled the plug, I stepped beside Chaz, then prayed, "Father, we ask for your favor and mercy. Chicago, keep breathing. You have family that love and need you."

The disconnect felt like a bolt of electricity darting from my feet up to my head.

Tears poured from all of our eyes, but no one cried more than Chaz. He faced me, then leaned his head on my shoulder and wept like a starving baby with a dirty diaper. I squeezed Chicago's fingers. If Chaz knew the truth, he'd blame this shit on me. Chicago was his only brother. Chicago was thirty-two. Chaz, thirty-one. I'd never seen a grown man cry so hard.

God, what have I done? I knew unless I confessed with my mouth and believed in my heart, the sins that I'd committed would never be forgiven.

At this moment I felt like I was going straight to hell.

CHAPTER 4

Tisha

Once a Christian, always a Christian, my ass.

I had nothing against the Lord or the people who worshiped Him, but some folks went too damn far with their phoniness. Being a saint wasn't in one's DNA, like being black or white. Young or old. Tall or short. Loretta talked the talk. The only reason she was a child of God was by default. News flash, Loretta. *We all are!*

Friend or not, she was one of those churchgoers who had started to annoy me by using God's name in vain. They felt as long as they worshiped the Lord and prayed for forgiveness, they could justify burning down the tabernacle with every living soul in it. Why was she adamant about taking Chicago from Madison? God loved Madison too.

As far as Darryl was concerned, I couldn't give my husband away. God knows I'd tried. I'd said, "Lord, wherever he lay, let him stay." But Darryl kept showing up at my front door at all crazy hours of the night, like he was the most eligible bachelor in Houston and I was his live-in maid.

The house of the Lord wasn't a place that I'd frequented. Treating people nice, working to hold my friendships together, struggling to take care of two point five kids, I did that every day. Money was a blessing and I gave thanks for every dime. Having a husband, but still being a single parent, wasn't why I'd signed the marriage certificate.

My life revolved around my kids and the two best friends I never wanted to lose—but constantly had to fight to keep.

A cloak of sorrow weighed heavily on my shoulders.

There were layers that I wished I could peel off and toss away, like a stripper taking off a thong. There were whole sections that I hoped I could burn at both ends. This way, I would never have to think about those things again. Like, I wished I'd done away with my fallopian tubes after birthing my second son—I knew I didn't want more kids—but there was something so final about having surgery. I was scared I wouldn't feel like a woman. Or what if I met a man, walked down the aisle, and wanted to give him the gift of life? The third time might be my charm.

Then there was Darryl. The man I wanted to—but couldn't—forget.

He didn't make my life miserable. I did, and I was going to change it. Darryl was no longer my priority. My boys were most important. Being there for Loretta and Madison was next. I didn't give a damn about Darryl anymore. Wish I'd realized he felt that way about me before I said, "I do."

Approaching an empty waiting room at the hospital, I opened the door. I sat quietly for a moment with my thoughts.

My mother warned me not to commit so soon. She suggested I wait until Darryl got a steady job. She'd told me, "A woman should never keep a man who can't earn his own keep."

Before I reunited with Darryl, I was happy. My boys didn't want for anything. I had my girlfriends to hang out with on the weekends. Life was enjoyable. Then along came Darryl.

I was hanging out at Carrabba's on Kirby one day. I was sitting at the bar with my friend drinking peach Carrabbellinis, snacking on fried calamari and shrimp, when I heard his voice. I stopped breathing for a moment. Stared at Loretta.

"What, girl?" she'd asked.

"Please tell me that's not him," I said, knowing it was. My heart instantly ached. I hadn't seen him in ten years. I'd wondered what he looked like. Was he with someone? Why did I care? It wasn't like our relationship had ended on good terms.

The last time we had a conversation, I'd graduated from college and was engaged to my now ex-husband. Darryl was twenty-four and single back then. Fast-forward ten years. I'd had two kids and was divorced. He'd gotten finer while away on a decade-long vacation for home invasion.

In Texas, a criminal could get more time taking a person's property than for attempted murder. Darryl's charges should've kept me away. A man willing to steal what someone else had worked for, instead of getting a job, was and always would be a thief. I married a thief. Only now, he didn't have to steal, because my dumb ass gave him everything he wanted. I mistakenly thought if I kept him happy, he'd do the same for me.

Neither Madison nor Loretta knew for sure that Darryl had done time. Madison suspected. She believed that men one step away from having a Dwight Howard or Superman physique, with no verifiable income, was an ex-convict. How did I end up shackled to the same man who had cheated on me the last time we were together? Was I that desperate to have a man? Or did I believe I could save him from himself?

Tired of sitting alone in the waiting room, talking with myself, I called my mother.

"Hey, honey. How's Chicago?"

"I haven't seen him yet." I didn't want to tell my mom about Loretta acting like Chicago was her husband, when I needed to tend to my own affair.

"Well, tell him I'm praying for him," she said.

"I will." I hesitated.

"What is it, Tisha?"

"I'm going to ask Darryl for a divorce."

I knew my mother would support me. One, because she never liked the way Darryl treated me. My mom never disliked people. She'd say, "Everybody can change. It's a person's ways you have to judge, Tisha." Two, she always gave me her unconditional love. I think God made all moms to save the world one child at a time.

"Good. Don't back out this time. Darryl is a man who pisses, but never put the toilet seat down. He never puts it down, because he doesn't like closure. Next time he's taking a piss, you put the seat down in the middle of his stream. He'll ask, 'What you do that for?'

Men are like dogs. They want things to stay the way they are, as long as you're cleaning up all their shit. Tell him he's pissed on you enough, and that's his last piss in your house. Mean it. Don't ask him to get out. Don't wait for him to decide when he's ready to leave. Put his trifling ass the fuck out, Tisha. When you don't like the way you're living, you need to change who you're loving."

Mom was right. She could've married my father, but she said he wasn't ready for a wife. She'd been proposed to several times. Said none of those guys were ready to settle down. "When the ring is more important than the man, say 'no' to both," she told me. Finally, when the right man asked for her hand, my mom was fifty; they've been happily married for ten years.

"Let me call you back, Mom." I ended the call and stared at the wall as if waiting for the wallpaper to speak to me.

Darryl had other girlfriends in high school and women on the side now. Like most Texas men, my husband had Southern hospitality. He spent my money on the finest clothes. Used cash to pay for his sexcapades so I couldn't verify where he was or whom he was with. If I put him out today, he probably had another place to move into tonight. Good for him.

I should've never invited him to my house. When he saw all that I owned, his eyes lit up like a kid on Christmas Day. I couldn't get rid of him. He started bringing more belongings than he took, including clothes and toiletries. When he started inviting his boys over to hang out at my place, acting like what was mine was ours, I put his boys out. Should've saved myself the heartaches and put him out too.

Before Darryl, I wasn't lying awake nights, wondering where my man was or whom he was with. I should've stayed single. Should've never gone to Carrabba's that day. Shouldn't have given him my new number. Shouldn't have agreed to go out with him again a year ago. And damn sure enough shouldn't have had sex with a man who hadn't had sex with a woman in ten years.

I was so in love, I married this man three months after getting back with him.

Unbeknownst to Darryl, Madison, Loretta, and my mom, I'd just found out yesterday that I was pregnant. I'd pissed on ten different sticks, praying for one negative. I didn't believe in abortion, but the last thing I wanted to do was have Darryl's baby. If I decided to keep it, Madison and I could raise our kids together. I sure hope Loretta was wrong and Madison's baby was from her husband, not from Granville. At least I didn't have that concern. I was 100 percent sure who the father of my unborn child was.

Searching to find answers to why both of my marriages failed, I began pacing the floor. Loretta didn't love Chicago. She hated that most men thought Madison was prettier. If Loretta truly loved herself, she wouldn't be in that room with Chaz, secretly loving Chicago. But who was I to judge? I needed a friend to talk to, but my friends had their problems to solve.

Exhaling, not knowing who needed whom more, I dialed Madison.

CHAPTER 5

Madison

Relieved to hear from a person who genuinely cared about me at a time when I was feeling my lowest, speaking into my Bluetooth, I sadly answered, "Hey, Tisha. I was going to call you later. Where are you?"

"At the hospi . . ." Her voice faded, then came in clear: "Hospital. Sitting in a visitors' waiting room by myself. Madison, I'm so sorry things turned out this way."

Had she called to give me the news? Was Roosevelt dead already?

"Me too. I mean I'm here sitting in the doctor's office. He went to deliver the news to Roosevelt's family and I've been in a daze since I," I said, then paused. When she didn't say anything, I continued, "I'm emotionally exhausted."

A tap on the door distracted me as Papa entered.

"My dad is here. We're actually heading out. Let me call you back."

She sniffled, then cried, "Madison, wait."

"Yes." I held my breath. If Roosevelt had taken his last, I'd stay and arrange his funeral. I wouldn't have to leave the country for a year with my mother. We could take a short vacation to Costa Rica or St. Lucia after my surgery.

I could terminate my dad's power of attorney. It wasn't that I didn't trust Papa, but I wasn't comfortable with what he'd do with Roosevelt's millions if he ever had access to the accounts. Would my dad make decisions in my best interest or his?

Papa softly asked, "Has he gone on to glory, sweetheart?"

Papa had reassured me that some of the best surgeons were in Brazil. Maybe that was true for my augmentation. America had some of the best doctors too. I loved my dad, but I needed to do my own research before letting any surgeon cut on me.

"Dad, give me that," I said, taking the document from him.

I held the power of attorney I'd signed for my father. For a moment he had the legal right to do all transactions on my behalf. Pinching the edge between my thumbs and pointing fingers, I prepared to do what I couldn't with the authorization to take Roosevelt off the respirator. I'd started to tear it in half.

Papa placed his hand over mine, then shook his head. I ripped it, anyway.

Aborting the baby was rational if Roosevelt was dead. That way, I could focus on me. The paternity wouldn't matter. I was only twelve weeks. A termination could save my unborn child from suffering through the stress of my recovery. Would the pain medication slowly kill my baby if I didn't? What would happen if I delayed having surgery until after the delivery? Could the cancer spread to my child and cause birth defects? I prayed my child would be healthy, but raising a miniature Granville scared the hell out of me.

Damn, if I leave the country, I hadn't considered who would make the funeral arrangements, choose the casket, contact the church, and pick out his suit, underwear, shoes, and plot. His mother could, but I didn't want to give her the satisfaction. Helen hated me, and the feeling was mutual.

"What did you decide?" Tisha asked, interrupting my thoughts.

That gave me the answer about my husband's status, but I didn't understand why she was crying. I handed the torn power of attorney to Papa. "Probably what I shouldn't have, but it's out of my control. If you're here to visit Roosevelt, tell him I love him."

Sending a messenger to a person on their deathbed was a bit careless, but sending one to a loving spouse that you wanted to die was viewed as ruthless. In my case I was being considerate.

"You've already said good-bye?"

"Not exactly," I told her.

"You are going to, aren't you?" Tisha asked.

I remained quiet.

"Madison, no."

Silence separated our conversation.

"Well, I don't know him that well, but I am going to see him today. It's the right thing to do. But I want to see you first. There's something you should know. Wait for me in the lobby," Tisha said.

"If you're trying to talk me into changing my mind, forget it. It's too late."

"Just a few minutes face-to-face, Madison. I'm getting on the elevator."

"I can't do this, Tisha. Not right now," I said, grabbing Papa's arm. I started crying. If I kept moving, there was no time to think about the fucked-up decisions I'd made.

Papa placed his arm around my shoulders. "It's not that bad, sweetheart. There are no mistakes. The events in our lives are predestined. I'm here for you."

Ending the call, I looked at my dad. "Papa, we've got to hurry. I don't want to deal with Tisha right now."

"You don't have to talk to her. My driver is waiting for you outside. I instructed him to take you to the house, pick up your mom and the luggage she packed for you, and take you guys to the airport. You'll take my private jet to Miami, stay overnight at the Viceroy, then continue on to El Salvador. Give me the key to your car."

El Salvador? "I thought we were going to Rio," I said, handing him my car key.

"I never said that. Where I'm sending you is better. Rio is too distracting. Not to mention dangerous."

And El Salvador was safe? I stared into his eyes. "Seems like you're taking advantage of my vulnerability. Is there something you're not telling me?"

Papa cleared his throat. His peppered hair sprinkled with scattered gray complemented his warm, walnut complexion. He stood six feet tall. Time definitely showed him favor. He was sixty, but he could easily pass for fifty.

"You've entrusted me to do what's in your best interest. Stop trying to control the outcome. You didn't have to tear up the power of attorney. I gave life to you. I wouldn't betray you." He kissed me, then continued speaking. "I want the best for my little girl. Give me your house keys too. I was going to store your car at my house, but I'll leave it at yours. I'll go by a few times a week, check on your place, and drive the car around the block."

Maybe it was best that I did leave. What exactly had I signed? Regardless of the fact that I'd taken back my power, I had to read every word. Handing Papa my house keys, I said, "Fine, but if you—"

The elevator door opened. Across from us, Tisha stepped off the opposite elevator at the same time.

"I'm so glad I caught you," she said. "Hi, Mr. Tyler. I need to speak with Madison in private, please."

"I'll go make sure the driver is outside, sweetheart," Papa said, walking away. "Stay inside until I come back and get you."

"We can sit over there on the sofa in the corner, away from the entrance," Tisha said, leading the way.

I sat with my back to the door, hoping no one would notice me. I heard lots of noise outside, but I couldn't tell what was going on. It wasn't my business.

Tisha stared at my legs. "Girl, do you ever have a bad day? Here it is, your husband might die today, and even with your being dressed in all black, you look stunning."

I gave my friend a half smile. "Thanks. I wish I felt as good. Have you ever felt that all of your decisions were so bad you couldn't find any good?"

Tisha patted my hand. "You will."

"You're saying that because you're my friend."

"I'm saying it because it's true. Good or bad. Nothing lasts. But what's up with your dad?" Tisha asked. "He's acting strange."

Why would she say that? She only saw him for less than two minutes. "I don't have much time. Papa's driver is waiting for me. What do you want to talk about?"

Now that I sat with Tisha, I suddenly felt like telling her everything. I needed to purge my guilt.

She held my hands. "Madison, you have to go back upstairs. Chicago is fighting for his life. We both know this wasn't his fault. That man deserves to live. If he doesn't make it, you know your face is the last one he wants to see."

I whispered, "He's not going to make it. And I can't watch him die."

"You should be by his side, not Loretta. Loretta is in love with Chicago and she's in his room."

"Tell me what I don't know. She's always in his room." The cold-hearted me spoke. "Not my problem."

Tisha shook her head, then gasped. "Madison, you're the first person I'm telling. My mother doesn't know yet." She squeezed my hands, then said, "I'm pregnant."

Where did that come from? But since she'd said it, I asked, "For that sorry-ass husband of yours? The one I told you not to marry. That's not my problem either. I've got enough of my own to deal with."

Tisha stood. "Why did I even bother?" She turned to walk away. She paused as if she was hoping I'd apologize or ask her to wait.

Why didn't I have compassion for Chicago, Loretta, or Tisha? I wanted to stop Tisha, but I didn't. I sat there and watched my last best friend leave through the revolving door. Maybe she needed some fresh air. I did.

What is wrong with me?

Rushing to my side, Papa said, "We have to go. Now." He acted like the building was about to blow up.

Exiting the lobby, I was confronted by press from every news station in Houston.

I stood still, then mouthed, "Loretta probably leaked my decision." I knew I shouldn't have lingered.

Desperately I scanned the crowd. I saw Tisha standing off to the side. Was this why she had to talk to me?

Our eyes met. Mine filled with tears. Tisha looked away. If ever I needed a friend, this was that time. All of these people hated me.

As my tears fell, a reporter shoved a microphone in my face. "Is it true that you signed the authorization to take Roosevelt 'Chicago' DuBois off of life support?"

Before I answered, another reporter asked, "Did you marry Chicago for his money? Is that why you want him dead? Is it true that Tyler Construction may file for bankruptcy? Is that why you married Chicago? To save your family's business?"

Fans started shouting from every direction. "Mur-der-er! Mur-der-er!"

Someone shouted above the chanting, "You didn't have to leave him for dead! You deserve to die!"

Another person shouted, "Let Chicago live!" and the momentum spread instantly until the new chant of "Let Chicago live" was so loud, I couldn't hear any questions. I only saw the reporters' mouths moving and their microphones waving. The woman who had interviewed Roosevelt and me on the news, when we had announced our pregnancy, was desperately fighting her way to the front of the crowd.

She shouted out, "Is the baby for your husband or the guy who shot him?"

My heart pounded, and my eyes widened. Loretta definitely made the call. I now wished I hadn't suggested that Loretta, Tisha, and I buy homes next door to one another. Loretta lived in between us. Seemed like a great idea at the time. We'd all been friends since we were five years old. Loretta's daughter was my goddaughter. Living that close meant I had to confront Loretta eventually. I didn't hate her, but my feelings were heading in that direction.

My dad wrapped his arm around me. "You can't stand here. Hurry, sweetheart."

He tugged in one direction. I pulled against him, staring at all of the microphones and angry faces of what I presumed to be my husband's fans in front of me. Maybe I deserved this. If each of them had a stone they could throw at me, I was certain they would.

Someone hurled an egg. My father blocked it. The cracking of the shell frightened me as the yolk splashed on my cheek and dress. Felt like someone had spat in my face.

"Let Chicago live!" they yelled louder and louder.

I covered my face and started crying. Did anyone care about me? No one came to my defense. Not even the police officers in uniform. Then I felt an arm around my shoulders. It wasn't heavy like my dad's.

"Come on, honey, let's get you out of here."

I opened my eyes and there was Tisha.

"I got you," she said. "Let's go."

CHAPTER 6

Johnny

Just because someone destroyed a deed to a house or a title to a car didn't mean ownership didn't exist. I had the original. Madison had torn up a copy.

While my daughter was meeting with the doctor and debating whether to approve the authorization that I'd told her to sign, I was out notarizing the power of attorney.

I thought by the time I got back, Chicago's body would be cold and stiff, but that cat was still kicking. Hopefully, not for much longer. With Chicago out of the picture, I'd have total control over Madison's assets and the millions she'd inherit whenever her husband died.

Women were intellectual, but they were also irrational. Madison was my child. In many ways I knew her better than she knew herself. I'd anticipated she'd change her mind. Not because she didn't want me to have control of her finances. She was a woman. Add that to her being pregnant and having breast cancer, and my daughter was an emotional time bomb on the verge of having a nervous breakdown.

A week had gone by since we'd escaped the media at the hospital. Madison hadn't left my house or the country. She hadn't stopped yapping about having an abortion, and my business was beginning to fall apart. I had to get her out of my home and on my private plane to Miami so I could stop tap-dancing around what I had to do.

I sat facing her. The rectangular coffee table separated the identical sofas. "Madison, sweetheart. If you're not leaving for another week, the least you can do is help me with the paperwork for the company. Go get out of that silk nightgown. Come, go to the office with me, make some phone calls, or something. The city's accounts payable folks are slow sending the payments and they won't return my calls."

My daughter stretched her back across my chocolate leather sofa; then she stared at the ceiling as though she was a patient and I was her therapist. Turning onto her side, she rolled her eyes at me, then focused on the flat screen above the fireplace. On the TV Judge Joe Brown was awarding the plaintiff $4,000.

"You don't run the company, Papa. I do. But you're so eager to get rid of me, you don't care that I have a doctor's appointment today. Handle it yourself. You keep saying a week. I've told you, unless it's for a vacation, I'm not going overseas. Stop calling, go down to the city, and find out what's happening."

Damn it, if this girl isn't as stubborn as her old man . . .

Rosalee sat at Madison's feet; then she gave me that piercing glance that silently said, *"Johnny, I've told you, stop messing with my child."*

Hmm.

She was being a mom. I was being a man. I didn't respond. I had to think this through.

"Her appointment is more important," my wife said, "and she doesn't need to be upset. She's about to go under the knife soon. Madison is right. You figure it out."

If the company folded and Madison didn't have insurance coverage, bet she'd be willing to help. My wife sat next to my daughter. My wife had her breasts removed years ago. My daughter was about to have the same done any day now. Who gave a damn how I felt?

If I wouldn't have to split my acquisitions fifty-fifty, I'd file for a divorce. I loved Rosalee, but I was no longer in love with her. We used to travel the world, go out on dates, and enjoy watching movies together. Not anymore. Rosalee had become a real homebody. Cooking and cleaning for our daughter. Eating and sleeping, when she wasn't cooking or cleaning, made her happy. Sex with my wife wasn't the same either. I bet when that baby gets here, that'll completely take Rosalee from me.

"The only thing I'm concerned about is my health," Madison said. "I wish you cared as much as Mother."

Cared as much as the mother who didn't care enough to tell her daughter she'd had a double mastectomy? The mother who didn't make sure her daughter had early breast exams even though she knew there was a family history? Rosalee needed to get off her guilt trip and stop babying Madison.

I was no fool. I wasn't going there. But I was getting tired of listening to them. I stood over Madison and said, "You already know your damn health status. You have breast cancer and you're pregnant. That's not going to change, sweetheart. You need to keep the baby. If it's Chicago's, we can possibly lock in more money when old man Wally, his grandfather, kicks the bucket."

A brilliant idea entered my mind. I had to find a way to pay off the lab technician that would process Madison's paternity test. Regardless to whose DNA the baby had, the results would show Chicago is the father. A giant smile grew inside me.

I didn't want to switch directions on my position. I told my daughter, "If you're not going to help me, you are going to El Salvador. And that's final."

"Johnny Tyler, you stop it right now!"

Madison dropped her forehead into her hands. "Leave me alone, Papa. Can you do that? Please . . . just go away."

I could do that. "Okay, after you take me to Chicago's condo so we can go through his statements and taxes. I keep telling you that you have the right to access his accounts legally. You're his wife. And we've got to do this before his family does."

Looking up at me, she answered, "And he's still alive, Papa."

Desperate to avoid my next move, I told her, "But not for long."

This time my daughter screamed, "What news have you been watching? He's getting better every day!"

"You can't believe what you hear on TV. Go up there to the hospital and find out for yourself. I don't understand you, Madison. You hold all the cards, and you don't want to do anything to help me."

This time she jumped up. "That's because I don't understand your motive!"

"Where are you going, little girl?"

"To my house, so you can stop stressing me out."

Oh no! Anywhere except her house. I hugged my baby girl. "I'm sorry. I don't want anything bad to happen to you or the baby. Stay here with your mother. Rosalee, calm your daughter down. I'm going to the office. I'll handle everything by myself. Call me after your appointment, sweetheart, and let Papa know how things went."

"I'm going to take a nap before I go to the doctor," Madison said, heading upstairs.

"Johnny, you've done it before. You can save our company again," my wife said. "Hire a consultant."

Rosalee was a housewife and hadn't worked one day for the business. She just didn't understand how strapped we were. Get a consultant with what money? I kissed her lips. We didn't open our mouths anymore. Didn't remember when that started, but I was not the one who initiated it. "I'll be back."

Getting into my Porsche, I phoned a different fraternity brother from the frat brother that did the notary, then cruised out of my driveway.

"Hey, Johnny. We still on?"

"I'm in motion. I'll meet you there in a half hour." I ended the call, then speed-dialed my wife.

Rosalee answered, saying, "You okay, honey?"

"I'm good. Watch Madison closely. Don't let her leave the house without you. Make sure she returns to our house after her appointment. I don't want her going to her place. She shouldn't be alone."

"She's already asleep. She's been napping a lot since she took her husband off of the respirator. I think she's going through depression, so you're going to have to lighten up on her. Oh, by the way, you look nice in your new suit."

"That's why I love you. Bye, honey. I'll see you tonight."

It had been years since I was going to the office every day. Turning the business over to Madison had kept me out of trouble. Hiring young, attractive, and smart girls as my secretary was legit. Putting personal assistants on payroll was my way of paying for pussy and their only job was to keep "big papa" satisfied.

Marrying Rosalee was the best decision I'd made my entire life. She knew her place. Like lots of wives in Houston, Rosalee was faithful to a fault. The man in me preferred it that way. My wife never talked down to me. Most of the time she had no idea what I was up to. When she did find out, I begged her to stay and she did. I loved Rosalee through her double mastectomy. That was genuine. Was glad she didn't get implants. Didn't want men getting stuck in my wife's headlights.

I didn't know what I'd do without her and never wanted to find out. Better to ask for her forgiveness because I didn't need her permission.

Leaving our home in River Oaks, I headed toward San Felipe and Post Oak, the location of my Westheimer project. My construction employees were hard at work—but not for long if I didn't get it together. I still wasn't clear on that Granville guy's involvement with my Madison and how it all started. Think I'd pay him a visit one day. Wasn't like he was going anywhere.

A few blocks and a couple of turns, I was at my destination. My frat brother was already there. I parked in Madison's driveway. We got out of our cars at the same time.

"Hey, man. Thanks for helping us out," I said, patting him on the back.

"Anything I can do to help, you know that. Shall we go inside?"

Unlocking the front door to my daughter's house, I gave him a tour. Showed him the security camera upgrade Madison had done. Oh, shit. I prayed she was asleep and not watching us on her cell phone. I went to the control panel. Turned off the surveillance system.

"Let's go upstairs," I said.

"I'm putting my ass on the line here for you, Johnny. You're going to have to do the same."

"Not a problem," I said, almost sounding like Madison.

"Sure you feel up to this?" he asked, following me up the stairs.

Opening one of the guest bedroom doors, I said, "Positive."

CHAPTER 7

Granville

"She took him off of that breathing machine because she thought he was going to die," No Chainz said.

"We keep going over this, but is he right?" I asked, looking at G-double-A. "Is he?"

The three of us were huddled at our usual round steel table, with those immovable stools. Lunch today was sausage link sandwiches and fries. A few inmates tried to sit in with us and listen, but I encouraged them to go elsewhere within the common area—if they didn't want my trouble.

I learned you could be decent up in here and stay out of trouble if you had what others wanted but couldn't get, didn't join a gang, and occupied your free time educating yourself on the law library computer by doing research for your case. I had a mini concession stand in my cell loaded with snacks. If an inmate didn't have money to buy his own, or his family and friends didn't visit, or if I wanted him to get off the computer, I'd let him have a treat. Some took advantage, pretending they were working on the computer just to get some M&M'S or Doritos. Long as I got what I wanted, feeding them didn't matter. Mama said sharing was having good manners.

"Maybe. Maybe not," G-double-A said. "If I keep advising you, we're going to have to work out a payment arrangement."

I stared at him. I wished the warden would hurry up and get that culinary class approved so I could cook a fancy meal for Madison when I got out. I sure was glad I had that tattoo of Loretta's name, which was on my chest, changed into a fire-breathing dragon. But I was glad it didn't resemble one of those gang tats. Here they housed lots of members of the same gangs together to cut back on fights, stabbings, all that.

I didn't need to attend no GED course. Already had my diploma. Wasn't interested in art, but some dudes drew shit better than what was in stores. Outside of earning seventeen cents an hour for doing laundry five days a week, my remaining time between eight in the morning to ten at night was spent talking on the phone or brainstorming with No Chainz and G-double-A.

"What did you just say?" I asked, biting a chunk out of my sandwich.

"You don't have to pay me. Let the court-appointed standby counsel have your back on this. Since Chicago is still alive, they might be able to help you convince the judge to set bail."

I frowned. They'd already set my bail at $75,000.

"Oh, that's right," G-double-A said, snapping his finger. "I meant to say the judge might lower your bail," as if he'd read my mind. "What you need to do is . . . Get a pen and write this down. I'm not going to keep giving you pro bono advice for the hell of it, and I'm not telling you the same shit twice."

Seemed to me he was the one who needed to write shit down.

No Chainz ran off.

"How much?" I asked.

"The going rate starts at two-fifty an hour, but I'll give you the family rate of fifty dollars."

No Chainz returned with his journal. "I'll take notes for you, Granville."

Beaux was putting change on the books for No Chainz and G-double-A so they could shop at the commissary. Recently the warden had approved iPods for inmates. The charging station was already in place on the second floor. I had my brother put enough cash into each of our accounts to make sure we were the first to get one. Finally I get to listen to my country-Western music. If I had to pay him fifty bucks an hour, I was deducting what Beaux had given him.

"Thanks, bro," I told No Chainz, still trying to make sense of why I had to pay this dude, since he was locked up like me.

G-double-A said, "As long as you're in here, the information you get on that computer to support your case is limited. They do that shit on purpose. I can get you access to *all* information. You feel me? The first thing you need is a 'get out of jail' exhibit list. The judge don't give a damn about what you say if you can't prove it. Consider your black ass guilty until the jury says otherwise, and even then the judge can overturn their decision."

I frowned. How was that? If the judge had that much power, what was the point in having a trial? I guess I did have to pay him. Maybe I should consider myself lucky to have a lawyer on the inside.

"It's true, dude," G-double-A said. "So don't get overconfident. Just when you think your black ass is on top, you may still end up doing life, because this whole town, including me, loves Chicago. And they want to see someone held accountable. Right now, all four charges are against you."

Why? If Chicago wasn't dead, then why should I serve a sentence at all? "I'm innocent."

No Chainz slapped the pen to the pad, then sighed heavily.

Putting No Chainz on pause, G-double-A said, "Shut up and listen. Granville, can you prove Madison had consensual sex with you?"

I'd been holding out on mentioning the video. I'd uploaded it to a site, but I was the only one with the password to view it. The password I'd sent Chicago had expired. We didn't have Internet access to the outside world. Our e-mails were scrutinized by staff. The only way to let these guys see it was to have Precious download it, then slip me the cell phone during visitation.

Reluctantly I said, "Yeah."

"How?" he asked.

I hesitated, then told them, "I took the videotape she recorded of us that night. I have it on, um, at my house." That was the truth, but I didn't want another man seeing my woman on film. That was personal.

"You're going to have to let us see that," No Chainz said, gripping his stuff. "Granville, you been holding out. What else you got, man?"

"Let's see. I bought Loretta an engagement ring. She wouldn't take it, but she introduced me to Madison. Madison invited me to her office, then to her house, and then she took all of her clothes off. She made me fall in love with her, and then she broke my heart by marrying another man. Isn't that alienation of affection?" I asked.

"Scrap that. That shit only works for women," G-double-A said.

"What about temporary insanity?" I was going crazy without Madison.

"That shit ain't temporary for you, dude. If your ass want to get out of here, you'd better think of a million reasons why the judge should let you out, and pray that one sticks."

Was he insulting me again? I rattled my head, hoping to come up with a good thought. The tape might work against me when they saw the ending. The judge would feel sorry for Madison, especially if the judge was a woman.

"I know Madison wants Chicago's money. That's why she pulled the plug."

"Prove it," G-double-A said. "You've got to find a way to prove you had justifiable cause."

I frowned. Didn't that mean I did it? I got quiet. *Think, Granville, think. Fuck!*

"I've got it!" I yelled.

"Don't keep the shit to yourself, nigga," No Chainz said. "What the fuck is it?"

"Bankrupt. Madison's dad's company is going bankrupt. Don't you remember the reporter asking Madison that question? Loretta went out with me, but she really didn't want to. She wanted me to date Madison, who was engaged to Chicago."

I was so glad we had three flat-screen televisions in our community area. Mainly, my group liked to keep track of the news.

"Yeah," No Chainz said. "Because they know a brother like you loves hard, and you're the kind of dude who would kill for his woman."

G-double-A slid his hand over his mouth and chin; then he started nodding.

No Chainz wrote so hard and fast that he'd torn a hole in the paper. I felt like a celebrity.

"They wanted me to show up at the reception and kill Chicago."

No Chainz stopped writing. "That's what I just said, nigga."

I continued, "That way, Tyler Construction would be saved and—"

No Chainz interrupted, "You'd be the sacrificial ham because most black folks don't eat no lamb."

"Now who's using big words," I told him.

G-double-A said, "Granville, I think your ignorant ass might have a case that will set you free and put these ladies behind bars. If you stage this right, a good lawyer on the outside might take your case pro bono."

My eyebrows lowered. If I got a lawyer on the outside, I'd have to pay two-fifty an hour. I wouldn't need to pay G-double-A. "You ain't slick."

" 'Pro bono' means 'for free,' " he explained.

"I know that," I lied. Was it "bona" or "bono"? I was frowning. "I don't care about Loretta going to jail, but I don't want my kid being born behind bars. Even if it means my doing time, I have to protect Madison."

G-double-A said, "Keep that kind of shit to yourself, dude. I'm not going to help you fuck up your case." He got up and left.

No Chainz followed him like he was dude's personal assistant.

I didn't want to get convicted. I chased G-double-A and said, "Fifty dollars an hour is cool, man."

He shook my hand. "You made the right decision. Let's do this, G."

CHAPTER 8

Loretta

Closure. That was what Chicago deserved from Madison.

Wish I could make her give it to him. I hated that she wouldn't annul their marriage. She was worse than an egotistical bastard. Madison was a bitch with balls who didn't have to piss to mark her territory. The more she ignored Chicago, refused to come visit him, the more he ranted about her.

"Fuck her!" I wanted to say.

Why were men stuck on bitches who dogged them out? When was he going to stop chasing a woman who didn't want him?

I sat in Chicago's hospital room and listened to him say, "I love Madison. I know you don't understand why, but she's everything I want in a woman."

Like what? You mean the fact that she hates your mother is cool? Or is it the part where she left you for dead that's turning you on?

I didn't want to, but I had to ask, "How did you guys meet?"

He smiled. "Madison didn't tell you?"

"All she said was she'd met the most amazing man at a fund-raiser. Then you showed up at Tisha's wedding and reception."

Madison had met the nine men—including Chicago—who had put a ring on her finger while she was traveling solo. Her exact words were "Women who roam in packs attract rats, Loretta. You should know that."

Perhaps I shouldn't have personalized what she'd said, but I did. That comment had given me one more reason to hate Madison.

"Indeed, we did meet at a fund-raiser in the Woodlands at the Club at Carlton Woods—"

I interrupted, "Madison doesn't know how to golf." She probably didn't even make a donation.

"Men don't care about that. When she strutted into the clubhouse wearing all pink to an all-white function, every single man and a few married ones did a double take, licked her like a lollipop with their eyes, then competed for her attention. She didn't have on golfing attire like the other women. Oh no! Madison had on a thigh-length dress, which clung to her breasts and booty, and stilettos. Her suckable toes were painted like cotton candy."

I hated when guys relived moments about women like the shit had happened yesterday.

"The two box office tickets I had for my suite, which were supposed to be for one of our team's football sponsors, I gave Madison one, then walked away. If she liked me, I knew she'd come to the game. And she did."

If I had walked into that country club, I doubt Chicago would've done the same for me.

Madison had his plug pulled two weeks ago. I'd been by Chicago's side for a total of six weeks and had never missed a day. Being at the hospital, I saw how people with money received the best treatment. If I had been admitted, instead of him, I would've been discharged a long time ago.

Most of the credit, I'd like to claim, but the doctor was awesome and the nurses were incredible. They barely left us alone. They had him breathing normally in less than seventy-two hours. His bandages were replaced four times a day. Honestly, Chicago was healthy enough to have gone home a week ago, but the doctor, who was also Chicago's fan, had insisted he stay a little longer.

"When I came to your house and asked you about Madison, why didn't you give it to me straight?" he asked.

Like whatever I would've said could've made you not marry her.

Whatever God had in store for this man had to be major. One would think after being on a respirator for a month, he would've had some degree of brain damage. Like Magic's response to having HIV, the doctors couldn't explain it; and I couldn't figure out why it seemed as though Chicago hadn't been shot. Had I not been here, I wouldn't have known that his having lots of money made a huge difference.

If he had been engaged to me, he wouldn't have questioned my character. "Truthfully, I don't know what you see in her."

Chicago looked at me. He quietly smiled. His eyes shifted to the corners. A short puff of air came from his nose. His lips remained curved. Then he closed his eyes and shook his head. "She's amazing."

I don't get it. What could she have done to cause him to respond like he was hypnotized? Was it her bedroom skills? Well, she won't be so amazing after she has her surgery.

My God, Loretta, what's wrong with you?

Hating on a friend who has breast cancer was low, but there was something so deep inside me and I couldn't explain why it was eating me up like a flesh-eating bacteria. Especially because Madison hadn't done anything to me to make me despise her.

"Loretta, my brother is lucky to have you. You're the kind of woman a man needs as his wife. Most men like shiny. We don't drive a Rolls that's stacked on sixteen-inch rims. We get twenty-fours that are flashy. The diamond Rolex on our wrist is there to impress the best-looking female. A man is attracted to a woman who makes all—and I mean *all*—of his friends envious. We want a woman who makes *us* shine."

Now I get it. I smiled on the inside. Chicago liked me a lot. That was why he'd kept me by his side. He was hesitant to tell me the truth because he was worried about taking me from Chaz.

Chicago continued speaking. "Madison is the shiniest. Madison is the type that every man dreams of as having as his wife. When a man gets the woman he's dreamt about, no matter how foolish it seems to others, he'll do whatever it takes to keep her."

I had a sudden urge to slap his face. I took a deep breath to conceal my frustrations. A part of me shared his view and the other side of me suppressed my sexual attraction toward Madison. I wasn't a lesbian; but at times, when I was around her, I felt urges in places that should be reserved for a man.

"Even if she leaves you for dead," I said, not caring how he felt.

"We don't know why she signed the papers. Maybe she didn't want to see me suffer. Or maybe she didn't want to compete with your being here every day."

"Don't leave out the part where you requested that I stay." I shouldn't ask, but I did. "Do you still love her?"

Slowly nodding, he said, "I'm in love with my wife. Why don't you tell me why you're so jealous of her. . . ."

I was beyond jealous. "If you want me to leave, just say so."

"I'll admit I've been selfish. You have my brother and your daughter to care for. Six weeks is a long time and you probably need to get back to work. I appreciate your supervisor doing me a favor and agreeing to give you the time off."

"I'm here, Chicago, because I want to be here."

"But if leaving is what you—" Chicago's phone rang.

CHAPTER 9

Loretta

A welcomed buzz came from Chicago's phone, giving me time to regroup from what could've been my biggest mistake. Looking at him, I tried to comprehend what was incomprehensible: Chicago's feelings for Madison. I wasn't giving up on making Chicago mine. All he needed was a little more time to get over his wife.

He smiled and answered, "Hey, boss"; then he put the call on speaker.

"Hey, Chicago. You sound better than when we saw you the other day. The whole gang is here. You got a minute?"

I recognized the voice from the days he was here. The owners showed their love and concern for Chicago during his recovery. One of them was here every other day. The man speaking had a controlling interest in the team. The last time he came in, Chicago didn't appear to be 100 percent coherent because he was under the influence of sleeping medication.

Chicago obviously trusted me. He hadn't asked me to leave, nor had he switched to his Bluetooth.

Chicago looked at me and mouthed, "Thanks."

"We're thinking about temporarily promoting Blue Waters to your position. It's just for the preseason, or until you get better."

A different person said, "Don't worry. We don't plan on replacing you."

I'd learned enough to know that might not be true. If Blue did an amazing job, Chicago may have to find another team to manage. If Madison had been here, she'd chime in on the conversation, on Chicago's behalf. I knew that wasn't my place, so I sat quietly taking it all in. If Blue got the job, Madison would probably become his woman. She was such an opportunist.

"Hold that thought," Chicago said. "I have a better suggestion."

The guy who would make the final decision spoke now. "You know we have the utmost respect for your opinion. Shoot. Damn, I shouldn't have said that. Let us hear it."

"I'm confident I'll have a full recovery. I'm not fragile. Actually, I'm doing better than you'd imagine," Chicago said with a short laugh. "Seriously, Blue is doing an outstanding job. That's why we need Blue to stay where he's at. He's great at holding things together at the ground level, but he's no GM. My brother, Chaz, can step in for me during preseason. From scouting to salaries, I've taught him everything I know. And if anyone has any questions, both Chaz and you guys can count on me to assist with getting the job done. Thanks to"—he paused—"a loyal friend, I should be back in full swing and ready to take complete control of all operations for the regular season's games."

My heart smiled on the inside. I was loyal to Chicago, but I definitely wanted to be more than just his friend. If the owners went along with his recommendation, I'd be upgraded to the girlfriend of the temporary general manager of our football team. For a short while I'd have access to the suite, and people would be asking for my autograph. Of course I'd have to get a makeover and hire a body image consultant. This could be my only chance to outshine Madison and I didn't want to mess it up.

The guy in charge said, "I'm going to put you on mute for a moment while we discuss this."

"No problem." Chicago looked at me, then winked.

My pussy puckered. I had the biggest grin on the inside. I flashed a small smile for him. Didn't want to seem overly excited, but God knew I was.

"Chicago."

"Yes."

"Have your brother, Chaz, meet us in your office tomorrow at noon. After the meeting we'll call you with our decision."

"Fair enough," Chicago said.

When he ended the call, he got out of bed, limped up to me, and gave me a big hug. He was scheduled to check out tomorrow. The doctor suggested Chicago wait a few days before starting home rehab, but he insisted on starting right away.

"Loretta, I appreciate your being here for me every day. You didn't have to do this. I know my family and my brother thank you too. It's because of you that I feel like I have a second life. All the daily prayers. Comforting my mother. The time you've missed from work and away from your daughter. When we get to my place, I'm going to write you a check."

I started shaking my head. "No, I will not accept your money. I did this because"—I wanted to say, "because I love you," but couldn't—"because you're a great man, and besides, what would your friends, fans, and family do without you?" I intentionally left out his wife.

Chicago sat on the side of his bed.

"You know Madison used to be involved with Blue Waters," I reminded him, "so you certainly did the right thing by not letting him get your position. You think they"—I paused—"Naw, she wouldn't do with Blue what she'd done with Granville. But if she has her baby could be his. She's never going to divorce you. And if you try to leave her, she's going to take you for your money."

I didn't know what the hell I was talking about, but I had to put ideas in Chicago's mind to draw him away from Madison. Now that he was close to a full recovery, I had to hold on tighter.

He shook his head. "Jealousy does not become you. Don't go there. I insist on writing you a check. If Raynard doesn't mind taking care of your daughter for a while longer, I hope you don't mind moving in with me until my rehab is complete. If you say 'no,' I'll understand. Think about it. I'll pay you for your additional time away from the pharmacy. Wait a minute. It just occurred to me. You haven't eaten all day. Go get something and get some rest. I'll see you tomorrow. I need to call Chaz and get him over here so I can prep him for his big meeting."

There was a God and He'd answered my prayers. Raynell would be fine. She wasn't with a stranger. She was with her biological father. And no matter what Raynard said, I knew his wife did not want full or primary custody of our child. I was moving in with Raynell's future stepfather. And once I was in, she could move in and we were never moving out.

CHAPTER 10

Tisha

Involuntary relocation. D-day had arrived for Darryl.

Two weeks had passed since Chicago left the hospital. Should've listened to my mother. Instead, I came home and told Darryl he had to move. He stopped speaking to me, but every night he showed up at my front door and slept in my guest bedroom. Whenever I mentioned our going to counseling, he laughed. The more I insisted he get out, nothing changed.

Since Chicago's release I'd only seen Loretta once. When I heard her car enter her driveway, I'd stood at my bedroom window on the second floor. Loretta had gone inside. My boys were at my mom's. I grabbed a bottle of champagne and went next door to welcome Loretta home. She passed me by, put a suitcase in her trunk, then sped off. No hello or good-bye.

Exhaling, I went back inside. I hadn't seen Madison since I'd rescued her from the media. Texting was our way of communicating. I hadn't called Loretta or Madison because I had my own housecleaning to do.

Darryl had dangled by his dick far too long. He was so trifling I'd decided he didn't have the right to know I was pregnant with his child. What difference would it make if I'd let him stay?

I bypassed the locksmith at my front door, sat the champagne on the kitchen counter, went upstairs to my bedroom, and called my husband. Soon as he answered, I let him have it.

"I'm not taking your shit and cleaning your kid's ass too. Wherever you've been all night, make arrangements to get real comfortable. Permanently! You hear me! I'm serious this time. You'd better give your parole officer your mistress's or your mama's address. You don't live here anymore!"

"Baby, what's the matter? You need your daddy to come over there and tighten you up? I'm on my way right now." He ended the call, talking to me like I was one of his side bitches.

Darryl was so self-centered he totally missed the part about my cleaning his kid's ass. I guess a part of me hoped he would've asked, "Baby, are you saying what I think?" Normally, I'd call him back. Not this time. Hearing him say "Come over there" confirmed he didn't deserve to use my house as his home.

The friendship we've had since high school and the sex between us were the only reasons he was still here. But I'd had enough. I'd rather fuck myself than open my legs again for his useless behind. My body shivered. The thought of Darryl penetrating me made my knees wobble.

I chastised my pussy. *We're done with that dick—you hear me? Shut up and let's go.* I left my bedroom and went downstairs to the living room. I'd almost forgotten I wasn't the only one home.

If Darryl had done some things right, I wouldn't be ending it all. We could've talked, got professional help, and tried to make our marriage work. He'd done wrong for so long that I had nothing to say, and he had nothing worth hearing. I'd cried my last tears. Made my final plea a long time ago for him to stay home, be with his family—hell, be a man and grow up. Hanging with his boys didn't pay bills, and neither did he. All of that was behind me. For real this time. Now I realized that we never wanted the same things. *Hell, other than wanting to be a freeloader, I don't know what that man wants.*

It was time to stop looking in my rearview mirror and focus on what was ahead. My husband was married to the streets and the women in them. I couldn't compete with that mentality. Maybe being incarcerated for ten years molded him into being an underachiever. Or he was one well before and that was why he got locked up.

Darryl had been out all night again, but that wasn't new. But today I was. I sat on the sofa, staring at the front door. There was a man there, but he wasn't my husband. I watched him, wondering if his wife was happy.

"Okay, Ms. Thomas, I'm all done," he said, handing me the new sets of keys and the reprogrammed garage door opener to my house.

The sound of my name was sweet. I'd never legally changed it from Thomas to Jefferson, but occasionally I introduced myself as Mrs. Jefferson to make Darryl feel good.

Tipping the locksmith a twenty, I said, "Thanks, I appreciate it. Have a nice day."

I meant that. Whenever I wished someone well, it was from my heart. I waited until he was gone; then I placed the sign I had made on the lawn: COMPLIMENTARY WHORISH PAROLEE FREELOADING HUSBAND WITH GOOD DICK AVAILABLE/NO RETURN 310-555-6969.

That fool had never taken a breath in Hollywood. His 310 area code was to impress women. Guess while he was in jail, he was one of those criminals sitting in a huddle, creating love letters to scheme females out of whatever they could get. Darryl had never been on a plane or outside of Texas. What was I thinking, walking down the aisle to him?

I went back inside, locked the door, tossed the new keys on my dining table, then headed to the kitchen. The dishes were still there from breakfast with my boys and my mother. After we'd eaten, my mom had taken my kids to her place for the weekend.

I busied myself loading the dishwasher, cleaning the appliances, and sweeping my kitchen floor. I vacuumed downstairs. Three hours went by. No Darryl.

Being alone wasn't what I wanted. I'd wished Madison or Loretta were here with me. I missed the way we used to get together at one another's home, sip bubbly, and girl talk.

Madison was at her parents'. The day her husband was released, she'd texted me, Long as that bitch is at Roosevelt's I'm not talking to him or her.

Loretta was being the hypocrite that she was by playing live-in wannabe wife to Chicago. All of my friends were disappearing for one reason or another.

My kids had become my company. I missed the sound of my boys' voices. I had to keep my babies safe, in case Darryl decided to be the fool that he was.

He'd have to show up eventually for a change of clothes, but this time there'd be no hot meal or puckering pussy waiting for him. All that he'd brought was neatly packed in boxes blocking the driveway. I placed the sign close to his things so he wouldn't miss it.

Darryl had exactly twenty-two boxes waiting for him outside. That meant he'd have to make several trips to get them all. His game systems, clothes, shoes, toiletries, the one television he'd dragged into my house, acting like he'd contributed to the household, and all the shit he'd bought with my money was waiting for him to take.

I didn't care about material things. Women who held on to items they'd purchased didn't honestly want the things. They wanted the man. They wanted to give him a reason to stay or come back. Not me. I was done with him, and he could have all his shit.

Putting away the dishes, I poured myself a glass of champagne to celebrate my new beginnings. I'd probably keep the child. Maybe. I wasn't sure, but I was positive that I needed a drink.

Slowly I sipped. *Tisha, what in the world did you commit to? This man literally did not have a pot to piss in. He'd been locked up for ten years. He didn't have a steady job. All Darryl did was talk a good game and slap good dick. Girl, were you that horny and lonely?* I asked myself, knowing the answers.

I felt like I had a lot to give and I wanted to share it with someone. What was the point of having this big house and not having a man in my bed? My place was a peaceful space before I let Darryl in. Honestly, I was beginning to feel at ease already.

I heard his car. Refilled my glass. Bubbles rushed to the top. Gliding toward the door, I took my time. Standing in the front window like a mannequin, I stared at him.

Darryl's car was parked on the street. He bypassed the boxes, as though they'd belonged to someone else, approached the door, and held his key. He tried to shove it in. It didn't fit. He tried harder. It didn't work.

Finally he walked to the window where I stood. Hurling his arms toward the moonlit sky, he shouted, "Tisha! What's up? Let me in."

I closed the curtain on his dramatic performance, turned, then walked away.

Darryl had exactly five minutes to start packing his things into the Benz he'd bought with my money, or I was calling the police. He'd had enough sense to ask me to pay cash for the car, saying, "I don't want a note." Without a job, he couldn't afford a car note.

Some men knew but didn't care how good they had it until a bitch pulled the rug from under his lying ass, rolled him up in it, and kicked his trashy behind to the curb.

CHAPTER 11

Madison

What a difference time made. For once, I was happy to be yesterday's news.

Since Roosevelt hadn't died, haters and the media had moved on. Houstonians were anxiously anticipating the free tickets to *Oprah's Lifeclass* with Pastor Joel Osteen. Rumor had it that Tyler Perry would be there too.

I had no interest in going to church, but I was thankful for the prayers, support, and outreach received from breast cancer survivors that didn't know me. Their caring helped me understand why some women gave freely with no expectations in return. It was their good nature.

Chaz had taken his brother's job for the upcoming football preseason. I'd bet no one could wipe the grin off Loretta's face. Blue Waters—who gave a care about his lying ass? My refusing to date him before my engagement to Roosevelt was no cause for him to tell my husband we'd had sex. That was a lie. Considering what I'd done with Granville, it wasn't worth my trying to convince Roosevelt it wasn't true. Why would Blue do that?

Reality was registering and I was feeling remorseful for signing that authorization. Guilt had kept me away from my husband long enough. I had to find a way to mend my marriage. Tired of hiding out at my parents' home, I opened the dresser drawer. I started packing the suitcase I'd emptied. The clothing my mother had at her house for the trip abroad was going home with me.

First stop was Tisha's, to pick her up. She'd agreed to go with me to my doctor's appointment. It was my pre-op, but I'd lied and told Tisha it was a routine checkup for my baby. The results from the pre-op would determine if I were ready to have breast surgery. After my appointment, we were going to my house and I was going to listen to my friend's concerns. My problems weren't going anywhere, and neither was I. I was sexy, beautiful, and alive.

I was determined to beat cancer.

Sleeping in my bed was what I'd missed most. My fluffy pillows, thousand-count sheets, soft silky comforter. My body relaxed at the thought of soaking in my Jacuzzi tonight, with a glass of champagne, surrounded by soft instrumental music and the sounds of me exhaling. No Mom checking on me like I was an infant. No Dad constantly trying to convince me to get on his jet and go.

He acted like anywhere outside of the Texas state line would be fine. I wasn't accustomed to doing nothing all day. Going back to work would've occupied my mind until I went in for surgery. My papa was a one-step-at-a-time, or jump-in-and-find-out-how-deep-the-water-was type of businessman. He'd done a one-eighty. At first, he wanted me to help him. Now, each time I offered to go to the office, he emphatically declined, saying, "Focus on your health, sweetheart. Papa has got things under control."

Granville's hearing was coming up soon. The reporters would be at his trial, but I would not. There were some advantages to some people not having lots of money. I was glad Granville's family hadn't posted his bail. If they had, I'd have to do like Loretta and get myself a gun.

"Okay, Mama. Love you. I'll call with the doctor's report." I gave my mom a kiss on the cheek.

She hugged me. "You sure you don't want me to go with you, baby?"

After the last visit I was certain. When the doctor explained the risks to my unborn child if I had to start radiation before delivery, Mama cried more than I had. All she had to do was share my history with me. If she had, I might not be in this situation. I hated to keep holding that against my mother, but it was the truth. I could've tested early to see if I had the gene, which obviously I do. Or if I felt like my mother was on my team and not straddling the fence with my father's wishes to send me out of the country, I'd let her go with me.

"Madison, please," Mama begged.

Rolling my suitcase out the door, I said, "I'll be fine. Love you. Bye."

Settling into the luscious Ferrari my dad bought me, I sighed. I inhaled the scent of fresh leather. It felt so good getting into my ride. Being out of my parents' house was liberating. I'd been there for two weeks and that was thirteen days too long.

The drive to Tisha's reminded me of the congested commuter traffic in Houston. I cruised along the freeway until I took the Westheimer exit, off Interstate 610. Bypassing my house, then Loretta's, I parked in Tisha's driveway.

Tempted to go home, I resisted. If I entered my living room, I'd go straight upstairs, get in bed, and miss my appointment. I was happy to see my girlfriend. I watched her lock her front door. She turned the knob, then pushed. Turned it again and pushed harder.

When she got into my car, I said, "Dang, girl, you act like you slept with Granville too." I laughed.

"Worse. I moved him in, married him, took care of him, put him out, and still can't get rid of him," she said. "He calls me every hour."

"Really?" I headed back toward Post Oak and turned left. "Send his trifling ass back to jail."

"I don't hate him. I don't want anything to do with him. Hopefully, it won't come to my having to bury him alive in my backyard."

"I'd say do the world that favor. I never gave a damn about Darryl. No sense in pretending that's changed," I said.

"Madison!"

Women need to stop being so damn nice to men who didn't deserve it. The one year Darryl had been with Tisha had financially set her back ten. The free rein she'd given him to her money, Tisha could've invested toward her kids' college tuition.

I looked at my friend. She was glowing. Her smooth, chocolate-colored skin was flawless. The whiteness of her teeth and clarity in her eyes shined bright. The spikiness of her Afro glistened at the tips.

"I was just kidding about burying him alive. How are you?" Tisha asked. "I can give you details on my changing"—she spread, then fanned her fingers—"all the locks on my house later. Darryl does not have, and will not ever get, a key again." When she said "a key," it sounded like she'd sneezed.

I laughed. "Oh, we have to talk about that. I know he's blowing up your phone because that's what men do *after* they fuck up a good thing. You were the best he'd ever had, girlfriend."

Tisha's cell rang. She held up her iPhone and pressed IGNORE.

"Good girl."

"Enough of Darryl," she said. "What's happening with you? You excited?"

Of course I wasn't happy about not knowing who my child's father was. I never imagined sympathizing with women on talk shows who had had sex with two or more men, but now I got it. If cheating men could get pregnant, they wouldn't be so damn quick to call a woman "slut."

I didn't want to focus on my fears. "I have to say you look amazingly happy, girlfriend. Like you're at peace."

"I am, but I can't say the same for you. You seem stressed. Are you worried about what to do with your marriage?" she asked. For a second, her eyes connected with mine.

I inhaled, long and deep. "Tisha, I haven't been completely truthful with you. This checkup isn't for the baby. Tisha, I have breast cancer. Stage two. Both breasts. Thankfully, it's not worse than my initial diagnosis. I'll find out if I'm healthy enough to undergo surgery and what to expect next. Whatever you do, please don't be mad at me for not telling you. When you told me you were pregnant, I couldn't be happy or sad for you because I knew taking Roosevelt off of life support was wrong. I can't have my last best friend hating me." I wanted to lean into my steering wheel and cry out, "I love that man!"

She looked out the passenger window, back at me, and then said, "How long have you known?"

"As long as I've been pregnant. The doctor said my having cheated with Granville might have saved my life. If I hadn't had sex with him, I wouldn't have had a reason to get a complete checkup."

I went in for a Pap and came out a mother-to-be.

"You've known for four months?"

I nodded. "Don't pretend you're surprised. I know Loretta told you."

Tisha shook her head. "It's kind of hard for her to tell me anything. We don't talk. But we're going to beat this. You know our councilwoman is forty-five years cancer free."

If attitude dictated the outcome, I'd live another thirty-five years, have a few grandkids, and die a billionaire.

I became silent. I was mentally ready for my pre-op. Parking in the garage, I recalled the time Granville had tracked me here using that GPS he'd secretly installed on my cell phone. I locked my car. Tisha held my hand—like we were a couple on a date—all the way into the doctor's office.

My oncologist said, "I'm glad you're not putting this off any longer. You're doing the right thing for your and your baby's health."

Tisha squeezed my hand like she'd temporarily forgotten about her baby.

Looking at Tisha, the oncologist said, "I'm going to have to ask you to go to the waiting area."

I gripped Tisha's arm. "No, I need her to stay."

"I'm not leaving her," Tisha said, holding me tighter.

The oncologist nodded then. "It's okay, Madison. She can stay. I'll be back in a few minutes."

When the doctor left, my eyes met Tisha's.

"Can you believe we're both pregnant?" she asked. "This could be a good thing."

She didn't have to worry about jeopardizing her baby's life. I did. She wasn't four months yet. I was.

As I was about to comment, the doctor returned. She showed us on the computer where the infected areas were. Fortunately, it hadn't spread to other parts of my body, but I was still having both breasts removed in hopes of the surgeon getting all the cancer. Plus, I didn't want to have to deal with multiple surgeries if my margins weren't clear after the first operation.

There were studies that showed having a lumpectomy was better. Opposing research indicated having a mastectomy was best. No study proved radiation or chemotherapy extended a person's life. I had to make the decision that made me feel most comfortable.

"Assuming your final tests today come back the same, I've already scheduled your procedure for next week."

Tisha went with me to the lab. When we met back with the doctor, we went over every detail. Some twice.

"She'll do everything you said, Doctor. I'll personally hold her to it. I know her tests will be favorable and I'll be back when she checks in for her procedure." Tisha gave me a long, comforting hug.

I needed someone to keep me on track. The drive back to my house was exhausting. Parking in my driveway, I said, "Thanks, girl, for being more of a friend to me than I've been to you."

"No such thing," Tisha said. "I'm just going to see you inside, let you get some rest, and then I'm going home to do the same before my mom drops off the boys. We'll continue our conversation later. Just think—we can raise our babies together."

Pushing my key into the lock, I laughed. It didn't budge. I tried again. "Your locksmith didn't change my locks too, did he?" I asked.

Tisha shook her head, went to her house, and returned with her duplicate set of my keys. Hers didn't work either.

I phoned my dad.

"Hey, sweetheart, where are you? How was your visit this time?" he asked, laughing.

"Daddy, I need you to come help me. I can't get into my house."

"Oh, sweetheart. I've been meaning to talk to you about that."

"About what?"

"I, um . . . we . . . Where are you right—"

I yelled, "At my house! All I want to do is get in!"

"Madison, sweetheart, we needed the money to save the company, so I—"

It was like someone pushed a dagger in one ear and out the other. A MUTE button turned on in my brain. I looked at Tisha. "I think my dad sold my house."

"With all your things in it? Don't think the worst. I knew something wasn't right with him but I'm sure he has a reasonable explanation."

"For locking me out of my own house! He can't explain that! He had no—"

"Well, you're right. There is no reasonable explanation. There's a misunderstanding." Frowning, she continued, "He wouldn't sell your house. Hear him out."

I did tear up the power of attorney, didn't I? I couldn't remember. "You'd better pray to God. . . . If you—"

My dad chuckled. "Don't do that. Give me a minute to finish this call. Madison, sweetheart, meet me at my house and I'll explain everything. I should've told you sooner, but I thought you were okay staying with us."

No way in hell was he serious. "You'd better not have my house online as a vacation rental. Don't you do anything else in my name!" I ended the call.

The nerve of him! Who is he with? What is he doing?

Tisha asked, "You don't really believe he's renting your house?"

I tried to unlock the door again. The key did not fit. "I'm not sure, but I'm going to find out."

"Come to my place until you calm down."

"Thanks, but I need to find out if I legally terminated that power of attorney. Right now, I think it's time I go home."

"You sure you want to go to your dad's?" Tisha asked.

"Not to my parents' house. My other house. I am Roosevelt's wife. His house is my house too."

Tisha's eyes grew the size of golf balls. She stared at Loretta's house, then back at me. Her mouth opened, but she didn't speak.

I hugged Tisha, then told her, "Loretta is playing house like we did when we were all six years old. Ken is probably the only man she'll ever get to propose to her, and she ain't nobody's Barbie. I should buy her ass a dollhouse and leave it on her doorstep. Contrary to what some people believe, I love my husband. Honey, he's only got one wife, and I'm all the woman he'll ever need. It's time I start acting like it."

I went to get into my car. Tisha stopped me.

"Madison, please. Come to my house. I don't want you driving while you're upset."

Maybe she was right. I left my car in my driveway and followed Tisha. "I refuse to spend another night at my parents'."

"You're welcome to stay with me as long as you want," she said, unlocking the door.

"I'll stay until I calm down. When I leave, I'm headed to Roosevelt's."

CHAPTER 12

Loretta

"'And you know this . . . man.' "

Leaning into Chicago, I nestled my head between his shoulder and his chest. We'd said it at the same time; then we laughed to the ending of one of our favorite movies. Chris Tucker was hilarious. Each day was a matinee with a different feature. Chicago and I had seen this picture three times since his release from the hospital. Laughter was healing and I loved the sweet sound of his hearty projection. I was so in love with him, a simple touch could give me a subtle orgasm.

I wished Madison knew that he was enjoying *Friday.* Or that I'd created Chicago's new preferred dish—stuffed chicken breast with Italian bread crumbs, mushrooms, and cheese, topped with a garlic creamy lump crabmeat wine sauce.

Their honeymoon destination had been a five-star resort in Bora Bora, but being here in Houston with Chicago was paradise. He'd reserved a bungalow with a glass bottom, where they could plunge directly into a pool and skinny-dip in the ocean water. A private yacht would've taken them on a cruise, where they would sip champagne and enjoy caviar. Roosevelt couldn't get a refund so I prayed one day he'd invite me to Bora Bora.

There were still times when he'd talk about Madison, but I'd learned how to shorten his words by changing the subject. I'd designed a spiritual, peaceful place he woke up to each morning. I'd brought the aroma of seawater to his daily bath by using soothing scented crystals that soften the water when they dissolved.

Madison's clothes hung in his closet. Her toiletries were on the vanity. Her fragrance was in the mattress when I changed his linen so I sprayed it with Febreze.

Sitting beside Chicago, my happiness faded. I imagined Madison laying on the beach in the sexiest two-piece swimsuit, with a pair of designer sunglasses covering her eyes. Her nails and lips would be painted to perfection; and no matter how hard the wind blew, she'd never have a hair out of place. How did she keep it all together?

"What's wrong?" Chicago asked.

Why did she creep into my mind all the damn time? I had to have this man, not his brother. I was glad Madison had screwed up. If she hadn't, Chicago would've taken her to Bora Bora and there'd be no chance for me to go.

Chaz could afford to take me there. The bungalows over the ocean's blue waters was a place I deserved to vacation but Chaz wasn't romantic. Money hadn't given him the same loving compassion as Chicago.

"Nothing," I lied, forcing the smile I had moments ago.

I picked up the empty popcorn bowl, took it to the kitchen, and rinsed the dirty dishes. Then I placed everything in the dishwasher. Men loved women who cleaned up after them. I bet Madison had never washed his dishes.

"Baby, you need anything?"

Whenever I asked Chicago that question, I prayed that in his heart one day, the answer would be "Yes, I need you, babe."

"I'm good," he said. "You can sleep at Chaz's tonight. I'm healthy enough to be alone. If I need anything, I'll call you guys. You're only a few doors away."

One night could turn into two, three, maybe a week. Eventually he wouldn't need me here at all. If Chicago and I broke our bond, I couldn't explain to my man why I'd prefer to sleep in his brother's guest room. Going to Chaz would make me feel as though I was cheating on Chicago. I had to stay where my heart was.

I knew Chaz had a set of keys to his brother's place, and he could walk in on us at any time. I didn't care about that. I had to make sure my keys to Chicago's condo remained in my possession.

"Okay, baby, I'll be right back," I told Chicago. "I've got to return this call to Raynell and take care of a few things."

My daughter wasn't the person I had to call. It was Raynard. Chicago didn't deserve to hear me talk about another man. Madison had taught me that men, in some ways, were insecure like women. Men didn't like a man's name coming from his woman's mouth, then resonating in his mind.

"Loretta, please stop calling me that," Chicago said. "It feels too intimate hearing you call me 'baby.' Chaz wouldn't like it either. But you don't have to leave to call your daughter. If you need privacy, go in your bedroom."

What difference did it make what I called him? Who did he think helped him to walk normal again on his own? Not his wife. Not his mother. Sure, Helen came by to visit us a few times a week, but she didn't make any attempts to cook or help wipe Chicago's ass when his leg was hurting so bad he could barely move. I wouldn't label Helen as a prima donna, but there were clearly things she was not going to do.

Giving Chicago a half smile, I said, "I have to run a few errands. I'll bring you something back for dinner." Then I left.

I stepped into the hallway. Maybe I was trying too hard. I'd honor his request, praying he'd eventually call me "baby."

Waiting for the valet at Chicago's condominium to get my car, I called Raynard.

"It's about time," he answered. "You done kissing Chicago's ass? You think his brother is going to marry you because you're playing nurse? You need to come and get your daughter. We—I mean, she misses you."

There was no need to be arguing with him. "I'm headed to the Galleria. I have to pick up a few things. Can you meet me at Bar 12 by 51Fifteen in two hours?"

"What? You're his personal assistant too? You've got to do his shopping? I'm buying for Raynell while you're spending money on another man."

His assumption was just that. "Two hours exactly, Raynard," I said, then hung up.

My cell immediately rang again. I answered, "What, Raynard?"

"It's not Raynard, bitch. It's his wife. You need to come pick up your whining-ass kid. I'm tired of taking care of her. I'm not her mother. You are."

Oh, she doesn't have a problem with Raynard taking care of her kid, but she has a problem with him taking care of mine. What if something happened to me and they had to rear my daughter. I knew that would never be the case, unless I died, but it wasn't going to kill Gloria and Raynard to keep Raynell a little longer.

"Give me my phone, Gloria!" Raynard shouted.

"Hell no! That bitch needs to come now! I ain't no damn nanny."

School was over. I wondered where Raynell was. Listening closely, I didn't hear her or Raynard Jr. in the background. The argument transitioned between Gloria and Raynard. I hung up again. If I got another call from his number, I was not answering.

Parking in the garage at the Galleria mall, I made my way to Nordstrom's and shopped for men's exotic underwear for Chicago. Wasn't as though I was directly spending my money. He'd compensated me generously with a hundred grand for taking a temporary leave of absence from my job to care for him. My supervisor was the biggest Houston's football fan. She liked Chicago and told me, "Take as much time as you need. Your job is secure."

I was sure she didn't mean take forever, but if Chicago asked me to marry him, I could quit. If Chicago didn't need me any longer, I'd have to go back before I was ready.

The reason I had to get Chicago new underwear was I was throwing away the old pairs. I didn't want him wearing the ones Madison had bought or any pair he'd worn for her, which was probably all of them. In my position Madison would do the same.

Saks men's department on the top floor was my last stop. I had everything gift wrapped and placed in a big tote bag so Raynard couldn't see what I'd bought.

I ordered a glass of Deep Sea Chardonnay; then I texted Chicago: Would you like the bacon, egg, and cheeseburger from Bar 12?

If Raynard wasn't here in twenty minutes, then I'd order to go so I could get back home to Chicago.

He responded: That sounds great! Have the bun wrapped separately so it doesn't get soggy.

In my mind I added "baby" to the end of his text.

"What's up, Loretta?" Raynard said, approaching the bar.

Happy to see he hadn't brought our daughter, I scooted to the right side of my bar seat as he pulled out a stool and sat to my left.

"Look," he said, staring at me with narrowed eyes, "I don't want to go through with this custody battle, but you need to be realistic."

"What would you like to drink, sir?" the waitress asked.

"I'll have what she's having."

Hadn't heard him say that in years. Before Raynell was born, I used to love this man more than I loved myself. Now he was sitting one foot in front of me and I prayed neither his leg nor hand touched mine.

If we didn't have a baby together . . . I wished I were pregnant with Chicago's baby. I laughed to myself. Now that would be an immaculate conception. I'd seen Chicago naked, sexed him in my dreams until I came, but I'd never felt him deep inside me. Not yet. But if Chicago gave me that opportunity, I was opening wide, taking him all in, and praying to have his child.

"Raynard, stop acting like you want custody. Admit it. Gloria is making you drop the case."

"What difference does that make? Bottom line—you need to come get her. When Gloria ain't happy, nobody is happy, and that includes Raynell. She cries for you all the time."

"You're her daddy. I know you're not telling me you can't stand up to your wife to protect your child. Oh, that's right. How could I forget? You're the same man who still hasn't given me closure on our relationship. Maybe if I was a bitch like your precious Gloria, we wouldn't be having this conversation."

Raynard scanned the bar. "Loretta, please. Keep your voice down. Why you running around caring for a man who has a wife, when you supposedly got a man? Things were perfect before you got involved with this dude. Now you're putting dick before your daughter?"

I almost choked on my wine. "My daughter? Mine? That's just it. Maybe you need to keep her for a year and see how it feels to have to plan your life around your kid. Excuse me, waitress."

"Yes."

I ordered Chicago's burger and said, "I'll also have the ceviche to go."

"Like that, Loretta? You cutting me short?"

"This ain't about you! You've had a long enough break playing part-time daddy every other weekend, don't you think? I'll let you know when I'm ready to get Raynell. She's six and you have her seventy-eight days a year. Three hundred sixty-five days minus your time, and I have her how long? You do the math. And if Gloria does anything to hurt, as you said, *my* daughter, I will come to your house," I whispered in his ear, "and pistol beat her butt first, then yours."

Raynard drank most of his wine, paid for his drink, and then said, "You have to get a gun first."

I tipped my glass toward his ass as I watched him leave.

CHAPTER 13

Johnny

"You'd better not have my house online as a vacation rental. . . ." Blah, blah. What was Madison going to do if I did? Tell her mommy?

Knowing my daughter, she wasn't sitting in her car outside her home waiting for me to show up.

"I told you to be quiet when I answer my phone. Playtime is over, honey cakes. I've got to go check on my sweetheart's house." I had to make sure Madison hadn't had her locks replaced.

If she had, that would be a violation of my agreement with my frat brother. Madison could lose her home and I'd still have to pay him back. I promised to leave everything "as is" until I repaid him in full. Right now, I owed more than I owned, and I had no idea how I was going to settle my loans without getting into deeper debt. Utilizing Chicago's resources was my best recourse, and my daughter was my biggest obstacle.

I'd admit that sex influenced bad decisions. I should've left hours ago when Madison discovered she couldn't get into her home. I was still at the office, lounging in what used to be hers. Now it was mine again. Should've never given it up completely. I'd left the furniture and paintings she had and added an executive leather sofa-sleeper for my sexcapades.

Monica, the receptionist whom Madison had hired, was sent home early. Whenever I had my personal assistant come by, there was no need to have two women on payroll, when only one was putting out.

"Aw, come on, Johnny. Her house isn't a trailer. It's not going anywhere. Let me suck your dick one more time," the pretty young thang said, moaning and begging at the same time. She got on her knees, then looked up at me with those beautiful brown eyes.

For the love of money, fame, or material things, all a man had to do to keep a mistress happy was give her what she desired. If a woman said, "All I want is you," she was a liar. That was why I made sure my PAs didn't expect me to leave my wife. We had a business arrangement with a signed nondisclosure clause that if she breached our confidentiality agreement—which included telling her friends or my wife—I had the right to sue her. Her salary, her gifts, I wouldn't hesitate to take all that I'd given her back, plus whatever else she owned.

Johnny might be old, but I ain't slow.

The naivety of a twenty-two-year-old who hadn't gone to college or been outside of Texas was beneficial in some ways. To them, $20,000 a year was a lot. I'd spent more than that on vacation. What I loved about my tender was there were no wrinkles on her face or between her legs. No gray pubic hairs. Her breasts didn't require help from a bra to stand out. The youthfulness of a woman made old men like me feel rich beyond money. I guess mature women didn't need that kind of comfort from a younger man.

Rosalee hadn't completely given up on pleasuring me, but I could see she was content with having very little sex. I was not. Should've made her sign a contract before we got married, promising to give it to me whenever I asked. She didn't care to do it more than twice a month. How does a woman go from every day, to a few days a week, to once a week, then to twice a month? Soon I won't be having sex with my wife at all. She was too old to blame it on menopause and I too frisky to be faithful.

I wanted to slow screw until the day I died. Having a heart attack while ejaculating inside a young vagina, with a stiff one, wasn't a bad way to go. Embarrassing maybe. Divorcing my wife was never happening. I didn't want to croak from a broken heart or leave the person who had been by my side when I didn't have a dime. Retiring from fucking wasn't happening either.

Leaning back on the sofa spreading my thighs, I watched my PA wrap her thick, lovely lips around my dick. "Damn." What man wouldn't want this? "Lick it for me." *Keep this up and I'ma have to pull out this bed.*

Her pretty smooth tongue extended. Opening wide, she pressed the tip against my balls; then she slowly wiggled up my hard shaft. She went back to my nuts, licking her way to the top this time. Plunging downward, her mouth twisted side to side. Then she moved up and down, massaging me with the insides of her jaws.

"Go a little slower, but not too slow." Even if I never came, the sensation was so incredibly amazing. It felt orgasmic.

Her head bobbed, knocking her throat against the top of my dick while her lips landed next to my balls. Every businessman should have a personal assistant and her only job should be to pleasure him. American entrepreneurs could learn a thing or two from men in other countries and how women service them during meetings. Blowjobs. Hand jobs. Those guys received pleasure while talking business.

Pulling out, I said, "Save some for tomorrow. Go get me a hot towel." The private restroom was adjoined to my office.

She stood, then wiped her mouth. Jiggling her breasts before buttoning her blouse, she said, "Okay. But when I get back, I want to know why you sold your daughter's house."

That's what I get for talking freely in the presence of this girl. I waited for her to return, and then I explained. "I didn't sell her house. I used it as collateral for a business loan. I temporarily had to give up possession, but no one is living in my daughter's house. Once the loan is repaid, she'll get it back. It's leveraging."

Gently cleansing me off, she said, "Well, when I did a title loan against my car, I got to keep my car. Since you're giving free rides, if you want to *leverage* Madison's Ferrari, I'll gladly enjoy that."

Nothing in life was free. People who expected handouts without earning theirs should play the lottery. I was already paying this girl for sex. I wasn't going to waste time getting her to understand the value of bargaining, especially when she had nothing left to barter. Every woman had a pussy, and most foolishly gave it away for free.

The movement of the towel felt good. Having her hands on my manhood made my erection overshadow what was coming out of her mouth. If I didn't have to leave, I'd stick my dick between her lips just to shut her up. The Cialis was kicking back in. Kissing the head, she dried me off.

Pulling away, I squeezed my shaft to make it contract. "The problem is, you can't afford the insurance, let alone the cost of a luxury automobile, my dear. If you could, you wouldn't be my personal assistant," I said, buckling my pants. "Stay out of grown folks' business."

Women with money didn't compromise themselves for a few dollars. That was why I made sure Madison had the best of everything growing up. Money attracted money. Wealthy, beautiful women attracted rich men—the kind of men who would put a ring on her finger. This young girl would have to suck a lot more dicks before she realized no man would walk down the aisle with an underachieving girl who would suck a dick for a dollar.

"I'm smarter than you think."

I didn't doubt she was telling the truth. Her being smarter than I believed she was didn't take much. Most women thought they were more intelligent than men. Some were. But not this one.

"And I'm more successful than you'll ever be. Be quiet, get dressed, and let yourself out. In that order."

After my PA left, I sat thinking how I could get a sweet six figures for Madison's car. Pounding my fist on the desk, I said, "If she would've left the damn country like I'd told her to . . ."

Women.

If not for me, Madison wouldn't have that mansion. I bought her that convertible Spider. I couldn't afford to let my business fail. My daughter was indebted to me. Pawning her property wasn't going to generate enough income to solve our financial problems but it did provide temporary relief. Her husband was my only viable option.

If Chicago didn't die, I might have to find a way to kill him.

CHAPTER 14

Madison

The valet attendant where Roosevelt lived approached my car. I handed him the keys, entered the building, and bypassed the concierge counter. My timing was impeccable. The huge frosted double doors, which provided authorized access only, parted as someone exited.

"Excuse me, Mrs. Tyler," the doorman said, following me to the elevators. "You need to come back and wait until I phone Mr. DuBois."

"What you need to do is show respect. And get it right. I'm *Mrs.* DuBois. Not Ms. or Mrs. Tyler," I said, flashing my wedding ring. "I have a legal right to be here, and if you," I said, pointing at him as I entered the elevator, "value your job, I suggest you get back to work and add my name to the list of owners."

How I missed being the boss at the office. In time I'd return and take over. I didn't get to where I was by asking for permission or letting men dictate to me. As I exited the elevator, my finger traveled toward the door and stopped fractions of an inch from the buzzer. I hadn't come this far to give advance notice.

Roosevelt was truly the best man I ever had. I never stopped loving my husband. Maybe I should thank my dad for giving me a reason to stop prolonging coming back to Roosevelt. I prayed that when I looked into his eyes, I would see that his feelings for me were the same as when we stood at the altar exchanging our vows. That would let me know that I was forgiven for all that had happened at and after our reception.

Hoping he hadn't changed the lock, I inserted my key to Roosevelt's condo. It fit perfectly. Quietly I entered and stood in the foyer. There were so many candles on the dining, coffee, and end tables, as well as the kitchen granite countertop, I flipped the switch to make sure his electricity was working.

"Hey, where's the beef?" Roosevelt asked from his—make that *our*—bedroom.

I didn't respond. I got a bottle of champagne from the refrigerator, two glasses from the cabinet, and filled each flute.

"Hey . . ." Roosevelt stood still when he saw me. Whatever words that were probably intended for Loretta became lodged in his throat.

Firmly I told him, "We need to talk."

I walked up to my husband. He looked amazing, like none of those bullets had penetrated him. I wanted to see his naked body. Kiss his wounds, wherever they were. When was the last time I'd made love to this irresistibly gorgeous man? I craved Roosevelt's stiff manhood sliding inside me. Making love one last time while I had my real breasts was what I needed. I took a deep breath.

"You need to leave," he said.

Handing him a glass, I put it in his hand. "If you let go, it'll be your fault. I'm not going until I get ready."

Holding the flute, he turned away. "Madison, don't make me do something I'll regret. I don't care why you came but you can't stay here."

From the side I saw the tears filling his eyes. He blinked several times, then swallowed. I wanted to walk to him, stand behind him, lean my head against his back, and hold him. Tell him to let it all out. We were going to be okay.

Instead, I said, "Why? Because Loretta is playing housewife? You're my husband, Roosevelt. And *I'm* your wife. That's why I'm here."

He sat on a bar stool facing the kitchen. He placed his flute down on the counter, then pushed it away as though I might have poisoned his drink. I wouldn't do that to my husband.

"Honey, all of this is a misunderstanding. It's Loretta's fault. She—"

Roosevelt stood and thrust his fist forward. Then he jabbed the other. Back and forth he boxed the air in front of his face as he said, "She what? Stayed at the hospital every day until I came home . . . or she helped me through recovery when I didn't know where the fuck my wife was or what man she was fucking!"

In midstream of the next punch, he pulled back and grabbed his shoulder. He smacked the bar stool, sending it crashing to the floor. He slapped the flute across the kitchen. I watched it shatter against the stainless-steel refrigerator.

That's right. Get it all out.

He had every right to be upset. But until he knew the entire story, his conclusions were premature.

"Baby, I'm home. I brought you"—Loretta paused—"What is she doing here?"

Roosevelt said, "Leave the door open. She's on her way out."

Touching my stomach, I said, "I told you, I leave when I get ready." I sat on the leather sofa, picked up the remote, and then turned on the television. Pressing the mute button, I slowly sipped my champagne.

Loretta took the glass from my hand; then she stood over me. "Madison, Chicago is right. You need to go. *Now.* If you don't get up and get out, I'll be forced to call the police."

I scanned the stations, not caring what was on. "And tell them what, Loretta? That you wish my husband were yours? That you're so desperate to have a man, you've abandoned your daughter. That you"—I stood in front of her face, yelling—"don't live here! I do! This is my house! And my husband! And you're the one leaving!"

Touching my stomach again, I leaned forward a little. There was nothing wrong. I did it to gain Roosevelt's compassion. Carefully stepping over the broken glass, I picked up the bottle, filled another flute with champagne, and then sat on the couch. Roosevelt picked up his stool; then he sat on the sofa beside me.

He took my glass and asked, "What do you want from me, Madison? I gave you every ounce of my love and you signed those papers and had me taken off of the respirator. You wanted me to die. But God had a different plan."

Even I couldn't argue that point.

"Amen, thank You, Jesus," Loretta said. "Hallelujah!"

I ignored her performance and responded to my husband. Softly, I said, "Baby, it was time for you to breathe on your own. I did that because I love you. Not because I wanted you to die." Shamelessly, I took part of the credit for my husband's survival. "You could thank me for your recovery. If I'd left you on that machine, you might still be there."

"Madison, you are full of shit!" Loretta said, standing behind us.

The hate that was heading in her direction had arrived. "Really, bitch. Really?" I turned and looked over my shoulder at her. "You tell Roosevelt about the bet you made me? Tell him the truth about why you dragged me off the dance floor at Tisha's wedding reception right after he'd proposed to me. If it weren't for your jealous ass, none of this shit would've happened."

Her jaw got tight. Eyes narrowed. Where were her Hallelujahs now?

"For real, Loretta? What is Madison talking about?" Roosevelt asked.

Suddenly Loretta wasn't so boisterous. "Nothing," she said.

"That's a damn lie to deal with on another day, bitch, but right now you're the one who needs to get out!"

"Madison, please stop calling her that."

"Fuck that bitch! She walk up in here, calling my husband 'baby,' and I'm supposed to be nice. And you let her call you that! What the two of you got going on?"

Roosevelt shook his head; then he held my hand. "Nothing. I don't want her."

I darted my eyes at Loretta, then winked. *Bitch, you are about to strike and get kicked the hell out.*

"Roosevelt, I didn't know how to cope with my problems and be there for you at the same time. And even when I did want to come see you, I wouldn't come to your room because she"—I pointed at Loretta—"would never leave your side. Feeling guilty, Loretta?" I asked, then added, "For being the real reason my husband was shot."

Oh, she was getting her just due: one slap in the face at a time.

Loretta stormed into Roosevelt's bedroom. "Don't sit your ass down in there!" I yelled to her. "Pack your shit, bitch!"

Roosevelt shook his head. "We don't sleep in the same room. She sleeps in the guest room," he said. "She's not going anywhere. Finish what you got to say, so you can go."

I forced tears to my eyes, but I didn't sniff. I stared at the television, then at him. "Roosevelt, I have stage-two breast cancer in both breasts. I'm sure Loretta didn't tell you. I couldn't bother you with my problems while you were recovering. I did what I thought was best. I can't blame you if you don't support me. I didn't want you to die, but knowing I might not have long to live, baby, I wasn't in my right mind. You know I'd never do anything to hurt you."

Loretta walked a straight line from Roosevelt's bedroom to the guest room. En route she said, "Give it a break, Madison. You and your daddy wanted him to die so y'all could get his money." She shut the door to the guest bedroom.

"I'm so damn confused right now," Roosevelt said, scooting away from me.

This wasn't about Loretta, and I wasn't going to let her interrupt my conversation with my husband. Loretta had made it harder for me to tell Roosevelt that my father had leveraged my house and I didn't want to stay at a hotel or at my parents'. Basically, I had no place else to go except for Tisha's, and I didn't want to be there. Every house didn't feel homey, even if it was your best friend's.

I moved closer to him. "Loretta is jealous. She'll say whatever she thinks will divide us. Now that we're back together, we can't let that happen."

He held my hand gently. "Madison, you went about this whole thing wrong. You should've told me everything."

"Told you when? Told you what? I wasn't the woman you fell in love with? My perfect body was not perfect. That I have to have the boobs you love chopped off, and I might die before our baby is born? What was I to say?"

Tears fell from Roosevelt's eyes. This was the time to let mine fall too.

"Don't say that. I love you for more than your body. I wish you would've told me, baby." Roosevelt wrapped his arms around me.

Softly I said, "She needs to go. I'm home now."

CHAPTER 15

Granville

This was not a vacation resort. Prison was not going to be my residence for the next twenty-five–plus years.

The judge forced some counsel upon me. I could've nipped and tucked my case away without going to trial and been on my way home to sleep in my bed. But *noooo,* she had to do it by the book.

G-double-A told me not to worry, that I should be glad that they hadn't thrown everything at me. He said, "Stop looking a gift horse in the mouth." I wasn't sure exactly what he meant by that. I heard my mom say it too. "Granville, they could've charged you for every person at the reception."

How was that? I didn't have enough bullets. Wasn't like I had a semiautomatic weapon. I had a little snub-nosed revolver. But no one could prove that, 'cause they hadn't found it.

Somebody had to be held accountable for Chicago being shot. They'd come to the conclusion that I should be charged with two counts of assault with a deadly weapon and two counts of attempt to commit first-degree murder because two shots missed Chicago and his brother, and the other three hit Chicago. I told G-double-A, "It should've been five charges. They can't even count."

He explained, "Dude, they charge you by the person, not the number of bullets."

So I could've fired a million times on one person and get charged once? Or the five shots could've landed me two hundred and fifty charges. That didn't make no damn sense. Two people meant I should've had two charges, not four. Right?

It's all bullshit! Now I had to sit across from this prosecutor dude, who probably didn't know much more than I did about the law, and listen to him try to get me convicted. I wasn't impressed with his stack of papers on his table.

My appointed counsel said, "Your Honor, my client pleads not guilty on all four counts."

Sitting in front of the judge, I was dressed in an orange jumpsuit; I hoped she found me attractive. I'd let the prison barber trim my hair and shave my face extra clean. I figured the judge would see I didn't belong behind bars and she'd have a change of heart. Wish I'd had some cologne. A good-smelling man always aroused women.

I stared at my short, young black lawyer. Doubted if he was thirty yet. Dressed in a dark suit, white button-down shirt, a skinny blue striped tie, and some weird black leather shoes, he stood beside me. The prosecutor had on a gray loose-fitted suit, with cheap black-looking shoes that made me uncomfortable. He must've lost a lot of cases to have to dress like that.

I knew I could represent myself better than the dude they'd given me. I spoke up. "Excuse me, Your Honor. Besides the fact that I'm innocent, I don't understand why I'm being charged with four counts. Wasn't but two people in the pool that I allegedly shot at."

They used the *a* word a lot. Figured I'd use allegedly too.

She was beautiful. Her full lips were coated with a chocolate lipstick. Her hair covered her ears, but it didn't touch her shoulders. I wondered what she was wearing under her black robe. Maybe, no panties. What lucky guy was hitting that? Or was she one of them pussy-licking judges? I wanted to unzip that cape, wrap it around my shoulders, and impress her with what Madison had taught me about how to eat pussy.

Trace the capital letters of the alphabet with my tongue. Always lick and suck the clit between letters. All these years I had no idea it was that easy to please a woman with my mouth.

"Mr. Washington, be quiet. You are not allowed to speak to me unless I ask you to."

Some of the inmates on my unit said that during visitation the room was so crowded on the weekends that they actually got to stick their dicks in their girlfriends long enough to bust one. Madison would never let me do that to her. Precious would, if I could figure out how to do it.

My brows drew together. I didn't empty the thirty-eight snub. I only hit him three, actually two times. The bullet that grazed his shoulder shouldn't count. I wasn't trying to shoot him at all. Well, that was a lie, but I didn't have a clear shot at him after he jumped into the pool. Why was she counting the fact that his brother jumped in the water too? This should be a mistrial.

The judge said, "Your trial is scheduled thirty days from today." She looked at her courtroom assistant and asked, "What day is that?"

"Your Honor, why so long? Can't we get together before then?"

My attorney shook his head when he should've been nodding. Wasn't like he was the one locked up. I asked him, "You wanna trade places, bro?"

"Mr. Washington, let your attorney represent you. It's not my job to explain to you what you don't understand." She banged her gavel, then said, "Next case, *Hernandez* versus *Perez*."

Tilting my head side to side, I mumbled, "It's not my job to explain to you what you don't understand." Then I asked, "Your Honor, what about the gun? They find it yet?"

"Get him out of here," she said, banging that gavel like she was upset.

"What about bail? How much is it again? Can you reduce it?"

"Out!" she said, then banged harder.

I thought she was going to break the handle on that wooden thing. I knew when a woman had had enough.

My attorney said, "Your Honor, may I have a few minutes with my client?"

Snapping my teeth at him, I said, "You're fired, dude! I'm going to represent myself."

The judge mumbled, "Heaven help us all."

Forget her. I turned toward the door, then looked to my left. I didn't know they'd come. Mom was seated in the first row with Beaux. Her white dress was pretty, but she'd lost weight the two months I'd been in here. Now she had to wait another month for my trial. Four weeks might not be enough time for me to get my case together. I should've asked for ninety days. G-double-A was going to probably charge me extra if he had to rush.

I hope I wasn't the reason Mom was melting away. Stress had shed a few pounds off me; and that was hard to do, since I was mostly muscle. I knew I'd just fired him, but I whispered to my attorney, "Can I see my mother and my brother for a few minutes?"

My attorney whispered to the deputy.

"I'll check with the judge," the deputy responded, leaving me in a small, cold room, which was hidden from the people inside the courtroom.

Guess that meant "no." Just like Loretta and Madison, that judge hated me, and she didn't even know me. An armed guard kept watch over me. Just like the rest of the world, people went about their day, not caring about me. I was human too.

I was shocked when the deputy returned with Mom and Beaux. "Ten minutes," he said, then left us with the guard.

"Granville, what have you gotten yourself into, baby?" Mom asked, opening her arms.

Placing his arm between us, the guard said, "Excuse me, Mrs. Sarah Lee. You can give him a quick hug now, and another brief hug at the end. Same for you," he said, looking at Beaux. "No touching is allowed during the visit."

Mom's eyelids lowered halfway. It was good to see her.

"When I get out, I want some fried catfish, Mama," I said, trying to cheer her up.

"Oh, Granville."

"It's okay, Mama. I have to follow their rules until I get out. I'm innocent. I got me an in-house lawyer, who ended up on the wrong side of the law. I'ma win this case."

Beaux shook his head, then nodded toward the guard. What did I have to lose? That guard wasn't defending me.

"I think that dude is taking you," Beaux said.

"You just keep sending his family what I tell you. He's legit." If my hands weren't cuffed behind my back, I'd swing on him. "How you doing, Mama? You don't look so good." I knew what would make her smile. I said, "I'll be home for Halloween for the birth of your first grandchild." My lips curved so far, my face hurt.

Mom was quiet.

Beaux said, "Mom has the big C. We need you to get out soon." My brother's eyes locked with mine. "Soon, bro."

Fuck! When did they find that out? I hadn't been in *that* long. My eyes filled with tears. I wanted to pick up my chair and slam it against the floor until there was nothing left in my hands but the metal bar that the seat was attached to. My fingers curled into fists, the way they used to when Beaux and I fought—except this time they were ten times tighter. I didn't want Mom to see me cry, but I'd cried every night since I'd been locked up. Now I had—but didn't need—another reason to shed tears.

I stood and told the guard what the judge had indicated a few minutes ago. "Get me out of here."

CHAPTER 16

Tisha

Every day I was sick and scared.

This one must be a girl. I was never this ill with either of my boys. Since I'd gone with Madison to her pre-op appointment, I didn't know why, but my stomach ached so bad I couldn't get out of bed.

Crackers didn't help settle or keep anything down. I couldn't feel any worse. I'd started putting the wastebasket next to my nightstand, in case I didn't make it to the bathroom in time to vomit into the toilet. I wished my mother had warned me about the hardship having children could bring, instead of encouraging me to marry my first husband and have her some grandbabies.

I couldn't do this again. It was easy for parents, friends, and strangers to give advice. "Tisha, he's fine. You better say 'yes' to that rich-ass man's proposal." They made it seem like a ring was golden and having a husband was priceless.

I learned that a woman without the ability to make her own decisions would forever live with regrets. She'd wonder what her life could have been if she hadn't listened to . . .

I was heaving over the basket; nothing came up. That's it. I dialed Madison.

She answered, "Hey, hon. How are you?"

I should've asked how she was doing, but I had to let her know.

"I've decided to have the abortion. I'm keeping the appointment I scheduled before I change my mind. Can you go with me?"

Without hesitation she said, "Of course. When?"

"I'm keeping the one I scheduled, in two days. I know your surgery is in three days, so I'm going to ask Loretta too."

"I'll pick you up. Let me call you back and get the details. Bye." Madison ended our call before I could thank her. It was probably my mentioning Loretta that had made her upset. We'd all been friends for thirty years. I had to include Loretta.

I'd promised to take my boys to the local carnival today. They'd gotten up an hour early. Every fifteen minutes they'd peep in to see if I'd gotten out of bed. Not wanting to disappoint my kids, I called their father.

He answered immediately. "Hey, Tisha. Is everything okay?"

That was a valid question. I seldom called him before noon, unless it was important. "Things are fine. Look, I was hoping you could take the boys to the carnival."

"Sure, when?"

My body was weak. I struggled to say, "Today."

"Oh, no, Tish. I can't do it today."

"Then, is tomorrow all right?"

"I'm leaving for Australia in a few days. Taking my soon-to-be fiancée there to propose to her. The last time I was in Sydney, I found the most brilliant pink diamond. Couldn't resist getting it for her."

I leaned over the bucket and heaved. Nothing came up. Why did Lance Thomas have to throw his fiancée in my face? That was probably the only reason he'd answered the phone.

"Never mind."

"You okay?" he asked.

I sat up. "I will be. But you could take a more active role in the boys' lives, Lance."

"If tomorrow isn't good, I can take them next month, when we get back."

"The carnival won't be there when you get back. Why don't you take them to Australia? I need a break."

"I gave you what you wanted. Should've thought about being a single mom before you divorced me. Besides, where's your husband? Let him take them."

That was not his business. "Why do you always say you don't mind doing something with the boys, but then when I ask, you're conveniently too busy to commit?"

"Tisha, I pay you twenty thousand a month. If you need time away from the kids, hire a nanny. Don't question me. Oh, and just a heads-up. I'm filing for a reduction from twenty to ten thousand. You're right. I'll step it up and share more time with my boys, but it's time for your husband to support you."

Support? Alimony from an ex-con without a job was a wish not worth making. I had to make sure my divorce was finalized before Lance filed for a reduction.

My four-year-old walked in with a bowl of Raisin Bran. His brother had a cup of milk in one hand, and a cup of orange juice in the other.

"Morning, Mommy," they said in unison.

"Put everything on the nightstand." I smiled, then switched to speaker. "Say hello to your dad."

Their faces lit with smiles. "Hi, Daddy," they said.

"Hey, guys. I'm coming to get you next month and we can go wherever you want in the world. How's that?" Lance asked.

He could see our kids once a month or twice a year—it didn't matter to the boys. Their daddy could do no wrong. I had them almost every day and though I knew they loved me, it wasn't the same kind of love they had for Lance.

They jumped up and down. "I want to go to Disneyland!"

"Disney World!" our other son shouted.

Lance said, "Disneyland and Disney World it is. I'll arrange it with your mother. Be good. I love you guys. Take good care of your mother. I'll see you next month. Tisha, we'll talk about that financial matter when I get back. Take care of yourself."

Not wanting Lance to hang up on me first, I quickly ended the call as our boys were yelling, "Bye, Daddy!"

Lance gave me the dose of reality that I needed. My mind was made up. The forty-eight hours could not come soon enough. It was hard raising two kids by myself. Although, I'd love to have a daughter, I was not going to be a single mother of three. I refused to have a baby by Darryl and give him a reason to keep begging to come home. Darryl didn't need to know, and he didn't deserve to know I was carrying his child.

Rolling over, I realized this was the hardest decision I'd ever made. I was definitely having an abortion. That was final.

CHAPTER 17

Loretta

Madison was a real *b-i-t-c-h*. She'd coldheartedly ended my honeymoon with Chicago. I was trying to wait her out, but she'd been here with us—all day—for two days. Thank God, her surgery was today, so things between Chicago and me could get back to normal.

I tossed all night in the guest room while she slept in the bed with him. She'd probably thrown out the gift-wrapped packages of underwear I'd spread across his bed the other night.

The few things I had at Chicago's condo, I neatly folded, then packed in my suitcase. Tears soaked into my shirts, pants, and panties. My packing wasn't to appease Madison. She wanted me out before she left for the hospital. Chicago wanted me to stay. Maybe I should embrace my religious principles and let her have her husband for this one day. I could come back tonight.

Just like that. I had nursed him back to health, and she twirled in like a ballerina and swept me under her tutu. Why hadn't God given me a tutu? That way, I could've twirled too. Who was I fooling? I wasn't as graceful a liar as Madison.

I couldn't accept being second to her again. It was time for me to move on, focus on my relationship with Chaz. He'd given me more than ample time to help his brother recover. My loyalty to Chicago made Chaz love me more, but I'd rather be with Chicago if only he would choose me.

If not, there was still an opportunity for me to shine with Chaz and make Madison fade into my shadow. Chaz was doing an excellent job as advisor to Chicago. None of the owners, Chaz, or the fans wanted Chicago replaced. Everyone loved Chicago, but no one loved him more than I did.

My God in heaven, I asked Him aloud, "What's the lesson here?"

I wanted Him to answer me. He didn't. Maybe it was time for me to redirect my affection, accept my perks, and show my face in the GM's suite at our home game later this evening. Perhaps I was looking in the eyes of the wrong man.

I'd dressed in hopes of pissing Madison off and wishing Chicago would give me "the look"—the one that would make Madison jealous. I wasn't sure if seduction was something a woman put on or turned on to get a man's attention.

My jeans weren't the normal ones I'd wear. They were fitted like a second skin. My blue-and-red jersey clung to my breasts. I was sorry Madison was having hers removed today, but mine were healthy, real and perky. I stepped into a pair of three-inch red heels, then fluffed my hair, which was normally pulled back into a ponytail. I stroked on eye-shadow, brushed on mascara, stroked on an extra coat of raspberry lip gloss.

I knocked on Chicago's bedroom door. "I'm getting ready to go."

"Okay. Thanks for everything. You can leave my key on the kitchen counter. I'll call you later," he said.

Really? Like that! I went through all this preparation for him to dismiss me from the other side of his door. I should kick it in.

"Loretta, thanks, girl," Madison said. "We're busy right now, but Tisha and I will meet you at the clinic for Tisha's procedure today."

I'd forgotten about Tisha's appointment. Her abortion was today? *Damn!* That meant Madison's surgery was tomorrow. I had so much to be thankful for; Madison was in bed with Chicago but she should envy me. I did not have to have surgery.

If I walked out Chicago's door, I couldn't stay in the building and go to Chaz's condo. He was probably already at the administration office at the arena handling business; and unlike Chicago, Chaz hadn't given me a key to his place. I had to call before stopping by even when

I was only a few doors away. What was I trying to prove? It was too damn early to be dressed up for a game. I started to feel foolish.

Not ready to leave, I dragged my suitcase back into the bedroom, closed the door, then removed my clothes. The lime green bra and panties looked great, but I should've put on come-fuck-me red. I sat on the edge of the bed and turned on the television.

Knock. Knock. "Loretta, you in there?"

I didn't answer her. I hadn't locked the door.

Knock. Knock. "Loretta, are, you, in there?"

Why should I respond? To give her the answer she wanted? Instead, I started changing channels.

Madison opened the door. I looked toward her, then back at the television.

Softly she said, "Loretta, you were supposed to be gone. Turn off the TV, get dressed, and get out before I throw you out."

I didn't know what made me ignore her. Maybe I wanted Chicago to rescue me? Perhaps I didn't care? But what I hadn't done was move.

"Loretta, I know you heard me."

Silence ended the words coming out of her mouth, until Madison gracefully ushered my four-wheel suitcase out of the room and opened the front door. The sound of her footsteps trailed into the bedroom, then stopped. I sat on the bed with my back to her. What was she going to do?

Ow! My neck snapped backward.

Madison's fists were wrapped around my hair. She dragged me onto the bed. I was at a disadvantage as she stood behind me.

"Bitch, let me go!" I yelled.

"After all the shit you put me through," she said, yanking my hair, "you're lucky I'm pregnant."

I locked my fingers around her wrist, then yelled, "Chicago!"

She snatched my bicep and yanked me from the comforter.

Whack! My hand landed across her pretty, little face. I hope she didn't think I was going to just let her assault me without my fighting back. Now I really hated her.

She snatched my hair again. I wished she had hair long enough for me to do the same, but she didn't.

"Bitch, even if he comes in here, he wouldn't help your ass over me. I don't know what you're trying to prove, Loretta, but you will never be me. If you don't get out of my house, your hair will be in the hallway with your other belongings," she said, slinging me out of the bedroom.

Her strength was unbelievable. It had to come from a place so deep that it resurrected from hell.

The tightening of her grip hurt. I felt strands of my hair detaching from my scalp. Chicago hadn't come to my rescue. It was time to concede before I ended up with a bald spot.

"Fine, Madison. Let me go. I'll leave."

She released her fingers. Strands of my hair were wedged between her fingers. I felt stupid fighting—not because she was pregnant. I contested those *Real Housewives* shows, where women were constantly attacking one another, but now I understood how things could escalate in a matter of seconds.

None of this would've happened if I'd left when she'd shown up. None of this would've happened if I hadn't made that stupid bet.

Wiggling her fingers, Madison sprinkled my hair, letting it fall to the floor. Her face, where I'd hit her, was beet red. I was turning into a person whom God wouldn't approve of. All of this because of a man.

I quietly went into the bedroom, put on my clothes, then stood outside the doorway. As Madison started closing the door, I said, "Oh, don't you want these," holding Chicago's keys in my hand.

"Keep 'em. I'm calling a locksmith." She closed the door.

I hurled the keys against the door, got my suitcase, and stormed toward the elevator. Madison had declared war by putting her hands on me. I was definitely going to get her back.

Heading home, I parked in my driveway. Instead of going inside, I went next door to Tisha's.

Opening the door, she said, "Hey, girl. You're early, but come in. I'm not allowed to have breakfast. If you're hungry, though, I'll fix you something."

I stood in her doorway. "I'm good. I just came by to tell you that I'm not going to the clinic with you. Aborting Darryl's baby is wrong, and your not telling him is worse."

"You have the audacity to pass judgment on me?"

"I'm not judging you. I'm your friend and I'm a Christian. I'm not a hypocrite. And it's not too late to change your mind."

Tisha didn't have to put me out, like Madison had done. I left.

CHAPTER 18

Tisha

Tears filled my eyes when I exhaled. "I appreciate your coming. It means a lot."

Madison sat beside me at the clinic, holding my hand. I wanted my mother here, but I needed her to watch my boys. I'd have lots of time to talk with my mother when Madison took me home. Mom would be staying at my house for a few days to care for us.

The waiting area was full. Abortion was not going to be my form of birth control but I'm glad it was my choice. This was my first and my last pregnancy termination. I was definitely having my tubes tied; until then, I'd use condoms and take birth control pills. I'd gotten rid of my husband, but I wasn't giving up sex with a new man. Nor was I waiting for my divorce to be final before dating.

Men, like my husband, used the reasoning "You're a married woman. You shouldn't be sleeping with another man." They never cared that fidelity didn't apply to them during their marriage. If Darryl's whorish behind tried that line on me, no explanation was warranted. I was so done with Darryl, I wouldn't let him kiss my ass. Didn't want to be that close to him again.

Looking around the room, I had no idea so many women weren't keeping their babies. We all had experiences worth sharing. Maybe I'd write my life story.

Marry Him for Money, Not Love. Since I'd had a rich husband and a poor one, I was wiser. Money was better.

If it weren't for Lance, I wouldn't have a beautiful home that was mortgage free. My kids might have to share clothes, shoes, a bedroom, and a bathroom. Lance could be a better father when it came to sharing time with the boys but I needed to thank him for being an excellent provider.

That should be the boys, Lance, and I vacationing in Sydney. I wondered if his soon-to-be fiancée was black. Was she younger? Prettier? Did she have kids? If so, would Lance do more for her children than he did for his own? Now that I was ending my second marriage, I realized my most memorable moments of our being a family were with Lance, and those times were good.

I had said "I do" to Darryl based on the love I had for him. He never loved me. When I analyzed both relationships, Lance had little time and lots of money. Darryl gave me no time and his butt was broke. My one-way streak of love had come to a dead end for Darryl.

I asked Madison, "You ever think about publishing a tell-all book?" I bet hers would be more exciting than mine.

"Absolutely not. Broke and vindictive women kiss and tell. I ain't there and I never will be that woman. You okay?" she asked, touching my knee.

I couldn't stop my right leg from shaking. I was there for Loretta when Madison wasn't. Was a friend to Madison when Loretta was not. I was always the one accepting my friends for who they were.

Loretta had changed. Regardless of how she felt, she should be here with us. Each time we met, she was different. Like she didn't know who she was anymore. She was vengeful toward Madison. I couldn't say she was "revengeful," because Madison hadn't done any harm to Loretta. Sure, Madison was confident; some would say "arrogant," but she never stopped being a friend to Loretta. Even when she'd refused to drive to Port Arthur to rescue Loretta from Granville, Madison did have a point. Loretta had gotten herself into that mess.

"It's okay to be nervous. You'll be fine," Madison said, drying my tears. "You're making the right decision. Wish I were as brave as you."

"Why did you decide to keep your baby, knowing it might not be Chicago's? What are you going to do if Granville is the father?" I asked.

Madison's eyes filled with tears. It was my turn to return the favor.

She stared straight ahead. I wasn't sure if she saw anything in front of her. Or, perhaps, if she was like me, lost in thoughts so shattering that all she could see were her own thoughts.

Slowly she shook her head; then she said, "I don't know, Tisha. There's a part of me that feels I may not have much time to live. What if my cancer spreads when they start operating on me? Or what if after I have the double mastectomy tomorrow, I won't love myself. I think God is punishing me."

"God wouldn't do that, Madison. Maybe He's testing you. Or blessing you with this baby. Either way, you're the bravest woman I know."

If God's plan was to bring Madison home, perhaps He was blessing Chicago by giving him his firstborn. I prayed my best friend's baby wasn't for Granville. Silently I asked God to forgive me for what I was about to do. Wasn't sure if I could repent in advance for premeditated murder, but I couldn't imagine having a baby by Darryl.

Madison gave a half smile; then she nodded. "I'm either brave or stupid. Guess I'll know for sure in five months."

A woman dressed in white scrubs opened a door beside the check-in desk; then she said, "Tisha Thomas."

Whether I was having a girl or a boy, I would've given the baby my last and Darryl's last names, Thomas Jefferson. A girl named Thomas. She would've been strong. I imagined her skin dark and smooth like mine. Her natural, thick black hair would've been just like mine. I would've homeschooled her, like I was doing with the boys. They knew their alphabets, numbers up to fifty, the multiplication table up to two, could spell and write their names and addresses.

I stood, sniffled, and then swallowed a lump, which hurt my throat. Madison stood and wrapped her arms around me.

"You'll be just fine, Mama. I'll be right here waiting for you."

I kissed my friend on the cheek. "I love you, Madison. Thanks."

Madison whispered, "If friends aren't there when you need them, then why do you need them?"

As I walked through the open door, Madison's words made me think about Loretta.

When the needle for the IV slid into my vein, I questioned, *Should I go through with having this abortion?*

CHAPTER 19

Chicago

Pow!

A bullet raced above my head; the second one was closer. *God, please don't let me die.* I jumped into the pool. My body plunged to the bottom. I fought to stay close to the bottom, beside my brother, Chaz. I didn't inhale. Water invaded my nostrils. I held my breath. Struggling to open my eyes, I couldn't. I jerked, praying I'd awaken before it was too late.

"Wake up."

I heard a voice, felt a hand shaking me. Still, I fought, knowing if I breathed, I'd drown.

"Roosevelt!"

"Huh? What?" Finally my eyes opened. Struggling to slow the rapid beat of my heart, I looked at my wife. She was asleep.

The sheets beneath me felt drenched with sweat. In my dream I floated in a pool filled with my blood. The only one who knew about my nightmares was Loretta, and now Madison.

Pulling back the cover, I sat beside Madison in our bed. She was absolutely the most beautiful woman I'd ever met. That used to apply to both inside and out. Despite her decisions, I still loved this woman with all my heart. I didn't understand why. Maybe God let me live so I'd be here for Madison.

I touched my sheets. They were dry. I leaned my back against the headboard. When I lay down to sleep, strange things came to life. Reality and fiction crisscrossed in my mind. My dreams at times seemed real. And what I thought was happening while I was awake was a flashback to when I was shot.

Madison mumbled, "I'm so tired," then added, "And scared."

I knew what it felt like to be afraid—to have a machine breathing for you. Madison would be on oxygen during her surgery. If all went well, they'd take her off the same day. It was more of a precaution for her. They weren't sure when they unplugged my respirator if I'd make it.

First I felt sweat, not everything is dry. I was alive, but I wasn't sure if I was awake. I touched my arms, then slapped my face. Yes, I was awake.

I didn't have to go under the knife and have body parts removed, like Madison would. But would we both be in shock when we saw her breasts were gone? For me, they took out one bullet, left one in, and the other one grazed me.

Was I being selfish to ask Madison to wake up because I needed to talk? What if the worst happened and she didn't make it?

"Baby, we need to talk," I said, nudging her. "It won't take long, baby. I need your attention."

"Okay," she said, propping herself up next to me.

I kissed her. She hugged me. My manhood crept down my thigh. Yes, I was definitely awake.

Except for her slightly protruding stomach, Madison's body was the same as the day I'd met her. She was four months. In five more months the kid would be here.

Staring into her eyes, I had to ask, "Madison, do you love me?"

Softly she exhaled. "Of course I love you."

"Are you sure?"

"Roosevelt, please. Just say what you have to say. I was up late last night with Tisha and—"

"I know, baby."

At least, Madison hadn't told me she aborted the baby inside her. If Darryl ever found out what Tisha had done, he'd have a right to be pissed; but he didn't have the right to make her suffer a lifetime if he wasn't going to do his part as a parent.

I wasn't upset, but I might be the biggest fool for what I was about to say. In my heart I had to ask her what she didn't ask me. "What do you need me to do for you while you're in the hospital? What are your final wishes? I mean, if you're placed on life support or a breathing machine, what do you want me to do?"

She kissed my lips. "I'm not sure."

Her answer wasn't helpful. "I don't want to decide for you. I pray I don't have to, but what if?"

She whispered, "Let me die. Promise to love our baby the way you love me. And I'll smile down from wherever I am. Roosevelt, I don't deserve you. We both know that."

I agreed. I deserved better. Just like in football, I knew teams never got what they deserved. They got what they earned. I wanted to give Madison the chance to win back my love while I was still in love with her. There was no way I could abandon my wife in her greatest time of need. I wanted her to fight for our marriage.

"But what about the baby? We have an obligation to make sure the baby is okay. What if they ask me to save you or the child? Then what?"

"Keep me alive long enough to . . . save the baby," she said as though she wished she were dead already.

What about me? Why didn't she choose to live? We could have another child.

"I was going to wait to bring this up, but I know your dad's company isn't doing well."

For the first time she looked into my eyes. "How do you know that?"

When I was in the hospital being taken off the respirator, my brother had told me, "Madison and her dad were asked by a news reporter if she married you for your money to save her dad's company. Chaz made a few calls and found that was true. Wanna tell me what's going on?"

Chaz was doing an awesome job, but I was getting bored sitting around my condo advising him. Once I was sure that Madison was fine, I was going back to work full-time. I wanted to be on the road with the team, but I had to make sure she . . . My thoughts went in a different direction with another question, which I wasn't ready to know the answer to.

"I don't want you to worry. I'll give your dad a call and meet with him. Whatever he needs, I'm sure I can help him out."

"I don't know, Roosevelt. I'm afraid my dad has dug a hole so deep, we'll never recover."

"Nonsense. That's like saying you've fallen and you won't get up. Setbacks are a part of business. I'll meet with him. Go back to sleep."

I wanted to ask Madison if the baby inside her was mine. Only God knew the answer, and the Christian in me didn't want to mistreat Madison. I'd wait to find out. Either way, I had to consult with my attorney on my next moves.

Kissing Madison softly on the lips, I told her, "Whatever you need, I'll take care of it, and you."

Madison softly said, "Roosevelt."

"Yes."

"Make love to me like it's our last time. I want to feel like a complete woman. One. Last. Time."

The last time we were sexual was before the reception. We'd stopped at Madison's after the wedding to change clothes for the reception. We were already late, so I had settled for a quickie. This time I was in no hurry.

Gazing into her eyes, I pressed my lips to hers and held them there. Then I told her, "I love you."

I trailed kisses to her ear; then I stuck my tongue inside. Her hands firmly embraced me. When she touched my dick, I moved her hand.

"Let me do what you asked."

Trailing kisses from her neck, I stopped above her collarbone and made a liquid necklace with the tip of my tongue. From her throat to her cleavage, I planted my lips, never letting them leave her body.

I gripped those hips, which rode me so well; the thought almost made me cum. I gently pulled her onto her back, centering her in the bed. My fingertip traveled to her Brazilian; then I made her pubic area my canvas. My tongue was the brush. I didn't wait for my saliva to dry. I cupped my mouth over her clit to keep her wet.

Just the way she liked it, I didn't suction the "little man" out of the boat. I lightly rubbed the tip of my tongue in upward strokes.

"Oh, baby. That feels so good."

Hearing Madison moan made precum ooze from my dick onto the

sheets. This wasn't about me, so I refocused. It was time to tug at the man in the boat. Not hard enough to pull him out. I softly sucked, pulling my wife to the edge of climaxing.

The "oohs," alternating with the "aahs," grew louder and closer together.

I inserted my middle finger into her vagina. It was tight, hot, and juicy. I had to taste her fluids. Placing my finger in my mouth, I savored her flavor. I'd almost forgotten how sweet she was.

Madison moaned, "Make me squirt."

Easing my finger back inside her walls, I slowly rotated the tip in small circles against her G-spot. Starting over, I pressed the tip of my tongue to her clit. Short, light, upward strokes grew into suctioning the little man. While applying more pressure to the G-spot to stimulate filling her reservoir with the fluids that would soon eject from her urethra, I never let my mouth leave her clit.

"Oh, my God!" she screamed, showering me. When she stopped screaming, her body rested heavily against the mattress.

I didn't stop pleasing her. I passionately caressed her breasts. Lightly brushing my hands around her beautiful, plump mounds, I swept back and forth across her nipples. I didn't pinch them, because I wasn't sure if that would hurt.

Instead, I kissed my wife's breasts until she cried.

CHAPTER 20

Johnny

"I'll meet you there, honey."

Rosalee was dressed and ready to head out hours before Madison was scheduled to go under the knife this morning. I had professional situations to tend to first. Sitting at a hospital, waiting until the surgery was over, wasn't going to benefit us. If something went wrong, there was nothing we could do to fix it. I was starting to feel that no matter what I did, losing my company was inevitable. But I had to keep trying.

My wife commanded, "Johnny, business can wait. I need you, and Madison needs us. Let's go."

I kissed her lips. "I'll be there before she gets out of surgery. Promise. You'd better get going before neither one of us is there for her."

Waiting for my wife to drive away in her Mercedes, I headed in the opposite direction in my Porsche. I stopped at a corner bakery café.

"I'll have a large coffee." Leaving the lid off, I sat alone, away from others.

Facing the window, I hung my head. Men weren't supposed to cry. That was my only child, my baby girl, my sweetheart. Tears fell into my cup. Family could forgive one another for failures, but death was final. I had to call Madison.

"Hey, Papa. Where are you? Mama said you weren't coming."

Damn that Rosalee. She couldn't wait and let me tell Madison.

"I'll be there. Don't worry. Your mother should be there any minute. Have you and Chicago left yet?"

"We're walking out now."

"I promise you, my face will be one of the first you'll see when you wake up. I love you."

"I love you too, Papa."

"Bye, sweetheart."

Leaving my cup on the table, I went to my car. I placed my hands on the roof and buried my face. This time I cried like a baby. It felt strange. I stopped, dried my eyes, and sat behind the wheel. Convinced myself all would be well. My wife had survived forty years cancer free.

At the pace Rosalee was moving healthwise, she'd outlive me. If she found out I was back to my old ways, she'd kill me.

I loved Madison, but there were times I wished she were a boy. Men related differently. When it didn't have to do with our woman, we were strong. We understood the predator that lived within us. And every predator had to have prey. Women wanted to save every living soul.

Parking in a space reserved for future homeowners, I saw that Madison was gone and the guy I was meeting was already there. I got out of my car and dropped the keys in his hand.

"Follow me," I said, leading the way to the garage at Chicago's condominium complex.

"How much you want for this lustful red Ferrari Spider?" he asked, starting the engine.

Madison's car wasn't worth the half million I wanted. No shrewd buyer was going to pay more than the blue book value. "I'll take two hundred thousand, cash."

Scanning under the hood, he laughed; then he told me, "Man, you got jokes. Do I look like a sucka to you? I buy and resell for a business, not a hobby." Carefully he closed the hood. Considering he was standing three feet from me and closer to my daughter's car, I couldn't say, "Yes, you do."

"I'm a businessman too. How much you want to pay for it?"

"Not a penny more than a hundred thousand. Final offer."

I felt like I was on a game show, but this guy wasn't kidding. Was it worth it? The title was in my company's name. I'd never sell my

Porsche. Wasn't as though Madison was going to need a car anytime soon. My wife didn't use her car that much. Rosalee and Madison could share until we got back on our feet.

Didn't want to give him time to change his mind. I showed him the title. Extending my hand, I said, "Let's go to the bank, baby. I'll have the car detailed and delivered first thing in the morning."

"I can polish it myself," he insisted. "Let's drive it to the bank. You walk out with the money. I'll drop you off back here. And I drive off in my Spider."

We left the garage and completed our transactions. He dropped me off, as agreed. How could I look Madison in the face after what I'd done? I drove to the office and gave Monica the rest of the day off. All I wanted right now was fellatio.

When my PA entered my office, I unbuckled, unzipped, and removed my pants and boxers. "I've got a lot on my mind. No talking. Just sucking."

Reclining on the sofa, I placed my hands behind my head; then I closed my eyes. Feeling her mouth on me, my body tensed. I wanted to shove her head down. Then I felt like pushing her away. I didn't touch her. What she was doing should have brought pleasure. The more she sucked, the angrier I got.

I thought, *I should be at the hospital.*

"Get up and get out."

It wasn't her fault. Madison wasn't responsible. I hoped my daughter would understand that I had to leverage her house, but how was I going to explain selling her car? They were material things that would eventually be replaced.

I cleaned myself off and headed to the hospital. Hopefully, Chicago was there. He could afford to buy Madison a new car, or she could cash in her engagement . . . I paused. Why hadn't I thought of this before I sold her car?

Making a U-turn, I called my frat brother, the one I'd leveraged Madison's house to. "Hey, man. I need to get my daughter's medical information from her house for her surgery. Can you meet me there with the keys?"

"Of course, man. Give me an hour," he said without hesitation.

"Thanks."

"Don't mention it."

CHAPTER 21

Granville

Nine hundred ninety-eight. Ninety-nine. One thousand.

My early push-ups were done. I rolled over. Did the same number of sit-ups. Keep this up and I could be on a cover for the sexiest man alive. I never had a gut, but for the first time I had abs that rippled like waves all the way down to those indentations that dipped toward my big dick.

I checked the posted roster. My name was on it.

I hated that we had to wear these ugly green uniforms that covered most of our body. Sometimes I'd pretend I was a doctor waiting to operate on a patient.

Dr. Washington, to emergency. Dr. Washington, you're needed in the emergency room.

Make believe was nice but I could never have been a doctor. The tools are too small for my huge hands. Some of my fingers were bigger than some dudes' dicks. I once finger fucked this woman and she told me, "That felt like the real thing." She made me feel good. That's when I realized, if my johnson ever stopped working, I had serious backup.

Shower time had become my favorite. I loved seeing myself naked. Stroking my sausage with lots of soap, I got a woody. Had to stop and rinse off. Didn't want to be late for lineup.

Wait until I showed Madison all of this. She was going to go wild, rubbing her soft, pretty, little hands all over me. My fantasies weren't as creative as my cellmate's. Every night I jacked off to the replay of the one time I had sex with the mother of my unborn child. After I came, surrounded by darkness, I cried.

Getting dressed, I sang, " 'I'm too sexy for myself.' " I cracked myself up to keep from getting sad. Prison was a dark place for a man who didn't deserve to be there.

I'd learned there were two kinds of inmates in here: the ones who worked out all the time to buff up big-time and had the type of muscles that made men jealous. Then there were the self-proclaimed professors who read everything from the dictionary to the Bible to impress others with their brand-new words and philosophies on life. It didn't matter what kind of man the man behind bars ended up being. A felon on the street or in jail attracted lonely women like shit did flies.

The seventeen cents an hour they paid me was an insult compared to what staff got broken off. What I liked was I got to spend time outside my unit working. I got promoted from doing the laundry to being in the kitchen. No more soupy mashed potatoes. The guys enjoyed my cooking. That made me feel good. Since they hadn't started the culinary classes, I figured in the meantime, I could experiment on these dudes.

I was standing in line because today was visitation for my unit.

The guards escorted us from the sixth floor to the first. A few guys had private one-on-one sessions with their lawyers. They sat behind closed doors with large windows. G-double-A entered a room, walking right behind this gorgeous woman, who had long, straight cinnamon hair. All the men noticed her. Since G-double-A was a lawyer, why did he have a private visit? Was she an attorney too? Or was that his way of sneaking a conjugal visit? Continuing my stroll, I thought, "That's slick dog." Wish I could do that with Madison.

A lady sat against the corner, talking on the phone, which was mounted to the wall. Inmates on the seventh floor weren't allowed face-to-face. We'd heard the warden had approved a videoconference, which would soon allow visitors and inmates to see one another without having the violent inmate leave the unit. That was good, but only if they didn't start using that for all of us.

I spotted Beaux and Precious sitting in the back of the room.

Good. All prisoners preferred sitting away from the guard at the door. One guard couldn't keep watch over all of us.

"Hey, bro. Precious," I said, exchanging a quick hug with both.

Beaux immediately said, "You need to come home. Mom is willing to put up her house for collateral. I can sell your stuff, take out a loan, and use what's in my savings to help bail you out."

Precious said, "I've been working two jobs and got two thousand to help."

She opened her legs. She wasn't wearing any panties. I got instant wood. My dick crawled toward my knee. When I saw the cell poking out of her pussy, I almost peed in my pants. My dick wanted to trade places with that phone.

I scratched my bald head. I'd never snuck in contraband. How was I going to get a feel and the phone without getting caught?

Staring between Precious's legs, wishing I could dial Madison, I asked my brother, "How's Moms doing?" Hopefully, Madison hadn't changed her number.

"Not good," he said, then looked away. He pressed his fingers deep into his eyes; then he cleared his throat. "But don't you worry. Let's focus on getting you out of here."

Beaux was the sensible one who had convinced me to save money. Things had to be bad if they were willing to risk everything for me to go home. What if Sarah Lee Washington, the strongest woman I knew, was waiting to see me before she'd let go? What if her not seeing me made her hold on? I didn't want my mama to die.

"I love you—and no matter what, I'm going to be here for you," Precious said.

"I love you too, Precious." A short time in the pen and lying came as easy as breathing.

I was an inmate who would say whatever I thought Precious wanted to hear. Some of these guys exchanged vows with women whom they'd never be with if they weren't in here. Others juggled three or four females for visitation, proposed to each one, and had all of them putting money on their books. Me? I was faithful to Madison.

"Don't let Mom sign over the house."

"She's not living there. I had to move her in with me."

"That won't last, bro. You know Mom. She was probably waiting for you to come here so she could get back to her house."

Beaux laughed, then said, "True dat. That's why I need you to let me handle your bail."

I pressed my fingers deep into my eyes to force back the tears. "Bro, I need you to send G-double-A's family a thousand dollars."

G-double-A's mom was taking care of his son until G-double-A got out. In a way, I was helping my friend and myself at the same time.

Beaux stared at me. "We just sent this dude's mom a g."

"Just do it. For me. Please," I pleaded.

"I don't trust this dude, Granville."

"I checked him out, bro. He's legit. He's going to get me off."

"That's my job," Precious said, spreading her knees, reminding me about the phone. She pushed it out a little, then sucked it back in.

Seeing a real pussy I couldn't touch was pissing me off. I wanted to bend her over, raise her skirt, yank out that phone, and fuck the shit out of her. I stood and motioned for the guards. "I'm ready."

"What about?" Precious's eyes moved in the direction of the cell phone.

"I need you on the out, not the inside. Tell Mom I love her, bro. See you guys next week."

I'd changed my mind about the phone. If we'd gotten caught, I might be sent to the seventh floor, transferred, denied visitation, or faced with a new charge. It wasn't worth it.

Happy to be back on the sixth floor, I sat on the stool at the table next to No Chainz.

"You got it?" No Chainz asked.

"Changed my mind."

"Probably best. Good move, G."

"You take care of that?" G-double-A asked. "Since I'm representing you when you represent yourself, we need to get your subpoena list together," he said, sitting on the stool next to me.

"Who was that woman you went in the room with. That's your wife?" I asked.

G-double-A shook his head. "That was Sindy. You can say she's my advisor."

"Who cares who she was? This nigga is always clocking dough," No

Chainz said, staring at G-double-A. "Besides, how many inmates you got on payroll?"

G-double-A looked No Chainz in the eyes, then answered, "Not you. But that can change."

I didn't miss that, but time was my money. I'd find out what the deal was with my boy later tonight when we in our cell. I cleared my throat and spread my thighs, then said, "Loretta Lovelace, Precious Dawson, Chaz DuBois."

No Chainz asked, "What about Chicago, man? And Madison. Don't leave out the groom and the bride."

I looked away from the list after G-double-A wrote their names. I didn't care about Roosevelt DuBois, but I was in love with Madison and she was carrying my baby. I named everyone I knew who was at the reception, then added, "Let's get a list of employees who worked that day."

"You're not so dumb, dude. That's going to cost extra, but that's an excellent idea. The more witnesses who testify, the greater chance you have for a mistrial. If their testimonies don't match, that could confuse the jury during their deliberation."

I smiled. "Really? That's how I'm going to get off?"

No Chainz patted me hard on the back. "Yeah, nigga. They still haven't found the weapon. Chicago can't say you did it if he didn't see you fire on him. This is Texas. Damn near everybody carries a gun."

G-double-A agreed. "I'll write, 'Did you have a gun on you at the time of the shooting?' and you make sure to ask each witness that question."

Wow, I was starting to feel better about being released. I'd hate for Moms to die while I was locked up.

CHAPTER 22

Chicago

Being in a hospital brought back memories.

I sat in the cafeteria with Mrs. Tyler, texting Loretta: Hey, I apologize for how things transpired. Let's get together and talk later this week.

She responded right away: I'd like that.

Mrs. Tyler was seated next to me. Her husband had come late yesterday after Madison's surgery, but he hadn't stayed long. He said, "I have to make sure the business doesn't go under while she's under." Then Madison's dad left fifteen minutes after he had arrived. He'd left so quickly—I didn't have time to ask how I could help him.

I texted Chaz: Where are you?

He replied: At home.

See you in a few to discuss the next game.

Johnny made me realize that emotional detachment was a real coping mechanism for some men. My grandfather Wally visited me once while I was sick. I knew men who avoided going to the doctor for routine checkups and postponed dental appointments until a toothache or abscess sent them running for help.

My dad was there for me, but no one physically had cared for me more than Loretta. Regardless of what I'd paid her, I couldn't put a price tag on what she'd done. I wanted that type of person for my wife.

"God will bless you, Chicago," Mrs. Tyler said.

Being with her made me wonder why I hadn't spent more time with Mrs. Tyler. Outside of the announcement of my marrying Madison, our families had never met. That day in my suite, during halftime Madison and I told our parents we were getting married. My mother hadn't hesitated to express she was opposed. But now that I think back, Mrs. Tyler's reaction wasn't good or bad. It was indifferent.

I expected more from Madison's mother right now. Didn't get why she was so down. What was done couldn't be undone. She seemed more sorry for herself than concerned about her daughter.

Good health was our greatest asset. Not money or material possessions. "He already has blessed me. I know a lot has happened, but I love Madison."

She started crying. I put my arm around her shoulders.

"It's all my fault. She blames me. I should've warned her."

This was not the time for Mrs. Tyler to become the victim. I should've said, "It's not your fault," but that would've been a lie. She should have told Madison that breast cancer ran in their family. If Madison and I had a daughter, we were going to make sure she knew everything and take her to get tested early as possible.

"I'm going to check in on Madison, and then I have to meet up with my brother. I'll be back tonight," I said. I'd barely touched my salad. I didn't have much of an appetite.

"Okay," Mrs. Tyler said, crying into her plate.

Walking away, I shook my head. Yesterday Madison's surgery was a success. While we waited for Madison to recover, I got to know her mom a little better. Mrs. Tyler was a nice woman, but she seemed sheltered. She didn't have any siblings, but where were her friends? Cousins? She didn't belong to any organizations. "Outside of my Madison and Johnny," Mrs. Tyler said, "you're my closest family. I can't wait until the baby is born."

Johnny didn't appear to be the isolating type. Men who made sure their wives didn't have a life or identity outside of them were big-time cheaters and/or wife beaters.

I thought about the two friends my wife has, or had—I wasn't sure. Neither of them had been to the hospital. Tisha, I understood her not coming. Loretta, not so much. I know she had an argument with my wife at my condo and I stayed out of it. They needed to release their pent up anger. But Madison hadn't done anything to hurt Loretta enough to keep her from being at the hospital.

Quietly I entered the room. I wiped the drool from my wife's face. So many little things kept reminding me of what Loretta had done for me. I kissed Madison's forehead. "Baby, I'm going over to Chaz's place for a moment. Your mom is in the cafeteria. I'll be back later."

Sleepily she said, "Thanks, babe." She smiled, then closed her eyes.

The drive home was about forty-five minutes. The valet attendant got in my car as soon as I got out. I went straight to my brother's place.

Tap, tap, tap, tap . . . tap, tap.

Banging on the door or ringing the bell was not what we did. We had keys to each other's condos, but we didn't use them unless we had to. I'd forgotten to ask, but I hoped Loretta wasn't here. Some of what I had to say, I wouldn't in front of her.

"Hey, come on in." Chaz didn't ask if I wanted a drink. He poured two glasses of scotch. "Let's sit on the balcony."

I sat, sipped my drink and stared up at the sky. I sipped again. It was about seventy-five degrees and the sun was fading into an amazing blend of orange, yellow, and red hues. I inhaled real deeply, then held my breath.

Exhaling, I said, "Thank You, Lord."

I could walk. I could speak. I was in my right mind. I hadn't lost my job. And I was sitting next to one of the persons whom I never wanted to live without. My family and Madison were the others.

"Man, I'm grateful to be alive. I don't know why He spared me—"

"But I thank Him every day. I love you, Chicago. I was scared to death, man. Thought I'd die if you didn't make it."

Tears streamed down Chaz's face. We hadn't talked about the shooting since it happened. I stared at the sky as though I could see God in heaven nodding at me. I was sure He approved of how I was handling things.

My eyes watered. I whispered, "I feel you. You should know that I'm going to help Madison's dad save their company."

"Hold up. Wait." Chaz sat on the edge of his chair. "Are you crazy?"

"The Good Book says your wife is supposed to come first. Before your mother and everybody else. Do I live by the Word? Or do as I please?"

"You don't want me to answer that. And you might want to hold off on that decision until after the trial. A woman can destroy a man's life in a nanosecond."

"Correction, the *wrong* woman. Good women make us better. The right one makes us our best."

"There's no such thing as 'the right one,' and, trust me, you've got the *wrong* one," Chaz said.

"I used to believe good women didn't exist until—"

Chaz interrupted, "Until Obama became president, and—"

"Exactly. As I move forward, that's what I want."

Chaz scooted back in his chair.

The first family gave me hope of having the perfect marriage. I wanted a woman whom I loved so hard, I was willing to die for her. Not because she'd dated some crazy dude. Men should never defend a dishonorable woman. But this guy was someone my wife had lied to me about. She'd claimed she'd met him before she'd met me. Sexed him before she'd sexed me. I believed her. That was the only reason I didn't call off my wedding. I didn't care about that hater e-mailing me a videotape of him fucking Madison. I never watched the entire clip anyway. Finding out Madison was the liar—Chaz was right.

"Man, I still want to forgive my wife, but you're right. I might have to let her go."

"Damn straight, I'm right. You're not going to get the president's stamp of approval on Madison. And you sure as hell won't have the chance you deserve with Sindy—I mean, another woman if that baby Madison is carrying has your DNA. That could be dude's baby, man. Wake up!"

Chaz wasn't slick. He was working on hooking me up to get my mind moving in a different direction from Madison. He held my hand.

"Let us pray that the child inside Madison's womb is not a DuBois."

In a way I hoped he was right. A divorce would be imminent. I could meet someone new and start fresh.

Breaking his grip, I said, "I'm no fool, man. Whether the kid is mine or not, I'm going to do right by Madison through her recovery and delivery. She needs me."

If a man knew there was a possibility the child could be his, he shouldn't abandon the woman *until he was sure.* Some of my players would rather have a broken leg than hear a girl say, "I'm pregnant." The way I was handling my situation, regardless of the outcome, I'd have no regrets.

"No, Loretta is the one who *needs* you," Chaz said, dragging the word "needs."

In a playful way I said, "You sure say some dumb stuff, man."

We laughed and drank. Chaz refilled our glasses. We drank, then laughed.

"Mm, mm, mm." I flashed back to a moment with Madison.

Chaz broke our silence. "Out with it."

My smile grew wider. "Madison got me sprung. The way she French-kissed my asshole," I said, giving my brother intimate details.

"Mm, mm, mm," he said. "Look here. I don't care what she did to you. I don't trust Madison. So I'm letting Loretta end our relationship."

"After all she's done for me!" I protested.

"Apparently, the only thing she didn't do for you was French-kiss your asshole."

We laughed. Whatever came up came out, when talking with Chaz. Couldn't blame him for being honest.

"When did you know you were done with Loretta?"

"Date numero uno," he said. "Loretta is too stiff. She tries too hard to be likable. She's no challenge in or out of bed. I need a scintillating, sexy, sophisticated woman, who's a straight-up freak with bedroom skills beyond the ordinary."

"Good luck," I told him, chuckling into my glass.

Shaking his head, Chaz said, "Naw, man. She exists. Met her at this non-profit called *I'm Not Locked Up*, when I was upgrading their computer system."

My brother had put his business on hold to fill in for me with the team. I guess this was a favor he'd done for someone. Probably that Sindy woman.

"So you met a receptionist?"

"Hell, no. You'll get to meet her. Soon. But let's keep it real," he said. "Loretta did all of that shit for herself. I didn't interfere because she was helping you get stronger every day. Despite all she's done, something is wrong with that girl, but I'm not sure what—"

"And you're not staying around to find out, so you're going to piss her off enough for her to call it off."

Chaz smiled.

I reluctantly asked, "What are you going to do?"

"You know me. I've got it all planned. Let me handle that situation with Johnny Tyler too."

I nodded. We tipped our glasses together.

My brother said, "When I cut 'em off, you cut 'em off too. Deal?"

I didn't have ultimate control over what he did with Loretta. He could handle the situation with Madison's dad because I was probably too close to focus strictly on business. I felt comfortable knowing whatever Chaz did, I had the last word about my marriage, and I wasn't afraid to terminate it.

I nodded at my lil brother, then said, "Deal."

CHAPTER 23

Loretta

"Baby, suck my dick right now."

Again? Chaz's sex drive was in overdrive. It was my fault. I should've taken care of his needs, too, while I was taking care of Chicago's. I didn't mind accommodating Chaz; but if I had to keep this up, when was he going to put a ring on my finger?

Not wanting to ruin the moment, I knelt on the mattress, leaned my head between his knees, held his stiff shaft, and began licking his balls. My tongue circled his scrotum, then teased the sensitive spot below his sac.

"Lick my asshole, Loretta. I love it when you do that."

Since when? Chaz had this new request, which was making me uncomfortable. I'd never put my mouth on a man's asshole. If I was going to keep this man, I had to please him. Since taking over for Chicago, I wondered if Chaz was getting his new idea from sexing other women.

Spreading his butt cheeks, I inhaled. There was a light stench. I shook my head. "Babe, you need to shower first, if you want me to do that."

"Go get a towel."

"Let's do it next time," I said, not feeling him on this one.

"Now, Loretta," he demanded. "And hurry before my dick goes down."

I went to his bathroom. Soaking a towel with hot water, I smeared soap on it. Got a second towel to get the soap off. Returning to the bedroom, Chaz was on his stomach. I separated his butt cheeks, wiped him good with the soapy towel. I covered my pointing finger and pushed it inside.

"Damn, Loretta. What the fuck you doing?"

"Sorry." I wiped him a few more times without probing.

He rolled over and placed his feet flat against the mattress; then he tilted up his ass. Yeah, some bitch had done this to him. I could do it too, or leave.

I slowly started licking in an upward motion. I kissed his opening, but I didn't stick my tongue in.

"Baby, that feels incredible. Now stroke my dick, but don't stop licking my ass."

I sighed heavily and did as he desired.

"Suck my dick. Then slide your tongue down to my balls and lick my asshole again, then take it from the top."

I stopped. "I don't know where you got this, but I'm done."

"I'm sorry, baby. I got carried away. Bring your sweet pussy up here to my face and straddle me from this end."

Now I didn't mind doing that. Sixty-nine was much better. I buried my knees beside his ears, then lowered my clit to his lips. He held his dick, waved it, until I slipped the head in my mouth.

Chaz started thrusting himself in and out of my mouth as though he was inside my pussy.

"Damn, that feels so fuckin' good," he moaned. "Your mouth is amazing."

I lowered my pussy until I felt his lips against me, but the only movement was from my gyrating. Giving up on having him pleasure me, I stroked and sucked his dick fast and hard until . . .

He screamed, "Yes, Madison!"

I stopped. Got out of bed and stared down at him. "What did you say?"

"Babe, what the fuck! You don't leave your man hanging like that."

I picked up a towel and *smacked* him right across his stomach. "What the fuck did you say?" I asked him again.

"'Yes, Madison.' Why? What's wrong with that? I was fantasizing about her in my head. She's not in my bed. You are."

"You've changed since you took over for Chicago. I don't know who you are anymore."

"My bad," he said. "After seeing that videotape of Madison fucking Granville, while she was engaged to my brother, I thought you guys were into the infidelity thing."

Chaz got out of bed, bypassed me, and went to the bathroom. I followed him.

"What the hell do you mean by that?"

"Look, Loretta, I'm not a sucker like Chicago. You play games with me—*you* get played. Maybe you should've been the one bold enough to scream Chicago's name, since you were riding my brother's dick so hard. Admit it, you hate Madison. You want Chicago. You think I'm stupid?"

I started shaking my head, when I should've been nodding. I cried out, "That's not true!"

"Loretta, I'm done with your so-called Christian ass. Get out of my house. And don't come back," Chaz said, tossing me my clothes.

I was not getting physically thrown out. Putting on my jeans and jersey, I wondered, *What does all of this mean?*

Was my relationship with Chaz really over? Should I get my daughter and go back to being an overwhelmed single parent? Or let Madison defeat me from her hospital bed? Even if it was only in his head, Madison fucking Chaz was unacceptable.

I hadn't seen Madison since her surgery, but it was time for me to pay her a visit.

CHAPTER 24

Madison

My breasts were gone, and so was the cancer.

Staring into the handheld mirror Chicago had given me, I was as flat-chested as the baby inside my stomach. I'd done the right thing. My baby was safe.

I slid my hand over my hair. Since I wasn't having chemo, I didn't have to worry about losing my hair.

"Mama, I can't wait to get to the salon."

Ladies didn't wrap scarves around their head. They slept on satin pillows. Men loved to feel real hair, regardless of the length. A touch-up wasn't necessary, but a shampoo, condition, and style were. I looked into my eyes; then I placed the mirror on the stand next to my bed.

My mother sat in the chair staring at me.

The team of doctors closely monitored my post-op recovery and my baby's health. Too sore to wear any clothes, I wished I could remove these bandages and just let the stitches show while I was in my room.

"Mama, please go home. You don't have to sit here, not saying anything. Go get some rest. Roosevelt will be here shortly. Whenever they release me, I'm going to need you to take care of me during the day while he's at work."

My mother started brushing my hair. I thanked God many times for her. Some people had mothers who didn't care, mothers who gave them away, or mothers who had passed away. Mine was alive, and she was by my side, caring for me.

My dad was another story. He was on his way. He was always on his way. Sometimes he actually got here. I'd become accustomed to his lying. Did my mom have to deal with his false promises too? Whenever he did arrive, he had to knock first, then wait for me to say it was okay for him to come in. That was the requirement for everyone, except Roosevelt and my mom.

"Baby, you were right. If I had told you years ago that breast cancer ran in our family, maybe I could've spared you. I'm so sorry."

Not this again. I didn't want her to brush that negativity into my head. I raised my hand. "Enough, Mama. What's done is done. I'm good. And your grandbaby is healthy."

I wanted to say, "I'm sick and tired of hearing it!"

A knock welcomingly interrupted our alone time.

"It's Papa, sweetheart."

I exhaled, wondering what scheme he'd concocted with Roosevelt. I trusted my husband, but my dad was one of those men always looking for a way to get over—even when he didn't have to. I'd find out the details later.

"Just a minute," I said as Mama raised the covers to my neck.

"You can come in now, Johnny," Mama said.

"There's my sweetheart." He kissed me. Then he pressed his lips next to Mama's and handed me a huge bouquet of white roses. "Madison, Chicago is heaven-sent. I spoke with him and I'm meeting with him when I leave here. Everything is going to be okay. You'll have your house back. Your car back. Your rings. Everything! And we'll have our business running smoothly in no time."

Instantly my stomach ached with nausea. *My rings? My car?* "What else did you steal from me, Papa?"

"I know, sweetheart. Don't look at it as stealing. You've been made whole. So I borrowed from you to save our company and it worked. It worked! Here's your real power of attorney. You can legally terminate it. I don't need it anymore." Papa twirled Mama around, then kissed her, long and hard.

Mama said, "Johnny, what's gotten into you? What foolishness are you talking about?"

I stared at the last page of the document. "I don't know what you did, Papa, but this isn't real. This is fraudulent. I did not witness this before a notary."

I'd heard every word. If it weren't for Roosevelt, my baby and I would've been stripped of all my possessions. I wasn't well enough to deal with my father, but he had it coming. I was not going to have mercy on him. Loretta was a bitch. My father, he was a straight dog. Their day was coming.

"Nothing you need to worry about, Rosalee. I've got it all taken care of. I'll give you guys the details tomorrow. Bye, sweetheart," he said, kissing me on the forehead.

"Johnny, wait," Mama said, following him to my door. She paused. "Madison, I'll be back. I'm going to get something to eat. You want me to bring you anything?"

"Go home, Mama! I'm fine." Slowly I got out of bed and placed the flowers on top of the food tray. I didn't have much of an appetite since the surgery. I'd lost fifteen pounds. That was a lot for me. One meal and two snacks were more than I desired to digest, but that was all I'd eaten yesterday.

The door opened a few minutes later. "Mama, what did you for—"

"Hello, Madison."

I recognized the voice but couldn't see her face.

"How did you get in here? You need to leave." I sat on my bed, close to the alert remote, then emphatically said, *"Now."*

Loretta removed the hood covering her head, grinned, then blocked the door with the food tray stand. Her eyes were glossy and dark. "Hello, baby, sweetheart, can-do-no-wrong Madison. I like your roses." She picked them up, sniffed. "Nice. But the color is wrong for you."

Quick as I could, I reached to page for help. Loretta slammed the flowers on the tray then rushed toward me. Slapped the device from my hand.

"When we were kids, I thought you were cute. When we all turned thirteen, I looked up to you. When we went off to college, I knew I was the smartest of us all, but you would always say something to make me feel stupid. After we graduated, I watched you get nine engagement rings to my zero. But I get it now. You surround yourself with girlfriends who can never outshine you. One day you're going to come face-to-face with a bitch who looks better than you, and then what are you going to do? You don't have to put Tisha and me down so you can stand out. Yes, I'm jealous. Yes, I'm in love with your husband. But I've never put my hands on you. Give me one reason why I shouldn't beat your ass. Just one," she said.

My body was too weak to fight back. I wished I had the strength to pick up the mirror and slap her with it or raise my foot and kick her. "What are you trying to prove? I can't control your lack of self-esteem. I won't ever be the woman *you* want me to be. Face it, you hate me because you hate yourself."

The back of her hand landed across my face. She snatched the pillow; then she covered my face. I couldn't breathe.

"Admit it. You don't think I can keep a man."

Why did it matter to her what I thought? If she uncovered my face, I'd tell her the truth. She couldn't. I scrambled to grab her hair. It was in a tight bun.

"You don't think I was dumb enough to let you get me twice," she said, briefly uncovering my face.

I gasped. She slammed the pillow into my face again.

"Chicago won't be able to bail you out of this, and no one will ever believe I did this."

Did what?

Loretta lifted the pillow. Her fist was raised in front of my face. My cheek was burning from the prior slap. My eyes widened in disbelief.

Heaving, I struggled to breathe. "You . . . wouldn't"—I choked on air—"dare. You're a pathetic bitch, who wished you were me. You could never be me."

Wham! Her fist landed in my left eye.

I screamed, but it was so faint that I barely heard it myself.

Loretta laughed. "Next time you decide to open your legs, make sure it's not for my man. I don't want to be like you, you tramp."

Tossing the pillow on my head, she unblocked the door and left.

CHAPTER 25

Johnny

Some consider me cocky. I say I'm confident. I was a black cat with ninety-nine lives, and I'd only used two.

One was lying to my wife by not telling her I was cheating on her again. If I got this big financial break, I should come clean. The other horrible thing I'd done was not being there for my daughter. After today both would be different.

Right now, nothing—not even getting my dick sucked—was going to prevent me from showing up for this face-to-face that was about to change my situations for the best. A few more blow jobs were understandable, if I was going back to being faithful. The thought of having mediocre sex, twice a month . . . aw, hell no. I might have to hang in there with my PA until I got caught.

When things were great, people overlooked the bad. That was how it should be. If I gave them what they wanted, why shouldn't Johnny do what made Johnny happy? That's what I needed all three of my girls to do. Love me for who I am. A provider.

I was glad Rosalee wasn't a nagger, like some of my frat brothers' wives, or I would've divorced her years ago. I hate naggers. They're miserable. They want their man to be miserable. And they don't add value to the relationship. All that damn fussing and when they wake up the next day they still have the same damn problems.

Dark clouds spread across the sunless sky. Daylight looked like midnight. The crackling of thunder followed streaks of lightning. The downpour created a flash flood, which was inches from overflowing into my Porsche.

I drove up to the valet and handed the guy the keys to my car. Stepping onto the sidewalk, my gator ankle boots and the hem of my pants were submerged in water. During the short distance from the stand to the door, the attendant held an umbrella over my head. My hair was dry. My feet were soaked. Nothing was going to ruin my day.

I'd arrived at Eddie V's, at West Avenue on Kirby, near opening time at four. Dinner started at five. My guest should arrive in a half hour.

Look the way you want to be and eventually you'd be the way you looked. The same held true for the way one would act. I used to be comfortably rich: plane, luxury cars, traveled the world for business and pleasure. Not necessarily in that order. Had my dick sucked by beautiful women in every country I visited. Look at Johnny now. With the exception of my wife, I was struggling to maintain all that I owned.

It was time to be a jet-setter again, baby! I felt so damn good about this meeting—I had the swag back in my step. I busted a James Brown move and spun around. I didn't care who saw me. I did it again. Pretended I had a cape on my shoulders, then simulated tossing it off.

I'd worn my best designer suit, a Rolex watch, a platinum tie clip, a diamond ring, and my $10,000 cuff links. I hung the price of a house on my fine physique.

Hopefully, Chicago wouldn't cancel due to the storm. He was one special guy. I didn't understand why he was extremely loyal to Madison after what she'd done to him. Damn. She'd better not have told him it was my idea to take him off the respirator. Just in case I had prepared a response to deny any involvement.

"Not my style. Not my place. Madison is your wife and she makes her own decisions. You should know that." Naw, I'd better change that last sentence. "We both know that." Yeah, that is less offensive.

The tone and structure of a few words could make the difference in getting what you wanted, or blowing a deal.

Waiting for Chicago to arrive, I went to the restroom, emptied my bladder, dried my boots, then washed my hands under the free-flowing unisex fountain. This was the oddest arrangement I'd seen. Once you were inside, there were designated sides for the men and women but no separation of access to the private stalls. The women used the same water to cleanse their hands; and if one wasn't aware, you couldn't see but could accidentally touch the fingers of a stranger. I wasn't sure who thought that was a good idea, but it made me a little uncomfortable. I put my hands under the blower for a few seconds, rubbed them together, left the restroom, and then scanned the dining room for Chicago. I didn't see him. I checked my cell. I didn't have any missed calls.

The restaurant was quiet. The after-work crowd hadn't started to pack the place. One couple was seated at the bar, another at a highboy in front of the grand piano, where a band would soon perform.

"Hey, Johnny. Good to see you."

The general manager had become a friend. His artistic love was modeling. He had that Hollywood flair. Blond hair. Blue eyes. The right amount of facial hair gave him that smooth, edgy look that made women wet. He was definitely in shape. Young. One day I expected to channel surf and see him in a commercial or a movie.

I had skills, but I hadn't tapped into my talents. If I had, instead of getting married I would've explored my desire to become an adult entertainer. Quiet as it may be, Houston had more strip clubs than Atlanta. If this deal with Chicago didn't prove lucrative, maybe I should stay on the business side, sell my construction company, and invest in a members' only joint for successful men over sixty with dancers under thirty. Afterall, strip clubs was a billion-dollar industry and I was not going to die broke.

"Hey, Drew. I'm glad you're here. Look, man, I have an important meeting today with Chicago DuBois." I stood tall, adding a little bass to my voice so I spoke with authority. "We're going to need a table that's private and away from all of the patrons who might come in later. And we have to be away from the band, so we don't have to talk too loud."

Normally, I'd make a reservation, but I was a regular and always received stellar service. Plus, with the bad weather I doubted many guests would come through.

Drew smiled. "Not a problem, Mr. Tyler. It'll be great to see

Chicago. Haven't seen him since the accident," he said, leading the way.

The secluded location in the corner, near the ceiling-to-floor custom-built wine rack, was where I was seated. "This is perfect."

"I'll bring Mr. DuBois over as soon as he arrives. Your usual?" he asked.

"Not today. Send over a bottle of your finest scotch," I insisted. "This promises to be a celebration."

"You got it," Drew said, walking away.

There were no subpar items on their menu. The crab cakes and lobster tacos were my favorite appetizers, but I'd wait to order until my potential business partner arrived. My cell phone buzzed. I removed it from my pocket.

"Hey, sweetheart, I'm here waiting on Chicago. How are you?"

My daughter cried into the phone, "Papa, you're not going to believe what happened! I've been calling Roosevelt, but he hasn't answered his phone. When he gets there, tell him I need him to come to the hospital right away." She was crying.

Relieved that she didn't ask me to come right now, I said, "Whatever it is, it can't be that bad. Is it? You're already at the hospital. Can it wait until after I get the details?"

Silence ended our call. *Women. She'll be okay.*

Glancing up, I saw two persons instead of one.

"I didn't know you were bringing your brother with you," I said, standing to greet Chicago and Chaz.

Chicago extended his hand. Chaz sat without saying a word. He was unfamiliar to me, but I wasn't underestimating his influence on Chicago.

"This won't take long," Chicago said. "I'm not here to build a friendship. I'm here because you're the father of my wife."

Chaz said, "Let's get to it." Then he placed a legal document, about twenty pages thick, in front of me. He remained silent.

"Okay," I said. Apparently, they'd predetermined what they wanted. I should've done the same.

Drew returned with the bottle of scotch. "I'll get another glass," he said, leaving right away.

Chicago tapped the document. "Everything is here. Have your lawyer look it over and get back to us."

Us? Hmm.

"What is it? Are you divorcing Madison?" I joked. This stack of papers was high. I thumbed through it.

"He should," Chaz said. "Would save us time and money. She's a liability with a big ass, but she's no asset to my brother."

Chicago cut his eyes to Chaz.

Chaz leaned back. "I apologize."

Good. I was relieved that I didn't have to defend my daughter. Drew placed the glass on the table then walked away.

"Johnny," Chicago said, "I would address you as 'Mister Tyler,' but I see where your daughter gets her ways. The house. The car. The business. Is there anything else you need to tell me?"

And I saw where they got their disrespectful ways: from their mother.

I didn't want to speak too fast. I should've asked for extra money to get Madison's engagement rings from the pawnshop, but that would make me seem greedy. I waited a moment; then I shook my head. "No, I've told you everything," I lied.

Chaz rolled his eyes, exhaled, then shook his head. "He's lying."

I prayed they didn't already know. That would make me look sleazy. I kept quiet.

Chicago said, "As cold and as callous as Madison is sometimes, what you did to her was cruel and unnecessary. If it weren't for the possibility that she might be carrying my baby, we'd have nothing to discuss. I'll get straight to it. One, I'm settling the debt to get Madison back her home."

"I saw that."

"Two, I'm buying her a brand-new luxury car of her choice."

"I saw that too."

"Three, I'm willing to bail your company out in exchange for fifty-one percent ownership. Four, if the baby is not mine, I'm taking complete ownership of Tyler Construction. It's not negotiable. Take the package, or lose everything you have left."

"Whatever that is," Chaz added.

Shut the fuck up, Chaz.

Chicago must've meant control, not ownership. That's the way I'd interpret it. I'd hold forty-nine percent? Guess I'd read that wrong.

What was I to do? I'd read how much cash this contract was putting in my pocket for that fifty-one. It was a million dollars, cash. That would leave me with way more than enough to get back Madison's engagement rings from the pawnshop.

"How long do I have to think this over?"

"Eighteen hours," Chaz said, then stood.

I despised that man. No doubt, the sentiments were mutual.

Chicago pushed back his chair. "Your time starts now."

Guess this wasn't a good time to mention Madison wanted Chicago to call her. He'd find out eventually. This was my big chance to save my business and recover Madison's property. She'd thank me later.

"Wait." I couldn't risk having him change his mind. I dug deep into my jacket pocket, pulled out my Montblanc pen, signed the document, then handed it to Chicago. "I trust you."

Chicago shook his head. Chaz quickly took the contract.

A man dressed all in black—hat, shirt, shoes, slacks—approached the table.

"Cancel this bottle of scotch," I told him. "We didn't touch it."

He looked at me, then turned to the brothers. "Roosevelt DuBois, Chaz DuBois," he said, handing them both papers, "you've both been served."

Unfolding the papers, they stared at one another; then they strolled out side-by-side like Otis and Blue did when they left David Ruffin's place in the movie *The Temptations*.

Whatever it was, I sure hoped it didn't mess up my deal.

CHAPTER 26

Loretta

I had no remorse. That *passé blanc,* light enough to pass for white, black bitch finally got what she deserved.

Next time, I bet, Madison won't think about touching me—let alone pulling out my hair. Turning down the opportunity to leave work early yesterday and deliver a package to the hospital where Madison was, I'd left the pharmacy at three in the afternoon, at the end of my regular shift.

Dancing around my living room, I felt the ballerina inside of me curtsy for the first time. I finally had gotten the courage to tell Madison how I felt. I tried standing on my tiptoes. "Ow," I said, falling to the floor. I rolled on the carpet with laughter.

Get it together, Loretta, I told myself. "Stop acting silly. What you did was wrong."

I regrouped. For a moment I allowed myself to release my frustrations, as opposed to holding it all in. Madison didn't hold back. Neither did Tisha. Why did I care so much about what others thought about me? Because I'm a Christian that didn't mean I was a saint.

Yesterday was the perfect storm. More accidents and additional trauma meant hospital staff was busier than normal. Doctors were writing prescriptions. The pharmacy was insanely backed up because more people than usual needed meds.

After picking up my daughter from her school, I went to an ATM, knowing the surveillance camera would capture me making a withdrawal. The timing would be a little off; but if Madison pressed charges, and she wasn't sure of the time I'd arrived at her room, I could use being at the ATM to my benefit.

Bad weather terrified my mother and increased the odds that she'd be home. I couldn't leave my daughter in the car by herself in a parking lot at the hospital. I wasn't that crazy. My parents' house was a little out of the way, but it was worth the trip.

I'd asked, "Mom, can you watch Raynell for an hour? I need to run a quick errand." Of course my mother had agreed, as she was happy to have the company.

My next location was room 911. How appropriate. But before I got there, I'd texted Chicago: Haven't heard from you. We really need to talk. He was the one who had initiated an apology and had suggested we get together, but I hadn't heard from him since he'd sent me that text.

He texted back: At the office, headed to a meeting, then I have to visit Madison at the hospital.

Men always gave too much information to their mistresses. Not enough to their wives. I was actually surprised he'd replied. Obviously, he was avoiding me. He should've given me options for another day or time, but it was easier for him to reply *but not* commit? Chicago and Chaz cutting me off added to the reasons I'd paid Madison that visit.

Simply explaining that I was at work or with my daughter wouldn't keep me from being arrested. If I was sentenced, I'd probably lose my job and my house—and I'd barely see my family. For a moment I felt sorry for Granville. His mama being sickly and he couldn't be with her wasn't right, but that was his fault. In case Madison decided to press charges against me, I prayed to God for a foolproof alibi.

Chuckling, I jumped in the air, kicked my feet back, and then let down my hair, like I was a vixen in a music video. I'd better stop acting a fool before I awoke Raynell. By the time I'd picked her up, my mother had fed her. I'd helped my daughter with her homework, made her take a bath, and then I'd tucked her into bed early.

Recalling my striking Madison, I covered my mouth. "Oh, my gosh." I bet based on her skin color, Madison probably bruised easily. Had I hit her hard enough to close her eye?

This is one time I imagined she wished she were my complexion. I didn't mean to hit her; she made me do it. Told myself she was defenseless. Hadn't recovered from her surgery. If she had been healthy, out of hatred, I could've bashed her three times.

I only slapped and hit her once. That was her fault. She should've kept her mouth shut and she shouldn't have put her hands on me that day at Chicago's. I was taught that if a person strikes first, I had the right to fight back. For Madison, the timing wasn't right, but the strikes to her face was warranted.

It was cool that Madison had said, "You wouldn't dare." But when she told me, "You're a pathetic bitch, who wished you were me. You could never be me," she made me hit her.

I hate her. I hate myself for hating her. But I wasn't sure why I felt this way. Abusing a sick person or anyone wasn't in my Christian nature. I had to pray on what I'd done and ask God for forgiveness for my hitting that whore.

Chaz and Chicago could screw Madison at the same time, for all I cared. Wasn't like she was faithful to Chicago, anyway. They'd probably already had a threesome. I wished Granville was the father of her baby.

My cell rang. I stopped dancing and pranced to my phone. *Yes!* I was grateful for the interruption.

I smiled, then answered it. "Hey, baby. You're done at the office?" Seductively I moaned, "You wanna come over tonight?"

Chaz firmly asked, "You at home?"

The tone in his voice sent chills through me—not the kind that normally made my pussy pucker. I'd hoped he'd call to apologize for putting me out the last time we were together but I feared he knew what I'd done to Madison.

"Yes. I'm home. You okay?"

"Stay there. I'll be there in ten," he demanded, then ended the call.

Ten what? It was virtually impossible to get anywhere in Houston in under a half hour. I took a three-minute shower, brushed my teeth, coated my lips with raspberry gloss, then slipped on a sexy, strapless white cotton dress. I checked on Raynell. She was sound asleep.

Part of me realized I shouldn't have anything to do with Chaz after he'd disrespected me but I was a Christian and it was my duty to forgive. If I could stay close to Chaz, I'd still have a chance with Chicago.

Skipping the panties, I trotted downstairs, opened a cold bottle of champagne, got two glasses, and set up everything in the living room in time for his arrival.

A stiff drink and a hard dick were what I needed, and not in that order. I wasn't in the mood for French-kissing his butt again; but if that was what he wanted, I'd do it to pleasure him.

When I saw him get out of the car, I prayed, *Lord, please don't let this be about Madison.* Shaking my arms, I took a deep breath. I bent over, fluffed my hair, flipped it back, and fanned my dress. Then I opened the front door.

Damn. Chaz was the hottest I'd ever seen him. This was a change from his casual pullover polo shirt and slacks. The scent of his masculine cologne greeted me first. Dang, I'd forgotten perfume. Madison would've automatically put hers on.

Motionless, I admired his deep cranberry button-down shirt, blue tie with cranberry stripes, with a blue tailored jacket and matching slim pants. His dark wavy hair was freshly cut and his face glowed like he'd just had an amazing facial. I had to start taking better care of my skin. There was no way I could let my man outdo me.

"Hey, baby," I softly said, bracing myself for the unknown. "I'm glad you finally came to see me. We need to talk."

Chaz stepped inside. Slammed the door.

I opened it. "If you came to fight and not make up, get out."

He always wanted to have sex with me. I was ready to pick up where we'd stopped. My breathing rapidly increased. I wanted him so bad—I'd lick his asshole without him asking.

Regretting what I'd said, I did not want this man to leave. That was a stupid statement to make to a millionaire, who was dressed the part. Madison wouldn't have said that.

"What in the hell is going on, Loretta?"

Stepping back, I replied, "I don't understand. Be specific. Isn't that what you used to tell me?" I picked up the champagne bottle and a glass. Tilting the flute in my direction, I held the bottle while keeping my peripheral vision focused on Chaz. I didn't want to hit him upside his head; but if he was here to defend Madison, he was getting some of this too.

He shoved papers toward me. I couldn't take them. My trembling hands were full. What should've been the catalyst to a toast was now my assault weapon. Raising the bottle to my mouth, I poured a mouthful of bubbles, then swallowed. Was Madison suing me? Did she still believe she'd won the bet and I owed her my house? What was I thinking? She couldn't have papers drawn up this fast. I'd just left her hospital room about five hours ago.

My fingers locked around the neck; I lowered the bottle beside my thigh. I asked, "What do you want?"

Chaz stared at me and bit his bottom lip. He didn't blink. "You're one pathetic, demented, deranged bitch. I have no idea who you are. It's because of you that Chicago and I are subpoenaed by Granville. I know you're somehow involved with this shooting. I just can't prove it!"

Why in hell was he yelling? If he knew so much, why did he come here? Why not call or text? Or continuing to ignore me would've sufficed.

I yelled back, "Keep it down!" Then I lowered my voice. "My daughter is sleeping." I frowned, trying to make sense of what was his purpose.

Shaking my head, I whispered, "What do you want from me?"

"Oh, wow. I think you know the answer to that question. Did you do the right thing for my brother believing he'd leave his wife? I think you just always need somebody to take care of, but your motives are all screwed up."

I was tired of this conversation and him. "Just leave, Chaz."

He said, "Yeah, Madison—"

Before he spoke another word, and before I realized what was happening, the bottle in my hand was in motion toward his head. Chaz swatted the bottle away and grabbed my bicep. The glass shattered against the travertine tile.

"*Ow!* Let me go!" Now I was the one screaming.

Thankfully, the door was still open. I prayed my baby didn't come downstairs. I yelled again, hoping Tisha might hear me if her windows were open.

"You want me to hit you? I'm not that kind of guy. But if a man were to beat your ass, I'd understand. You're not worth it, Loretta. You need professional help. I don't know what sick games you're playing, but stay the fuck away from me, my brother, my family, and the stadium . . . or I'll get a restraining order against you," he said, letting me go.

I followed Chaz outside. "Go fuck Madison for real this time!"

He got into his car and drove off. How did confrontations escalate out of nowhere? Could this have been dealt with in a respectful manner? Maybe, if Chaz hadn't shown up at my front door, already angry.

Another car pulled into my driveway. I didn't recognize the driver or the vehicle. A tall, handsome man dressed all in black strolled up to me.

"Loretta Lovelace?" he asked in a serious tone.

"Yeah" was all I said.

He pulled papers from his back pocket, then handed them to me. *Oh, I get it.* Chaz is in on whatever this is. Maybe. I couldn't be sure, but I refused to reach for the papers.

I yelled at him. "What? Is she suing me? Or is this from my baby's daddy and his bitch?" I wanted to hit this arrogant guy, who was staring down at me.

Suddenly I realized that I'd offended so many people, this could be from a number of individuals. If Chaz hadn't blocked my blow, he could've left in an ambulance.

My body felt like a pot of bubbling water on the verge of erupting into a vigorous boil. Scalding water would be more effective in peeling away this guy's layers than my scratching his eyes out.

Dropping the papers at my feet, he said, "You've been served."

"Fuck you too!" I yelled to his back before picking up the papers.

I read the subpoena in disbelief.

Was he serious?

CHAPTER 27

Madison

"That demon has got to be destroyed."

"Loretta is a nice girl. I can't believe she'd do such a thing."

"Papa, you've got to trust me. I wouldn't lie about something like this. I'll text you a picture." I pressed a few buttons and sent a photo of my swollen eye.

He sighed. I knew he didn't believe me. Anyone who knew Loretta from a distance couldn't imagine violence had become part of her fake Christian character.

"Roosevelt hasn't called me. He didn't come by yesterday. Did you meet with him yesterday? Did you give him my message?"

"Of course," Papa said. "Some guy came into the restaurant after our meeting and handed Chicago and Chaz some papers. Maybe he had other business to 'tend to. Sweetheart, what really happened to you?"

"I'm telling you the truth. She did this to me."

"Hey, babe. Who are you talking to?" Roosevelt asked, entering my room. He glanced around. "Better yet, who are you talking about?"

"Papa, let me call you back."

"Oh, I didn't realize you were on the phone," Roosevelt said.

My dad continued, "Your mother and I will be there later to bring you home."

Somehow I doubted he'd show up. Why was he avoiding talking

about what had happened to me? "I told you, I'm going to stay at Roosevelt's."

"Sweetheart, that's not what he—"

"I know. He's here. I'll call Mama when I get settled in, and then you guys can come over. Bye, Papa."

"I love you, sweetheart."

"Love you too. Bye."

"What in the hell happened to your eye?" Roosevelt asked, touching my cheek.

Happy to see the man I loved, I smiled at my husband. Didn't take much to cheer me up after what Loretta had done. My dad had done what worked best for him. Avoidance. Signing Roosevelt's contract wasn't a well-thought-out decision for my dad. I didn't agree with him giving up 51 percent of our business, but he couldn't have given it to a better person. And since I was still legally married to Roosevelt, I technically owned 100 percent.

After I got better, I wanted to go over that contract my dad had signed. Help save his dignity before he'd become desperate again. He could be a foolish man at times, but at least he was a faithful husband and loving father. I didn't appreciate his not coming to visit me that much, but I understood. Men were not as strong as they appeared. What was most important was he'd done what was best for his family. Interesting how when you're sick, you need to know people care about you.

One of the nurses peeped in. "You okay, Mrs. DuBois? Oh, I see your husband is here. You let me know if you change your mind about reporting that incident. You should."

Again I smiled. "No, but thank you." After my surgery, I found myself being kinder to others, especially the nurses.

"I'll have your discharge papers sent in shortly for your review. Take care," she said, closing the door.

My doctor reassuring me they'd gotten all of the cancer was my biggest relief. Even Loretta assaulting me didn't kill my joy. So-called Christian. More like a hypocrite. Soon as I had this baby, she'd get hers.

I answered Roosevelt, "Loret—"

Holding up his hand, he said, "Stop right there. I don't want to know. Madison, I'd be a damn fool to get involved in whatever has and is happening between you and Loretta."

"Do you think this black eye is my fault? Baby, she's crazy."

Roosevelt's piercing stare went through me. His lips tightened. I felt his thoughts traveling back to the day I signed that authorization to take him off the respirator. Had he honestly forgiven me for that?

"I came to see how you're dealing without your twins. You okay?"

Hell no! That was like my asking him if he was good after being castrated.

I calmly replied, "I'm weak. It's like I have no energy. Yesterday was better until this happened," I said, pointing at my eye. "I don't know what's worse. I've heard chemo can be draining, but this recovery without treatment is too."

In order to keep my husband's sympathy, I'd never say, "I feel great."

Roosevelt stood beside my bed and held my hand. "Hopefully, when they test you after the delivery, you'll still be cancer free and won't need radiation or chemo. That's just a precaution, anyway. Next to my mother, Madison, you're the strongest woman I know." His grip was softer than usual.

"Wait. What do you mean you came to see how I'm doing? Did you forget I'm being discharged today?"

He exhaled, and then sat on the side of my bed. "You should take your mom and dad up on that offer."

" 'Offer'? The last time we spoke, you said you were—"

"I know."

My happiness faded. "Know what? Why did you wait to the last minute to drop this on me? You didn't come by yesterday. You didn't call. Now you show up to tell me this at the last minute?"

Sliding his hand from the top of his head to the nape of his neck, he said, "Things are changing. And I don't want to lie to you. There might be someone else in my life soon."

"Are you telling me you're cheating on me, or you're thinking about it?"

Men. One minute they are sure about who it is they want. The next moment my husband is confused? I expected that from the baby in my womb, not a grown man.

"Madison, I married you because I loved you unconditionally. Being in love with you and loving you unconditionally aren't the same. You changed my love. And no matter how hard I try to overlook what happened . . . Look, I'm not abandoning you. I'll always do right by you. But—"

"But while I'm recovering from breast surgery. Double mastectomy. One. Two. Count 'em"—I slid my arms out of my gown. I stripped away my patches for him to see my stitches—"You tell me this." I started crying.

This time I was not faking. Despite my ill will toward him months ago, Roosevelt had made me feel safe and loved. I was changing because he'd shown me how a real man treated his wife. I did not want another woman to steal this man from me.

He kissed the stitches on both of my breasts. "I'm not cheating. I haven't had sex with anyone but you since we've been seeing one another," he said, then paused, knowing I couldn't say the same.

But I'd only screwed up once. "I thought you'd forgiven me. Why get my house back and buy me a new Bentley? Why the mixed signals of affection?"

He kissed my forehead; then he stood. "I restored you because I have forgiven you. I haven't met this woman yet. Chaz thinks I should open myself up to moving on, just in case the kid . . . Honestly? I'm confused. I'm not even sure if I can go out with her. But I'm not sure I can do this with you either. I'll call you later," he said, letting go of my hand.

I watched my husband walk out on me when I needed him most. Covering my breasts, I started weeping into my pillow. I couldn't stop crying. I wished Loretta were here to hit me again so the greater pain could overpower my broken heart.

I heard the door open and prayed he'd come back to tell me he'd made a mistake. I'd forgive him.

Staring at the tall, handsome man dressed all in black, I dried my eyes, thinking he had the wrong room number. "Can I help you?"

"Are you Madison Tyler DuBois?" he asked.

Reluctantly I answered, "Yes."

Handing me a set of papers, he said, "You've been served"; then he left.

CHAPTER 28

Granville

This was the most important day of my life.

I didn't go to sleep at all last night. I prepared all day yesterday. G-double-A and No Chainz drilled me on what to do and say. They reminded me to sit high and stand tall. Always speak clear, but not too loud. Don't frown or show a mean face. Don't smile, because I would appear condescending.

"If they think you're dumb, you're done, dude." Those were the last words No Chainz spoke to me this morning.

"Yeah, man. You're big, black, and ugly as ever," G-double-A added.

I should've never introduced him to rap music. Keep it up and I'd take back the iPod I'd bought him. Make him get his own. Hell, I'd paid him five g's already. I hoped he wasn't a white guy trying to become black behind bars; then whenever he gets released, he'd act like he couldn't relate to us.

Being escorted to intake and discharge, I was one of those dudes that didn't change. But was I ugly, for real? That bothered me. Or was G-double-A joking? Maybe that's why it took me so long to get a woman and have my first seed growing. Women found me unattractive?

Did my mama lie to me all these years? I did overhear her say, "An ugly man makes a pretty baby," but I thought she was talking about my dad or Beaux.

Last night I'd practiced in the darkness of my cell. I paraded a short distance, back and forth, pronouncing my words clearly so the judge or the witnesses wouldn't have me repeating myself if they didn't understand what I was saying. I didn't want to risk confusing the jury.

Inmates in other cells shouted questions and formulated strategies. We had sixty-two cells—124 beds—and the majority of the prisoners in my unit were serving the maximum of three years. Then there were the ones, like me, awaiting trial, then sentencing. If I got life, I'd have to be transported to the state. Walking out of this place, I felt like a slave being freed. I didn't want to come back to FDC after my trial, but I knew I'd have to take off this suit, put on that green prison gear, and be shackled like my ancestors.

This morning my standby counsel was seated next to me, but I was on my own during the testimonies. Since I was representing myself, he was only allowed to speak with me when court wasn't in session.

At first, I thought he was too young, and I didn't want an intern giving me advice. After consulting with him outside of the courtroom, I realized I had another advantage. Someone else had to pay him to advise me. He knew the law that applied to my case; and if he didn't, he did his research. I wasn't sure, but I believed that both of us were up all night preparing for this moment.

I wished G-double-A and No Chainz were here with me. I felt smart in my new designer suit and cowboy boots, which Beaux had bought me. I should've listened to G-double-A and worn shoes, but my boots made me feel so sexy. Too late now.

Beaux checked on my apartment every day to make sure nobody stole my stuff. He paid my rent and bills on time each month. Since I refused to bail out, my brother said he was working on a backup plan. I wasn't ready to return to my life on the outside. If I were out, I'd find Madison then lose focus on building my case. G-double-A wouldn't be able to advise me every day. I'd made the right decision.

Looking over my shoulder, Beaux, all the people I'd had served, plus Raynard were here, and Madison. I liked her sunglasses. She was more beautiful than I remembered. I had to get a picture of her pregnant. She was sitting down, so I couldn't see if she was showing. Didn't look like it. I stared at her, then looked away. Did she kill my kid? If she did, I might press charges against her.

Mom had decided not to attend the trial. I probably made her feel bad in the letter I wrote:

Dear Mommy,

Why did you wait for me to get locked up to find out you're sick? Why didn't you go to the doctor when Beaux and I wanted you to? I miss sitting in Dad's chair, talking to you. I miss bringing you crab, shrimp, catfish, and all the stuff we used to spread over the table. Mama, I need you. Don't do this to me. Don't you dare die while I'm locked up. Hang in there for your grandbaby.

Love you, Mommy,
Your son

That was the first letter I'd written my mom, ever. I was concerned, though. Actually, I was scared, not knowing if I'd see her again. I had to get out. I nodded at Madison; then I motioned to turn forward and looked back over my shoulder. That woman with the long cinnamon hair was seated on the last row beside, "Oh my goodness," the sex therapist with a large red Afro. I wondered if G-double-A sent the long haired woman to take notes on my case and if Loretta sent Numbiya. My dick went limp.

I faced the jury. They were my peers, I guess. Half were men; the other six women. Eight were black; four white. They all looked like they had jobs and kids. They might feel sorry for me and let me off easy. I didn't care how I got off. I just wanted out.

The judge entered the room. I smiled. She was black and stunning. She wasn't the same judge I had before but I was glad she was black. This one was light like Madison. I hoped she wasn't going to be mean to me. Maybe I could charm her into dropping my case.

Uh-oh. What if she thought I was ugly?

"All rise. The Honorable Judge Owens presiding," the courtroom deputy announced. Once the judge sat in her seat, he said, "You may all be seated."

She explained her philosophy and background. Said something about ice cream and how everybody had a favorite. Mentioned something about how she liked Blue Bell. Compared that to how the jury should be aware of their biases and not allow that to influence their decision.

Blah. Blah. Blah.

Her beauty distracted me. I wanted her juicy lips all over me. Wow, was she educated and hot! I hadn't had sex with a woman since I'd been locked up. I got a woody and flashed back to when I prayed for the teacher not to call me up to the chalkboard. My dick was huge and long. That's why Loretta wanted me to share it with Madison. I'd never been to college, not a real one. Almost went to Lamar State College in Port Arthur. Finishing construction school got me in the door with my first good-paying job, and I'd worked my way up. I wondered if that deputy dude had a degree.

I missed working more than I missed having sex. Laboring made me feel like a man. Sticking my dick inside a pussy made me cum. Took being behind bars to make me appreciate both. Being a fast learner, I'd worked my way up in the jail's kitchen from washing pots and pans, scrubbing floors, and whatever else had to be cleaned to cooking. I was on my way to becoming a self-made top chef. Maybe I could get on one of those shows when I got out.

Seemed like it would be against the law to pay me a little stipend—especially one that didn't compare to the almost $100,000 I made working for Madison. They needed a pay scale. Inmates with good jobs should get paid half of what they made on the outside. In some cases the labor value was the same.

At least I had my brother to put enough money on my books so I could shop online at the commissary and get junk food, my own drawers, and nice white socks. That's how they knew the socks were mine. They didn't issue free white socks inside the joint.

The judge asked me, "Mr. Granville Washington, are you prepared to present your case?"

I stood. "Yes, Your Honor. I'd like to thank you, Your Honor, for inviting me here today. I appreciate your hearing my case. I'd like to thank the jury for making time to be here with me. Y'all look nice. And I'd like to call my first witness to the stand, Chaz DuBois."

That high-yellow chick banged her gavel like she was tenderizing a piece of meat. My dick shriveled up fast. "Mr. Washington, you will not make a mockery of my courtroom."

"Yes, Your Honor. I apologize," I said, not sure of what I'd done wrong. Then I remembered to stand at attention.

Chaz raised his right hand, took the oath from the deputy, and then sat on the stand.

"Thank you for being here," I told him.

"Mr. Washington, enough of the pleasantries," the judge said.

Oh, now I get it. "Yes, Your Honor. I apologize," I told her; then I asked Chaz, "Do you recall what happened the night someone shot your brother?"

"That someone was you," he answered.

I admired his tan suit and expensive watch. His button-down white shirt was fresh, but he wasn't wearing a tie. How did this thirtysomething youngster have more money than me?

"Let's not jump to conclu—"

The judge interrupted, "Answer the question, Mr. DuBois."

"Yes."

Stretching my head toward the ceiling, I said, "Please explain in detail to the court exactly what you recall."

That dude sighed heavily into the mic. "It was the evening of my brother Roosevelt's—known to many as Chicago—wedding reception. I was in the middle of making the toast when"—Chaz pointed at me—"he pulled out a gun and pointed it at my brother."

"Did you see what type of gun the shooter had?" I asked.

"No. You were too far away."

" 'Too far away'? Hmm, did you see the shooter pull the trigger?"

Chaz grunted between closed teeth. "Man, why you going through all this when you know you did it? Just admit it and save the taxpayers' money."

I used to be a taxpayer before Madison broke my heart and fired me. Not sure which one came first.

"Mr. DuBois, answer the question," Judge Owens said.

"What was the question?" he asked, straightening his jacket.

I repeated, "Did you see the shooter pull the trigger?"

"Yes. It was you."

I knew he was hoping I'd slip up and admit my guilt. "Are you sure?"

"Absolutely," he said.

"Did you have a gun in your possession at the time of the shooting?" I asked him.

"No."

"Where were you when the first bullet was fired?"

Chaz exhaled again. "Standing at the top of the arch over the pool."

"What happened after that?"

"I jumped into the swimming pool after you fired the second shot."

"First I was too far away. Did you jump into the swimming pool before or after the second bullet was fired?"

He sat silent.

"Mr. DuBois, answer the question," Judge Owens insisted.

"After," Chaz said, rolling his eyes.

"Were you shot before you jumped into the pool?"

"No."

"Was your brother shot before you jumped into the pool?"

He sighed again. More heavily this time. "I'm not sure."

"Thank you. Your Honor, I have no further questions."

She asked, "Does the prosecutor wish to cross-examine the witness?"

He stood. "No, Your Honor."

Good. I continued, "I'd like to call my next witness to the stand."

I smiled on the inside. This might be an open-and-shut case.

CHAPTER 29

Granville

"Roosevelt DuBois," the deputy called out.

This was going to be a match between two bulls over one golden cow. Man versus money. Love over fame. He had more success, but my heart for Madison was literally bigger than his. My dick too. Standing taller and squaring my shoulders, I stared at him to prove I was the man.

There was no way I was going to let this chump take my Madison away from me. I watched him stroll up to the witness stand, take the oath, then sit. He had swag. Even as a man, I'd have to admit that. I wondered what it felt like to be a multimillionaire and if there was a way I could get my hands on some of his money to balance things out. If I won my case, maybe I could sue him in civil court.

Damn. I'd forgotten, based on what G-double-A had advised me, I wasn't supposed to stare at him like that. A smile stirred in my stomach. Concealing it, I asked him, "Do you recall what time you arrived at your wedding reception?"

I had to throw him off. He probably thought I was going to ask him the same questions I'd asked his brother. There was definitely one question he'd have to answer like all the witnesses.

"No" was all he said.

"Roosevelt, do you recall if you arrived at your reception early, on time, or late?"

I cracked myself up on the inside. I felt like a real lawyer.

"Late."

"And why were you late for your own reception?"

His eyes met mine as he said, "Because I was making love to my beautiful wife."

My eyes narrowed; my lips tightened. He was messing with me. I looked to the prosecutor for an objection. There was none. The judge didn't say anything either.

Fine. Take his side.

"Did you have a gun in your possession at the time of the shooting?" I asked him.

"No."

"Did you know everyone at your reception?"

"No."

"Do you recall approximately how many people were at your reception?"

"I clearly remember seeing one uninvited guest who pointed a gun at me, and that was you."

Who made him GM? This guy couldn't even give the right response. I shook my head; then I said, "You didn't answer the question."

The judge told him, "Answer the question, please, Mr. DuBois."

Why she respecting him? Were they friends? Was she trying to send me to jail for almost taking Roosevelt's life?

He spoke slowly. "I think my wife had approximately two hundred on the list."

It seemed more like two hundred and fifty to me. "Is 'approximately two hundred' your answer?"

"Move on, Mr. Washington," the judge insisted.

What is up with her attitude? She's prejudiced. Fine. Be that way. I didn't need her to side with me. The jury was making my decisions.

"Do you recall what happened the night someone shot you?"

"My brother was making the toast. You pointed a gun at me, fired twice. I dove into the swimming pool, and the next thing I remember was being in the hospital on life support," he said.

I started frowning, then stopped. "So you never saw the person who shot you pull the trigger?" I asked him.

"No."

"Do you have any enemies or jealous women who didn't want you to marry Madison Tyler?" I asked, looking back at Loretta. Why was she sitting in the last row in the corner? Sindy was her name. The woman that met with G-double-A. She was on the last row across from Loretta.

I faced Roosevelt, awaiting his response.

"Not that I know of," he said, glancing at Loretta before redirecting his attention to me.

"Why did your wife take you off life support? Did she want you to die so she could get your millionssss?" I asked, dragging out the *s*, and then added, "And save her daddy's company?"

He looked at the prosecutor. The prosecutor, who hadn't said anything prior, stood. "Objection, Your Honor. He's leading the witness."

"Overruled. Answer the question, Mr. DuBois."

"I don't know. Ask her when she takes the stand."

"Did you see what type of gun the shooter had?"

Roosevelt said, "I have your bullet that was removed from my leg. One is still in my body and—"

Yadda, yadda, yadda, dude. I cut him off. My last question was "Do you have knowledge of your fiancée/wife having a sexual affair or encounter with another man at any time during your relationship?"

His exhale into the microphone resounded throughout the courtroom. "Yes."

"I have no further questions, Your Honor."

The prosecutor didn't cross-examine Roosevelt either. Wherever they got him from, I was glad. I'd fire him if he was my lawyer.

"The court will take a fifteen-minutes recess," the judge said, motioning for the prosecutor to approach the bench.

I sat beside my standby counsel and started reviewing my questions for my next witness. G-double-A and No Chainz would be proud of me. I had to use the bathroom so bad, I wanted to piss in my pants. I knew Roosevelt had to know that man who'd slept with his fiancée was me.

I knew it. I knew it. I knew it.

CHAPTER 30

Madison

Now I understood how a good case could turn bad. Even if he lost, by the time this was over, Granville's stupid ass would have exposed and humiliated all of us. I was a fool for sleeping with him. I blamed Loretta, but was it really her fault that I'd opened my legs?

She didn't invite Granville to my house. She didn't undress me and force Granville's salami dick inside me that night. She wasn't the one who impregnated me. But . . . yes, she was indirectly responsible for all of us being here today.

Soon as we got into the hallway, I grabbed Loretta's bicep; then I ushered her to the women's restroom. Tisha followed us.

Loretta pulled away. "Don't touch me. Don't you *ever* touch me."

Tisha closed the door. I adjusted my padded customized bra. It was the same DD-cup size and shape as the real ones I had a month ago. My baby was five months and one week. My stomach was starting to round out.

"If I weren't pregnant, I'd do more than touch you. I'd beat your ass." I removed my sunglasses so she could see my eye was still slightly bruised. The blood clot was slowly going away, but it wasn't completely gone. Black had faded to purple, and purple had turned to blue. "I should've pressed charges against you."

Loretta's eyes widened. "Oh, wow. It's still there. You sure I did that? If I did, Madison, I'm so sorry."

This was a time when I wished God would strike Loretta down for lying. "I agree. You are pathetic. Tell me something I don't know."

Tisha said, "You're not sorry, Loretta. And if we weren't at the courthouse, I'd beat you down for Madison."

Tisha didn't start fights. But she didn't run away from one either. If she threw the first punch, this would be a first. The two times she had physical altercations in school, no one messed with her afterward. She'd whipped one guy so bad, he was too embarrassed to return. He transferred.

I knew Tisha supported me. With her conniving, coward ass, Loretta wasn't dumb or brave enough to do her dirt in front of anyone. I didn't care who came into or was already in the bathroom, but it appeared to be empty.

"Let me make myself clear, Loretta. I have an ass whupping with your name on it. Soon as I drop this baby, you are going to wish you were a Christian bitch," I told her, shoving my pointing finger close to her face.

She stood there, staring at us.

"You satisfied with the chaotic mess your jealousy has created?" Tisha asked her.

Loretta folded her arms; then she hunched her shoulders. "Y'all done? This friendship should've ended years ago."

"You're right," I replied, then touched my stomach. I felt my baby twitch. I smiled. He or she was growing. Soon my baby would be kicking. This child was exactly what I needed right now. Hoped I felt the same after delivery.

"I'm not apologizing again," Loretta said, placing her hand on the door.

"Walk away. Because you're the only one who's not vested in this. I have to live with having cheated on my husband. And your ass gets your daughter, goes back to your job, and starts all over." I yelled in Loretta's face, "I hate your ass!" Then I started crying.

"The feeling is mutual. Same for you, Tish." Loretta left. She'd taken all of her problems to the Lord in prayer and left them there, I guess.

"Madison, she'll get hers," Tisha said, drying my tears. "We've got to keep you and"—she touched my belly—"this baby healthy. I love you, Madison. You're a good person. With all the things you've said, you've never done me wrong. Neither of us can say the same about Loretta."

CHAPTER 31

Madison

Granville trailed my every step. He stared at me with lustful eyes as I approached the stand. I felt his eyes on my stomach. I could tell he thought the baby was his.

Loretta was probably jealous that Roosevelt and Granville wanted me, and neither of them wanted her. She was stupid to let Chaz use her. What man in his right mind would want a woman like her?

Roosevelt was having a difficult transition; but as long as he continued to love me unconditionally—in time, if my baby was his—we'd stay together. If he had been done with me, he would've filed for a divorce by now. Men shouldn't stay married if they were unhappy.

I wasn't sure why the two women on the last row were here or whom they were with. They were too beautiful to be related to Granville but the one with the long cinnamon hair was somewhat familiar. I couldn't remember where I'd seen her.

"Hello, dear," Granville said. "You look nice. I miss you."

That fool was still crazy. My head snapped in the judge's direction.

The judge responded, "Mrs. DuBois, please remove your sunglasses. And Mr. Washington, do not address Mrs. DuBois in that manner."

The faces on some of the jurors were fixed on Granville. His love for me was genuine. I believed the jury felt it too. His was an obsessive kind of love I didn't want.

Staring at the floor, he said, "Yes, Your Honor. I apologize."

It was best for me to say as few words as possible. Not knowing what to anticipate, I did as the judge requested, then braced myself for his first question.

An overwhelming gasp came from those who had thought I was being stylish. Helen sat between her boys. Martin was next to Chaz. Wally sat beside Roosevelt. I was surprised to see Roosevelt's grandfather. He'd stayed away from the hospital when Roosevelt was there, but Wally had made his way to the courtroom. My parents were seated on the opposite side of the room from my husband's family. Tisha and Loretta were on the side with my family. Other than the two women sitting on Roosevelt's family side, I imagined that at my funeral the seating arrangements would be almost the same.

Granville looked at me. "Who did that to you?"

I shook my head.

The judge told me, "Answer the question."

I sat for a moment, recalling the oath I'd just taken: "Do you promise to tell the truth, the whole truth, and nothing but the truth, so help you, God"; before I answered, "I do."

The woman with the long cinnamon hair watched me intensely. Where had I seen her? Why was she here?

My cream-colored dress, which was slightly tapered, stopped right above my knees. I'd worn black shoes and a skinny black belt to accent the bulge in my stomach. I felt like a woman of honor and dishonor. I could lie for Loretta. With the exception of family and friends, no one knew a padded bra replaced my breasts. My hair was eloquently covered with a black wrap. No makeup. No lipstick. My only jewelry was my wedding ring.

Now I was the one looking down. I didn't want to get her in trouble. If I did, I would've pressed charges. Quietly I answered, "Loretta Lovelace."

Granville gazed over his shoulder. If looks could've killed her, he would've committed another crime.

"Mr. Washington, proceed with your questioning."

He faced me. I wondered if underneath it all was a good man with a foolish heart.

He stood tall and squared his shoulders. "Mrs. DuBois, did you have a gun in your possession at the time of the shooting?" he asked.

"No."

His suit was nice. I'd never seen him dressed up. I could tell from the formfitting attire that he had developed what I'd call a "prison physique."

"Mrs. DuBois," he said in a romantic tone, "why did you hire me?" His hoarse voice still annoyed me.

"I didn't hire you."

"But I worked for you, right?" he asked.

"Yes, but my staff hired you."

He stood taller, as though he'd suddenly realized he was slouching.

"Okay, then why did you fire me?"

"I didn't. Your supervisor fired you." I was indirectly responsible, but I didn't want him to drag me under his bus.

He followed up with asking, "Based on your recommendation?"

"Yes" was all I said, hoping it would all be over soon.

Glossiness coated his eyes. He seldom blinked.

"Why did you invite me to your house, cook dinner for me, serve me alcohol, then proceed to initiate sexual intercourse with me?" A tear fell from his left eye.

The entire jury leaned forward and stared at me. I was sure they were holding their breaths.

At that precise moment I couldn't choose which one I hated more—Loretta or Granville. I sat quietly for a moment. Again I reminded myself I was under oath.

The judge said, "Answer the question, Mrs. DuBois."

Roosevelt's mom, Helen, sat on the edge of her seat. I moved closer to the microphone and whispered, "It was a bet."

"Could you please speak up, Mrs. DuBois?" Judge Owens asked.

I repeated, "It was a bet."

"And exactly what was this bet?" Granville questioned.

Softly I exhaled; then I placed my hand on top of my stomach, hoping to gain sympathy from the jurors. "Loretta Lovelace dared me to have sex with you. So I did. For that, I am truly sorry."

Roosevelt knew some of what had happened. Today he might hear it all. I'd lied and told him Granville was my ex, someone I'd dated before we'd met. He knew that already. But he didn't know I'd cooked for this man.

Granville asked, "Who was your chauffeur driver on your wedding day?"

No, he *did not* bring that up! "You, but—"

He cut me off, and threw me off by asking, "What was the prize?"

Granville wasn't as dumb as I'd originally concluded.

"If I won, she'd sign her house over to me." I looked into Roosevelt's eyes, then continued, "If she won, I'd call off my engagement to Roosevelt DuBois." There, I'd spoken the truth in front of everyone. The worst was finally over.

"I'd like to show Exhibit A to the court, Your Honor."

Judge Owens announced, "The video is graphic. If anyone would like to leave the courtroom, you may do so at this time." She waited a minute. No one moved. The judge nodded at the deputy.

The lights dimmed just a little. Staring at the flat screen, I sat in disgrace as I watched Granville undress himself down to his wife-beater T-shirt. He dropped his clothes beside my bed as I removed my dress, then placed it on the chaise lounge in my bedroom. Next I lay down on my back and spread my thighs, inviting him to go down on me, giving him instructions on how to pleasure me orally.

Roosevelt had seen the tape before, but seeing him watch it in front of his family embarrassed both of us. It reminded us that I'd lied. Without turning my head I shifted my eyes and glanced in Loretta's direction. Her attention was glued to the video—so was everyone else's, including my parents', and the two women seated on the back row.

I couldn't win the bet without intercourse. I watched myself put a condom on Granville's long, dark, thick shaft; then I mounted him. His dick felt amazing. I came instantly. *It is only for a short while,* I'd thought, convincing myself to enjoy the ride and win the prize. He grunted as he came.

Thrusting my hips, I bounced higher and higher; until the last time I came down, I saw how his dick went inside my ass, but there was no condom.

Now Roosevelt could connect the dots as to why I couldn't have sex with him. I'd lied to him again. I'd told him I was suffering from an allergic reaction to coconut. I was never allergic to coconut. Since I was a little girl, I didn't like the way it felt inside my mouth.

Thankfully, there were no cameras in the courtroom. The condom that my gynecologist had pulled out of me the next day during my exam was Granville's.

I screamed. He shouted, "Yeah!" He was pushing himself deeper. My face was red. My ass was too, but it was covered in blood. The video stopped as I'd passed out. The lights came up in the courtroom. My husband also found out why I was at the hospital the night he couldn't contact me.

I wanted to kill Granville as he hung his head, then said, "Sorry, dear. I have no further questions."

The prosecutor looked at me, then raised his brows. "No questions, Your Honor."

Granville said, "I'd like to call my next witness."

Judge Owens stared at me. Her lips were tight; her eyes narrowed.

CHAPTER 32

Granville

I wished I hadn't shown that videotape of Madison to everyone in the courtroom. I wanted to make Chicago watch it—prove to him that no matter how much money he had, I was the stronger bull. Seeing Madison break down and cry as she left the stand broke my heart. I didn't want to, but I cried too.

Drying my eyes, I didn't expect much from Loretta's testimony.

Had second thoughts about subpoenaing her, but G-double-A and No Chainz had said, "Man, you *have* to call her. She's the one who introduced you to Madison."

They were right, but Loretta also had a restraining order against me. I thought that might hurt my case. Wasn't sure how that worked with the distance thing. Guess this was an exception.

G-double-A had told me, "Man, you never know what the jury is thinking. Things you believe will help your case will hurt you, and vice versa. Focus on creating reasonable doubt, dude."

Loretta took the stand. She was my last witness for today. Maybe Raynard was here to support her. I didn't care about him. The DJ and a few of the employees who worked the reception were coming in tomorrow and the next day. I wished this were the last day, because the jury might forget all of this by the end of the trial—especially if the gun turned up. I had to make sure my closing arguments included the key points from today's witnesses.

She raised her right hand and then sat. Loretta's hair was pulled back into that dreadful ponytail she wore most of the time. Guess she was too afraid to cut it off like Madison, or too lazy to style it, or maybe she believed looking homely would give people in the courtroom who didn't know her the impression she was a Christian. She'd worn a silver cross necklace. Every time I'd seen her, she'd worn raspberry lip gloss. Today her lips were dry.

My first question for Loretta was "Why did you go out with me?"

Sighing heavily, she pressed her lips together.

Damn, girl. This is the first question, not the last.

"I've been asking myself the same thing. To answer your question, I thought you were a nice person, but I was wrong."

I was ready to move on. She'd said what I wanted the jury and judge to hear. I was a nice guy. She left out that I was funny too. Women loved my sense of humor.

The judge said, "Explain."

Now my lips were pressed together. I realized I was slumping, so I stood tall, pushed my shoulders back, and waited to hear her response.

She calmly said, "Granville Washington has four protective orders against him."

"I object, Your Honor. That has nothing to do with this case."

"Overruled. How do you know this, Ms. Lovelace?" Judge Owens asked.

What she asked that for? She was the judge. Didn't she know my background? She was trying to set me up and make the jurors go against me.

"I went out with him for three weeks. We were on our last date. He tried to give me an engagement ring. When I refused to accept it and told Mr. Washington I didn't want to see him anymore, he angrily followed me to my car. I saw police and asked for assistance. The police ran Granville's license and told me he had three protective orders and advised me to file one too. Mine is number four. Before I filed, he kidnapped me, and my so-called friend Madison Tyler refused to help."

"I'm going to remind you, Ms. Lovelace, that you are under oath." The judge looked at me and said, "Next question."

Good. I didn't care what made the judge remind Loretta, but I was glad she did. Loretta had started this. Now I was going all in.

"Ms. Lovelace, you say you were kidnapped. Did I force you into my car?"

"No."

I had to hurry with my questions before the judge gave Loretta more time to explain. "While you were in my car, did you give me Madison Tyler's business card, knowing Madison was engaged to marry Chicago?"

"Yes," she said, heaving.

"Would you tell the jury why you gave me Madison Tyler's card? Was it because you knew how fast I fell in love with you, and you wanted to set me up to fall in love with Madison? Or were you so jealous of Madison that you wanted to ruin her engagement?"

Loretta answered, "I am not jealous of Madison. She's a grown woman. She had sex with you because she wanted to."

Hearing that made me feel good, but I had to say, "You didn't answer the question, dear."

Loretta stood. "Stop calling me that! I'm not your 'dear'!"

"Ms. Lovelace, sit and don't get up until I say so," Judge Owens said, then continued, "Mr. Washington, I'm warning you."

"I apologize, Your Honor."

"Continue, Ms. Lovelace," the judge said.

I expected the judge to scold me again. She was becoming predictable. But what I really wanted to do was make Loretta madder. I deepened my scratchy voice. "Would you kindly tell the jury why you gave me Madison Tyler's card?"

"She already told you. We had a bet."

"A bet you initiated?"

"And?"

I wobbled my head. "And admit it, then. . . . You're in love with, and wanted to marry, Roosevelt DuBois."

She stared hopelessly at the prosecutor. He didn't say a word. Was dude holding out to slam me at the end?

Loretta glanced at the faces in the courtroom. I didn't bother looking over my shoulder. I knew where everyone was sitting. I was glad Precious had listened to me and hadn't come. She would've dragged

Loretta off that stand by her cross. Precious didn't need convincing to defend my honor. I wished Madison felt that way about me. None of this would've happened.

Loretta's eyes lingered in Roosevelt's direction.

She whispered, "Yes."

"Speak louder so everyone can hear you," I said.

Loretta stood. "Yes! Yes! You satisfied?"

Banging her gavel, the judge instructed, "Be seated, Ms. Lovelace. I'm not going to ask you again."

"I understand your pain," I said. "Because of your jealousy, I fell in love with an engaged woman, who left me for her fiancé. So who is really the victim here?"

"It's not time for closing arguments, Mr. Washington. Do you have any further questions?" Judge Owens asked.

"Yes. One final question."

A puff of air blew from Loretta's nostrils into the microphone. "Thank God."

I expected her answer to be the same as the others, but I had to ask: "Ms. Lovelace, did you have a gun in your possession at the time of the shooting?"

CHAPTER 33

Loretta

Why did he have to ask me that?

Madison knew I owned a gun, but Tisha was the only one other than me who knew the answer to the question. Suddenly I regretted opening my purse in the dressing room at church and showing Tisha my gun on Madison's wedding day. I wasn't that tough now. When Madison told her assistant to hire security, I should've let her do that.

I wished I could question Granville. Congratulate him on kidnapping Madison on her wedding day, and then ask how did he screw it up? If Madison hadn't shown up, Chicago wouldn't have gotten shot, and I would not be sitting on this stupid stand answering questions for this idiot!

Madison was two hours late for her wedding and Chicago waited for her. We all waited for her.

Look at her, sitting there with sunglasses on. She didn't have to tell everyone in the courtroom that I was the one who had hit her. I should tell them she had started it by pulling out my hair. There was so much during a trial that needed to, but was never heard.

I prayed Tisha didn't hate me enough to rat me out. I got the gun to protect myself from Granville, but the only time I used it as a threat was when those women were taking pictures of Madison, Tisha, and me at that steak house restaurant. I wanted to send them a clear message not to mess with us.

The gun made me feel powerful. I dared anyone to disrespect me. Even when I didn't have the gun on me, the knowledge that I owned one gave me courage to do bold acts, like tip my glass toward Raynard's ass and punch Madison in her face.

I sat quietly.

"Ms. Lovelace?" the judge said. "We're waiting. Answer the question."

I should've been prepared for this. He'd asked it of Chaz and Chicago. But I didn't think he'd ask me; and at the moment I couldn't recall if he'd asked Madison. Guess my eyes and ears were too glued to her sex video. Obviously, Madison was enjoying cheating on Chicago. Granville's dick was the biggest I'd seen it. He could barely stay hard for me.

Suddenly, I noticed the woman seated on the last row with the gigantic red Afro was the sex therapist I'd sent Granville to. Was she here to testify?

"Ms. Lovelace," the judge said, "I'm not going to ask you again."

Inhaling, long and slow, I thought I was going to faint. Maybe that was my answer. Fake passing out so I won't perjure myself.

I don't know what made me say "no," but I did, thinking it would end like the other responses.

"That's a lie, Loretta, and you know it!" Tisha shouted.

"Be seated! This is my courtroom," Judge Owens said.

Maybe if I'd gone to the clinic with her to have her abortion, she would've kept quiet. Perhaps if I'd been a better friend and hadn't gone to the hospital and hit Madison in the face when she was in her bed recovering from surgery, our friendship bond wouldn't have been broken.

Madison had forgiven me for all I'd done—except when I'd hit her. And although she hadn't pressed charges, I still hated her. Look at her. The glow on her face outshined the mark I'd left on her eye. I prayed that was Granville's baby inside her and not Chicago's.

If I would've focused on the man in front of me instead of wanting the one Madison had, I know Tisha would've kept quiet. Chaz wouldn't have dogged me out if I hadn't fallen in love with his brother.

"She's telling the truth. Loretta did have a gun in her purse. We know because she showed it," Madison said.

Now who was lying? I'd never shown Madison the gun during the wedding or reception. Tisha must've told her. Or was Madison's outburst payback for what I'd just said about Chicago? Or was God teaching me a lesson?

Raynard stared at me. I couldn't tell what he was thinking, but I was sure he was hoping Tisha and Madison weren't telling the truth. His wife wasn't going to be happy raising our daughter. If I ended up doing time, he'd probably end up divorced.

"You be quiet. You've given your testimony," the judge said to Madison, then looked at me. "Loretta Lovelace, I'm going to give you one more chance to answer the last question truthfully."

I looked at Chicago, held my head down, then answered, "Yes, but I didn't shoot anyone."

"You've lied on my stand. I can't believe any of your testimony, Ms. Lovelace." The judge looked to the deputy and said, "Arrest her for perjury."

Raynard stood. "Your Honor, I have a videotape of the shooting."

"Oh, great," Granville said. "Just when things were going my way, you show up with a tape." He covered his mouth. "Oh, my bad. Did I say that aloud?"

This was starting to resemble an episode of *Judge Joe Brown,* where everyone was talking out of order in the courtroom.

This was one time I was glad Raynard was here. After the judge saw the tape, they'd see I was telling the truth.

The deputy approached me. "You have the right to remain silent. . . ."

Why didn't I think of that before I'd lied? I should've pleaded the Fifth.

CHAPTER 34

Chicago

Un-be-liev-able!

I felt like a fool. She had a gun? At my reception? Was she planning on shooting or protecting Madison? The confession that she was armed meant she knew something was going to happen. If Granville hadn't shot me, was Loretta going to kill my wife? Right now, I didn't know what to believe.

Watching Loretta being handcuffed, I thought the judge was being too hard. I waited, hoping to hear the judge say, "Let her go." She didn't. She allowed Raynard to meet with the prosecutor. I wasn't sure if they were going to accept his video as evidence, but I wanted to bail Loretta out before she was booked—but not before I saw that tape.

Why did Raynard hold on to evidence that long? They should charge him with obstructing justice. What made him decide to turn it over? Now that Loretta was suspect, maybe he wanted to prove she was innocent. Perjury was one thing, but if Loretta was involved in the shooting . . . She couldn't be.

After all she'd done to help me, I felt guilty for not being more sensitive. Once, Madison came home unannounced—I considered my condo Madison's place too—and I'd dismissed all that Loretta had done to help me recover. I'd let her walk out—more like get thrown out by Madison—and I never confronted Madison or apologized to Loretta.

Had I misled Loretta? I picked up on her feelings for me the first time I'd gone to her house. If I had known Loretta had initiated a bet for Madison to fuck that crazy guy, Granville, I wouldn't have asked my brother to go out with her. I wouldn't have cared about Loretta at all. There was a reason she'd attracted that man, and there was a reason he'd tried to kill me. Or was it Loretta who had fired the shots?

Since we were both Christians, I didn't want to condemn Loretta. She had things in common with me that I'd never have with Madison. Yet, Loretta could never be Madison. Had I known how deep Loretta's jealousy toward Madison was, I would've never befriended Loretta. *Never.*

You can't choose your fiancée's friends, but your fiancée's friends sure can screw up a good thing. The attraction Loretta had to me, I reluctantly confessed to myself, was mutual. But mine wasn't the kind that wanted to leave my wife for my wife's best friend. It was flattering, but I'd never interfere with what I'd thought was my brother's pursuit of happiness with Loretta. That would've been doggish. I prided myself on being a man my community and fans around the country admired. Most men strayed sometimes, but there were varying degrees. When a man's character was exemplary, regardless of his actions, most people still loved him. I was blessed that I was that kind of man.

What Madison had done—that was the bitch type of doggish. I'd never cheated on her. I had justification to treat Madison like shit after she'd left me for dead; but again, it wasn't about her. Just her luck, she married a real man.

My grandfather Wally, who'd come to court today, told Chaz and me a long time ago, "When you have the choice to take the high road or the low road, always do what's right. No one can fault you for doing the right thing. Real men don't dog, stray, act like a bitch, or tuck their tail."

What the hell was wrong with Loretta? She ruined my marriage because she wanted to be with . . . I shook my head, then headed out of the courtroom.

"Roosevelt, you got a minute?" A deep masculine voice resounded from behind me.

I knew who it was. "How can I help you, Johnny?"

"My daughter. You know she was framed, and not in her right state of mind. Please find it in your heart to forgive her," he pleaded.

Too bad Granville hadn't subpoenaed Johnny Tyler. I knew Johnny didn't pull the trigger. But he didn't know that I knew he was the one who'd encouraged Madison to sign the authorization. He was the one who thought I'd be dead by now. Would he be cool if Rosalee was the one in the video cheating on him?

Ready to move on, I asked, "That's it?"

He cleared his throat. "Can we meet later? Based on my lawyer's recommendations, I'd like to propose a revised business contract."

"Not happening. What you need to do is be happy you still have a job working for my company," I said, then started walking away.

"Papa, let me handle this. Roosevelt, wait."

I turned to see Madison. Her dad went in the opposite direction, shouting, "Tyler Construction is my company!"

Obviously, he was so eager to get the check I'd given him, he hadn't read the entire contract. Directing my attention to Madison, I saw that pregnancy agreed with my wife. I did not.

If I had seen that video for the first time today, maybe we could exit this courthouse, arm in arm, to confront the salivating reporters outside, all waiting to quench the media thirst for the breaking news. However, I'd watched part of the video before; and sitting in the courtroom today, seeing my wife enjoying sexing a man—who she lied and told me was someone she'd slept with before we met—it was the first time I'd seen all of it, and all of her. She was so hot, if the accident hadn't happened, she would've kept coming.

Chaz put his hand on my back. "Let's go."

"Chaz, please don't interfere," Madison said. "That's rude. Roosevelt can speak for himself. Stay out of our conversation."

"What, Madison?" I asked, staring into her eyes. Seeing my wife's bruise made me not give a damn about Loretta. But how could I not be there for Loretta?

"I know I hurt you," she said, lowering her eyelids midway.

I shook my head. "Embarrassed me? Yes. Hurt? No. There's nothing else you can do to break my heart. When I get on my knees at night and pray, I pray for you. I pray that God will keep you and the baby safe and healthy. I ask Him to give me strength to deal with you in a positive way." I cupped the palm of my hand to my nose, then slid it over my mouth and down to my chin. I blinked hard, trying to force my tears not to fall.

"I'll meet you at the house," Madison said confidently.

When I was in love with her, her confidence was attractive. Now it was annoying. Respecting Madison didn't mean I had to obey or accommodate her. Why I'd allowed her back in my house? I wasn't sure.

"Please don't come to my house tonight," I said. "I'm not asking."

Trailing me closely, she cried out, "Why shouldn't I come home?"

I shouted in her face, "Really! After what everyone in the courtroom just saw, you need to ask me that! You—" The embarrassment from the video suddenly hit me hard. "Stay away from me right now."

Madison gripped my arm. I firmly moved her hand. I squeezed her wrist tighter than I should have, then immediately let it go. I said, "I apologize," but I didn't want her touching me.

For the first time in my life, I wanted to hit a woman.

CHAPTER 35

Chicago

Chaz refused to let me keep talking with Madison. He told me, "I don't care what Loretta has done for you—you're *not* bailing her out of jail."

He'd insisted that I wasn't indebted and she had parents, a baby's daddy, and friends, if one could consider Madison and Tisha that. Plus, Chaz made me admit, "You're right. Loretta is not completely innocent." Her hands could indirectly have my blood on them. What if Granville, Madison, and Loretta were scheming to get my money and it backfired? Maybe Raynard was somehow involved.

"You're doing the right thing," Chaz said, parking his car at Eddie V's valet stand.

This time we sat at a private booth, near the bar. We sat side-by-side in the center so we could see the entire room and enjoy the live music.

For a moment we were both quiet.

Breaking the silence, I said, "There should be a reality show called *The Biggest Fool,* and I should be on it. This would've never happened to you."

Chaz's eyes watered. "Nah, don't say that, man. I admire you. Not many men would respect a woman like Madison. Don't dog her out now. Stay close to her until the baby is born, then create distance. If it's yours, it's all about my nephew. File for physical and legal custody.

If not, you've got to cut all ties with Madison—the same way I did with Loretta."

I smiled. "What do you know about physical and legal custody?"

"Man, I stay ahead of these women," he said, laughing. "Actually, I almost dated a girl with kids once, until I heard all the mediation drama between her and the father. She broke it all the way down on the first date. I didn't want to go in her house or get any. I couldn't wait to drop her off."

I didn't understand why I loved Madison so much. I had to pray for the answer.

"Are you going to let Mom take over Tyler Construction?" Chaz asked. "I say we do it."

"You know Hurricane Helen despises Madison and Johnny. If we let her storm through their company—"

"Correction, *our* company. Legally, Madison is still my wife, which makes her the only one hundred percent owner."

Chaz mumbled, "You did that on purpose. Wish we can find a way to get around that."

My motivation had been to help, not hurt Madison's family. "Mom will try to sell it from under them," I said. "I know we're going to replace Johnny, but let's keep Mom out of this, and let's wait until after the baby is born before we make a move."

Chaz nodded. "*The baby, the baby, the baby.* Man, what we got? Another four months?"

"About that," I said, smiling at my brother. "Changing the subject, I'm excited about your handling preseason. I'll be ready to take over everything for the season's opener."

"Cool. Long as you keep me as your assistant. I love this life, man."

"You got it." It was awesome working with my brother.

Drew, the general manager, approached our table. "Welcome, fellas. You don't have to ask—I've already alerted my staff to make sure you're not disturbed. Order whatever you'd like, it's all on the house tonight."

Eddie V's Prime Seafood was a five-star restaurant in many ways that kept us coming back. "Thanks, Drew," I said.

Chaz added, "Two tickets. Box suite or the fifty-yard line for the next home game?"

Drew smiled wide. "Never been in a suite or sat on the fifty."

Everyone we knew, and some we didn't, requested tickets. Before the season ended, we had a long list for the next season. Mom and her friends. Dad and his buddies. Friends of their friends begged more than family. I hadn't overlooked Drew. There were no seats to offer. Chaz had no problem saying "no" to anyone, including Mom and Dad. Depending on Drew's selection, someone was getting bumped.

I wasn't Mr. Nice Guy. I knew how to say "no." The difference between Chaz and me was that I was a man of my word. A commitment by Chaz was more like a promise that he had no problem breaking, especially when it came to women.

"Think about it, let us know before we leave," I told him.

"Oh, Chaz, I've been meaning to ask. Can you create an app for me? I need to find a creative way to connect with and increase my followers. I just landed a part in a movie. Nothing big, but it's a start."

"That's great, man. Congrats." I was excited for anyone who got an opportunity to pursue his dream.

"Straight up? Congrats," Chaz said. "Already got some things in mind. Call me next week."

Creating apps was my brother's first love and business. Maybe that's why we were different. Tech brains processed information like a computer did. When Chaz was in programming mode, his communication sometimes required decoding. After what happened in court earlier, I was glad we were relaxing.

"Who's giving up their two tickets?" I asked.

Two was quickly becoming a good number. The two gorgeous women that were in the courtroom earlier entered, then stood near the bar, scanning the room. The one I liked caught my attention immediately. She was striking. Her cream-colored, sleeveless dress hugged her curvaceous body. The neckline covered her collarbone. The hem stopped right above her knees. The diamonds and pearl necklace complemented her diamond earrings. I'd guess five-nine and a perfect size nine. I already saw her wearing a jersey with the number ninety-nine and nothing else.

"I thought you'd like her," Chaz said, motioning for them to come over.

Speaking between closed teeth, I asked, "What are you doing? I was just enjoying the view. Real men don't stray. Remember? You know I'm a married man."

"On paper. You said you were open to meeting someone, and there she is," Chaz said, then smiled. "You were so close to death—you deserve to live a little. Do like President Obama says, 'Move forward.' "

The president being the husband and family man I aspired to become, I was sure whatever my brother had in mind wasn't what Obama had meant.

When I saw her up close, I held my breath. I hadn't felt this since I'd met Madison. Butterflies zigzagged in my stomach. My hand trembled underneath the table.

Chaz stood. "Roosevelt, this is Sindy, with an *S, Single*ton." He placed emphasis on "Single," then continued. "And this is her friend Numbiya Aziz. Numbiya is my date," he said, flicking his brows up twice.

Sin, Sin, I thought, exhaling. Men exhaled too. But we never waited for it. It just kind of happened unexpectedly for us. I felt as though I was already cheating on Madison.

Not wanting to be impolite, I stood and then shook their hands, as though they were here for a business meeting. If Sindy was anything like Madison, sexual pleasure definitely didn't come with the initial acquaintance.

Numbiya slid in. My brother sat on the side next to her. I waited for Sindy to scoot over, and then I sat on the edge away from her. Before she placed her legs under the table, I'd gotten a good look at her open-toed leopard shoes, noticing her impeccable red polish and suckable toes.

"You can come closer, Roosevelt. I won't bite," Sindy said, swiping her long, straight cinnamon hair to one side. Her silver-and-gold Rolex watch, with diamonds, was like the one I'd bought and planned on giving Madison on our honeymoon in Bora Bora. That was the plan before we were married. The trip was nonrefundable; but when I told them what had happened, they said I could reschedule. If we hit it off, I'd gladly take Sindy on that vacation.

I loved a woman who could afford to buy for herself the presents I'd give her. I wouldn't dare give Madison any more presents. As the father of her baby, if it were mine, emotionally and financially I'd do right by Madison and my child. As my grandpa Wally would say, "Respect is for you, not the other person."

Suddenly I became sad, thinking about lying in that hospital bed, longing to see my wife. She never came with good intentions. I wondered if Loretta's support was self-serving too. Damn! Why did some women have to be so devious?

Chaz was right. I deserved to live a little.

Sindy whispered, "Hey, you. You good? You look like you could use a hug." Gracefully, she opened her arms.

Her mocha lips were inviting. She had a light complexion like Madison's. I prayed she wasn't from Port Arthur. I had a clear view of her face. Her eyes were golden. She smiled and I inhaled an amazing scent. Everything about her was womanly. Her French manicure was impeccable. There was a diamond solitaire on her left middle finger. Her ring finger was bare. I stared at Chaz. Regardless of his good intentions, I was not ready for this beautiful woman. I couldn't ignore her, but why had he invited them to the trial?

We embraced. I would never forget our first hug. She didn't pat me. Slowly she slid her hand up and down my spine as she gently scraped her nails against my back.

Forgive me, God! This woman excited me. Why was I too sentimental? Most men wouldn't notice how a woman felt, as long as he got between her legs. An erection was emerging. I had to let her go.

I saw the way Granville looked at my wife in that courtroom. Grown men don't cry in public over a woman. He was in love with Madison. Yet, he didn't have compassion for Loretta. When Loretta was handcuffed, he was happy. What made men not go the distance for Loretta when they'd jump overboard without a life-preserver for Madison or a woman like Sindy?

Drew placed a bottle of champagne in a silver bucket, filled with ice, at the end of the table. "Only the best for you, fellas. Suite seats, please." He left and a waiter arrived with four flutes, filled our glasses, then whisked away.

Answering Sindy, I said, "I'm good," and then I looked at Chaz.

He knew I'd like Sindy. Hopefully, there would be other times for me to get to know her. Changing my focus, I asked Numbiya, "What do you do?"

She smiled. Her natural chocolate lips exposed the whitest teeth. There was a sexy gap between her top front teeth. Her dark, radiant skin appeared soaked in shea butter. The bright red Afro was about five-inches high. She had an unconventional type of sexiness that resonated from within and beamed through her eyes. I saw why my brother was attracted. She was different.

"I'm a sexologist."

A what? He'd met her where? Glancing toward my brother, I frowned. I looked at Sindy, wondering if she was one too.

Chaz laughed.

I held up my glass of champagne. "A toast to Numbiya, the sexologist."

Wasn't quite sure what she meant; but knowing my brother, I was in for something, let's say, "jaw-dropping and eye-opening."

CHAPTER 36

Loretta

Yesterday had been the worst day of my life.

"It's time for your strip search," she'd said. "Come with me."

Flashing to the video of Granville's dick going inside Madison's ass, I had realized that it was my turn to be violated. I wondered how invasive the strip search would be. Tears had streamed down my face.

Why hadn't I just told the judge the truth? Ultimately I might have still ended up here, but I felt like a fool for being locked up for lying. I felt bad for what I'd done to Madison.

"Have a seat in the BOSS chair," she had said firmly.

I learned "BOSS" stood for body orifice security scanner. The chair would scan my entire body for all metal objects—cell phone, weapons, and contraband.

I sat in the seat. The arms, seat, back, and footpad were hard, boxy, and flat. I did as I was told. Didn't need any time added to my stay. The machine beeped, but I hadn't been sure why.

"Do you have any mercury or gold fillings?"

Damn. "Yes" had been all I said.

I had to place my jaw over a circular plate, which was attached to the side of the chair. It beeped.

"Open your mouth wide." She looked inside. "I don't see any fillings. Open wider," she had said, probing my mouth. Her fingers pressed my jaws outward.

She had started to annoy me, but I hadn't shown it. "I have two gold fillings in the back, which are covered with white porcelain."

Rubbing my gums, she said, "Okay, your search is complete. You're cleared."

The room that the chair was in doubled as a storage room. The walls were lined with racks stacked with tan and green prison attire, socks, blankets, and a few large brown cardboard boxes.

I had felt relieved then. I had thought after she'd put on those rubber gloves, she was going to shove her fingers up my vagina and rectum.

"Let's go," she had said, following me. "Turn right."

I walked a short distance in what they called the intake and discharge room. I envied the inmates checking out. She opened a door. There had been a woman waiting for me.

The room had been small. A desk. A chair. The worker. And me.

"Have a seat," she said. "You're being booked for perjury. After this interview you'll be given the clothes you must wear and a blanket for your bed. We can either mail the clothes you have on to wherever you'd like or you can donate them. Which would you prefer?"

Her pen had hovered over a piece of paper, awaiting my response.

"Someone is going to bail me out today. I'm sure of that. So can't I just wait in a holding cell down here?" I was scared. I didn't want a bed or a blanket or their clothes. I wanted to go home.

She smiled. "You don't get it. Judge Owens is tough. You have to serve a mandatory thirty days. No one is getting you out before then. And if you want to get out in thirty, stay to yourself."

My heart had stopped for a second. Was she serious? For telling a lie I had to do that much time? It wasn't like I was a criminal, had a record, or had even committed a real crime. A sin? Yes, one that I'd repented, and God had already forgiven me for it.

"You can mail my clothes to my parents' home," I said, giving her the address.

Someone had tapped on the door then, opened it, and handed me a short-sleeved tan pullover, tan pants, brown socks, brown underwear, and a pair of shower shoes. Refusing to touch any of it, I had sat there, staring at her. She placed them in my lap.

"Visitation is once a week, but your visitors must be on your list. Anyone you'd like to see?" she had asked, holding her pen in position.

Immediately I gave her my parents' names, then added, "Tisha Thomas, Madison Tyler."

I had thought about Raynard, but I decided I didn't want him to see me in here. I didn't know what was on the video he claimed he had, or if he'd used it to try and control me.

"Anyone else?" she had asked.

"Yes." I had to add his name to see if he'd return my favors. "Roosevelt DuBois."

She stared at me, shook her head, then put down her pen. "Let's go."

There had been three of us in a line. We were escorted to the women's unit on the sixth floor. I was shown my cell. The top bed was mine. Covering my bed with the blanket I was given, I got in and went to sleep. I hadn't wanted dinner or conversation with my cellmate.

Morning came an eternity after my lockup. It hadn't been twenty-four hours, but it felt like it should be my last day.

It was seven in the morning—wake-up call and count, and then breakfast was served. Most of us were allowed to eat in the common area. A few of the women who were notorious for starting fights had to eat in their cells.

I sat alone. Shuffling food from one side to another, I missed my daughter.

My cellmate sat next to me. "What you in for?"

"I'd rather not say."

"Word is, you and your boyfriend, Granville, across the floor, tried to kill Chicago."

What the hell? "I don't have a boyfriend, and I've never tried to kill anybody," I said, talking way more than I wanted.

Nodding upward, she said, "Eat your food."

"Make me" was what I wanted to say, but I wasn't looking for trouble or trying to add time to my stay. "You can have it."

"I don't want your food. I want you," she said. "Eat it, or I'm going to eat you tonight, Lovelace." She slid her finger along the side of my face, over my lips, and then left.

I ate everything, praying I'd have to take a really good shit right before bedtime.

CHAPTER 37
Granville

Two weeks of trial. Another two weeks of deliberation. My closing argument was probably the best the judge and jury had heard. I was confident that today I'd finally get to go home.

This was the last time I'd be told when to eat, sleep, and wash my ass. No more free labor for the state from me. Companies paid workers in China more than seventeen cents an hour. Well, they got a lil more than four months out of me.

Scrubbing my ass, I thought about all the times I stood at the window inside my unit, hoping to get a glimpse of Loretta dressed in prison clothes. I never saw her. She was used to wearing the boring black pants and blouse to her high-paying pharmaceutical job. Trading that for khakis every day shouldn't matter, but I bet having girls hit on her was new. All that yap about how my dick wouldn't work—what if she discovered she was into females and that was why she couldn't keep me happy?

We were on the same level now. I rinsed and then dried off my hot bod. Put on my prison gear for the last time. If I got a job and she was fired, she'd beg me to take her back. Imagining the look on Loretta's face the day they handcuffed her made me want to pee in my pants. The whole time she was here, she was directly across the hall from me. Our narrow, rectangular-shaped window faced one another.

Every day I took turns for the lookout with G-double-A and No

Chainz to get a glance of Loretta in her new uniform. If the guard thought any one inmate was lingering too long, they covered the window from the outside with a brown magnetic strip and blocked our view. I didn't see Loretta the day she'd checked in, but I'd heard this was her last day too. The judge was serious about making Loretta stay thirty days. Whatever sentence they felt I deserved should be given to Loretta for making that bet with my Madison and entrapping me.

I checked for the fiftieth time that my name was on the posted list for my verdict today. It was.

I couldn't wait to put on the new suit Beaux bought me with the money from pawning the $15,000 engagement ring I'd bought Loretta. Wish I had my favorite cowboy boots, but G-double-A said they were too flashy and the jury would prejudge me. I didn't understand what difference he thought that would make on judgment day.

Beaux had paid G-double-A's mom what I'd hoped would be the last grand for his helping me. There was $6,500 left over from the $7,500 proceeds of the ring to pay my rent and car note for a few months. Beaux had suggested I give up my apartment, move my furniture into his garage, sell my truck, and save the cash. He'd said, "Use your money to start over fresh when you get out, bro."

Precious had said, "I got my own spot. Come stay with me, boo."

Shacking with her was my last choice, but it was better than being homeless. The second I got out, I was going to pick up where I'd left off. I wasn't living at home with Mama, my brother, or Precious. Soon as the jury told the judge I was not guilty, I was going to my house.

Staring at my handsome, irresistible reflection in the window of my cell, I licked my fingers and smoothed my eyebrows. I kissed the picture of Madison that I'd taped to my wall. "Love you, dear. See you soon." I ripped the picture into tiny pieces. I didn't want no other inmate dreaming about my woman.

The barber had shaved my head silky smooth yesterday. I had him trim my skinny mustache extra thin for good luck.

The guard announced, "Granville Washington."

No Chainz said, "Well, G, this is it. I don't want to see your ass back here, nigga."

G-double-A patted me on the shoulder, and said to No Chainz, "He'll be back."

I frowned. "And if I come back, you givin' me my money back, or I'ma beat you like you stole somethin'."

G-double-A laughed.

He wasn't going to get me down. I hated this place. I heard state was worse, but I had to get out today, or I was going to lose my mind. Being caged like an animal wasn't natural—no matter how decent the facility was. My bed was too small, the cell too little, and there wasn't enough space to store my work and regular shoes. The steel-toed boots they gave me were so big, and I only had one other pair of tennis and shower shoes by my bed. No Chainz had five pairs, which took up the same amount of space as my two.

My fellow inmates wished me well as I left the unit, escorted by the guard.

When I arrived at intake and discharge, Loretta wasn't there. Maybe she'd messed up and gotten extra time. I stepped into the cage and changed into my suit.

A guard walked into discharge with Loretta. Her hair was pulled back in that awful ponytail. This was the first time I'd seen her edges nappy. No lip gloss. Her red eyes narrowed at me.

I ignored her. This was my day, not hers.

For beating up my baby, she should've done another two years and eleven months—the maximum inmates usually stayed at this location—or maybe Loretta deserved life for screwing up mine.

They cuffed and transported me to the courthouse. The ride was a few blocks. They brought me through the back, sat me in a cold room, and then took off the cuffs. Another guard stood watch over me until it was my time to go before the judge.

I had to have time on my book with God. Never asked Him for much. Sitting in the back room, I prayed for a miracle.

"Okay, Granville. It's time," the deputy said.

Entering the courtroom, I was shocked to see Madison, happy to see Beaux. The rest—Chicago, Chaz, their folks, Tisha, Raynard, Madison's parents—didn't matter. My mom wasn't here. That made me a little sad. I craved her hug. I was surprised to see Loretta. She must've come straight from jail. She sat in the last row, in the corner. This wasn't reserved seating, but it was the same place she was during my trial.

Oh, no. G-double-A's person with the long cinnamon hair wasn't here. I hope he wasn't right about my going back.

As the judge walked in, the deputy announced, "All rise."

Judge Owens did all the preliminary stuff. *Blah. Blah. Blah.* At least I didn't hear that ice-cream story again. I wanted her to get to the important part.

Finally she asked, "Has the jury reached a decision?"

After running her mouth, she didn't even let me say anything. What if it wasn't in my favor? I could change somebody's mind before hearing them read what was on that paper in that man's hand.

Standing, the foreman answered, "Yes, Your Honor."

Sitting high, next to my standby counsel, regardless of what was on that tape Raynard had, I knew there was no way the jury could find me guilty. Hopefully, he didn't have a clear view of my face. No one saw any of the bullets hit Chicago. As far as I was concerned, whoever fired those bullets was shooting into a pool of water. How would anyone have known people would jump in the way? That was stupid on their part. No one would charge a driver for running over a rodent that ran into the road. It happened to armadillos in Texas all the time. Plus, they still hadn't found no weapon, and I had proven reasonable doubt.

"On the first count of attempted murder, we the jury find the defendant, Granville Washington, not guilty."

I almost peed in my pants. I started tap-dancing in my head. Footsteps trailed behind me. I heard the courtroom door open, then close. It didn't matter who that was; I was next to leave here a free man.

"On the second count of attempted murder, we the jury find the defendant, Granville Washington, not guilty."

Now I was suppressing my laughter, but I was sure my happiness showed all over my face. I wanted to give my standby counsel, the jury, the judge, and the foreman a big country group hug.

"On the third count of attempt to commit first-degree murder, we the jury find the defendant, Granville Washington, guilty as charged."

My neck tightened, shrugged backward. How was that? I raised my hand. "Excuse me, Your Honor. I think he meant to say, 'Not guilty.' "

"Mr. Washington, don't say another word." She looked at the foreman and said, "Continue."

"On the fourth count, attempt to commit first-degree murder, we the jury find the defendant, Granville Washington, guilty as charged."

I wobbled my head, and thought, *He made another mistake.*

The judge banged her gavel. "The court will take a fifteen-minute recess."

Tears streamed down my face. I sat there, trying to figure out what had gone wrong. Looking over my shoulder at my brother, he hunched his shoulders. I stared at Madison. She stood, staring back at me. Her stomach had gotten bigger. She was beautiful pregnant. I was most disappointed in the verdict because I'd failed her. I wouldn't be there for her or the birth of our child.

I guess when I'd heard the door open and close, the woman with the cinnamon hair and the other with the red Afro had come in. But they weren't sitting on the last row. They were one row behind Chicago.

G-double-A had some explaining to do. If I'd beaten the first two charges, what went wrong with the last two? It was only a matter of time before they put those awful handcuffs back on me in front of my woman. I called out to Madison, "Don't worry, dear. I'ma file an appeal."

CHAPTER 38
Madison

Turn your big, fat meat head around, shut up, and stop staring at me.
Granville gave me the creeps. Finally he was going to get what he deserved, but justice had not been served. I stood to leave the courtroom. Granville faced the front. I sat down. When he turned around, and started staring at me again, his standby counsel tapped him, then motioned for him to face the front again.

We all sat waiting for the judge and jury to return and for Judge Owens to announce the sentencing date. Helen had left after the first not guilty announcement. Chaz left the room during recess, presumably to tell his mother the final outcome.

It was bittersweet for me. Roosevelt answered all my calls, but he didn't want to see me. He declined accompanying me on visits to my obstetrician. He didn't want to see the ultrasound graphics of my baby. He said, "If it's not mine, I don't want to get attached. I'll wait."

I was tired of waiting to have my husband back. I was glad he'd made love to me before my surgery, though.

Disappointed in the decisions I'd made about Granville, I was foolish to let a bet ruin my life. All the hope I had was growing inside me.

Tisha whispered, "This part will be over soon. There's no way they'll approve an appeal, and even if they do, that'll take years. By then, we could sell our houses and move our children to New York or California."

Granville could get up to fifty years. If he got the max, he'd be almost one hundred years old by the time he was released. I stared at the back of his head, wondering what he was thinking. If the baby was his, at the rate of prison pay I'd never get child support, and I'd never have to fight for custody.

I was glad to have Tisha by my side. Loretta should've done something better with her hair before showing up anywhere in public. Sitting in the corner did not hide her appearance. No one had anything to say to her.

"Yeah, L.A. sounds good. New York gets too cold. What about Miami?" I asked, not caring about moving.

The places I'd love to live weren't best for me to raise my child. Plus, there was my family business to operate. I was familiar with a big city. Houston was one of the largest. But free-spirited, fast-moving folks hailing taxis on one end of the country and half-naked women parading everywhere on the other coast weren't where I wanted to rear my kid.

Texas was America.

Time passed slowly. Fifteen minutes had come and gone.

"Excuse me," Loretta said, squeezing in between Tisha and me.

I scooted to the edge. My baby kicked hard, making me grab my stomach. My unborn child could sense Loretta had bad vibes.

"Madison, Tisha, please accept my apology," she said, touching my hand.

I pulled away. "Please don't."

"I wanted to pray real quick before the judge returned."

Tisha moved Loretta's hand from hers. "This is not the time or place, Loretta. Please move."

Loretta proceeded to talk. "First John, fourth chapter, seventh verse says, 'Dear friends, let us love one another, for love comes from God. Everyone who loves has been born of God and knows God.' I love you guys."

Chaz reentered the room with his mother. My eyes trailed them as they sat with their family.

I didn't believe Loretta. Neither Tisha nor I responded. I wasn't going to become the hypocrite my ex-friend was. Loretta stood to move.

I whispered, "Thank God."

The jurors reentered the room and took their seats. I felt stuck when Loretta sat back down.

When the judge entered, the deputy said, "All rise."

"Oh, great." Anger festered. Tisha was supposed to be next to me, holding my hand. Instead, Loretta divided us.

Granville hung his head. My heart dropped. Not because I was sad. I sensed the woman with the red Afro sitting behind Chaz was with him, and the gorgeous woman with the long cinnamon-colored hair was with Roosevelt. She tapped Roosevelt on the shoulder; then she whispered into his ear.

I watched my husband smile.

Chaz and Roosevelt were dressed nicer than I remembered. I understood why Chaz seemed happier without Loretta, but I didn't know why Roosevelt appeared comfortable with that woman.

Now I remembered her. I'd seen the young woman at a local event where her father publicly bragged about her engagement to this French billionaire. That moment was like the scene from *Coming to America.* She rushed out of the room in tears.

Judge Owens spoke and I could hear the people around me breathing.

"The defendant is acquitted on all charges." She banged her gavel once, stood, and then left the courtroom.

No one moved as Granville slowly walked out of the courtroom with his brother.

CHAPTER 39

Loretta

Being behind bars changed me in ways I hadn't imagined. Watching Granville walk out of the courtroom a free man scared us all. The worst part about his acquittal was he couldn't be retried for the same crime. What did the judge see that we hadn't?

I still had my gun; and if he came anywhere near me, I was going to shoot first and ask no questions. The world was a lonely place in jail, but I'd go back if he showed up at my door.

"Mommy, why did you leave me again? Did I do something wrong? Did I make you mad?" Raynell asked.

I sat on her bed, combing her hair. Every day since I'd been released, my daughter asked me the same questions. There were no excuses. I was locked up for thirty days, but I'd left her the day Chicago was shot. I was caught up with a man who would never love me. When I got her back after my breakup with Chaz, I never imagined going from court to jail. Thank God, all of that was over.

I gave her the same response. "No, baby. You did everything right. I was the one who was wrong."

Having someone tell me what to wear, when to shower, when to go to bed, when to wake up, and when to eat was horrible. Sitting around from eight in the morning until ten at night, listening to all those women claim their innocence, made me understand that I was guilty.

Having my pussy eaten for the first time by a woman? I hate to admit it, but I enjoyed it. If I hadn't gone to jail, that experience would've never happened. My returning the favor would not have happened either. Everything about her seemed softer. Her lips, tongue, touch, and—oh, my gosh—her techniques were better than any man's.

My cellmate had a few more months to do. I didn't need any new friends. I promised to visit. I'd lied. I wasn't going back to that detention center under any circumstances.

"Is Daddy coming to get me? I don't want to go back to his house. Gloria was mean to me, Mommy. She hurt me."

After I left the courthouse, my first inclination was to go to Raynard's house and beat Gloria's ass for mistreating my baby. No way I was going back to jail for something stupid. The best I had to offer my daughter was to be with her.

The women in the detention center awaiting trial for murder made me realize if I'd handled my situation with Granville differently, Chicago and Madison would be happily married. No one would've gotten shot. It was my fault. None of us were happy. I was most worried for Madison.

The way I'd treated Madison and Tisha, I wasn't being a friend. They weren't speaking to me, and I deserved that. But I wanted my best friends back.

"You're not going back to your daddy's house, baby." I'd say it as many times as I had to for my daughter to believe me.

"Mommy, you promise," she said, holding out her pinky.

Locking my pinky finger with hers, as we pulled in opposite directions, I said, "Mommy promise. Your dad should be here soon and I'll let him know you're not going with him."

Raynell hugged my neck tightly. It felt good to be in my house with my daughter. It also felt different. A certain innocence was gone. To eat, sleep, and go to bed when I wanted was something I'd never take for granted again. Now that I was on probation—not with the correctional officer, with my job—I had to do everything right to keep a roof over our heads.

The doorbell rang. I kissed Raynell. "You stay here, princess."

Trotting downstairs, I poured two glasses of champagne, set them on my dining table, then opened my front door. Raynard was dressed in gray slacks and a nice T-shirt with OISEAU across his chest. He held a shopping bag with Saks printed on the side. It was spilling over with dresses for Raynell. He handed me an envelope.

"Hey, Loretta," he said, stepping inside.

I opened the door wider and scanned the inside of his car, which was parked in my driveway. "I should've known Gloria wasn't in the car, if you're actually speaking to me," I said, closing the door behind him.

The clothes and what was probably a check for $5,000 in the envelope reminded me of the way he used to be. Before I started dating Chaz, Raynard always took complete care of us. Now that I was back to being alone, he was back to normal.

"We need to talk," he said, standing in the living room.

Leading the way to the dining room, I sat and started sipping champagne. "That one is for you." I didn't touch it.

Raynard picked up his flute, then sat next to me. He straddled his legs wide. My knees were now between his thighs. I didn't move away. Looking him in the eyes, I said, "Before you get started, what was on that tape?"

"You can have it and see for yourself," he said. "Obviously, it wasn't enough to convict him, but it definitely cleared any suspicions they may have had of you."

I smiled and gently kissed him on his lips, then said, "I'm listening."

"You know the only reason I surrendered that video of the shooting was because I didn't want to risk your doing time for a crime you didn't commit. You made a few bad choices. You never should've dated that Granville guy."

Okay, here we go. I knew he wasn't done with letting me know how he did it all for me. I was thinking more like I never should've had your baby. What good was the tape if it didn't get Granville convicted? It might be why he'd gotten off. I kept quiet while I continued drinking.

"We both ended up with the wrong people. Listen, Loretta, I want us to be a family," he said, holding my hand. "I've never given you that, and you deserve to be my wife." Raynard showed me the most brilliant diamond ring I'd ever seen.

Why couldn't he have done this sooner? Like six plus years ago.

"Wear this. And when the time is right, we'll do it right."

Shaking my head, I told him, "Raynard, too many things have happened since we had Raynell. I don't love you the way I used to." I should've added, "And neither does our daughter."

He nodded. "I deserve that. Let me work on winning you back. Can you wear this and do that?"

I remembered what Tisha had told me: "When the ring is more important than the man, say 'no' to both."

I could accept his ring, but I didn't want to. "Raynell is uncomfortable being at your house, so let's trade places for a while." I lowered my voice, then said, "I appreciate your keeping her while I was away."

I didn't want him to hear the word "prison" or the name "Chicago" come out of my mouth; I was sure Raynard didn't either.

He blurted out, "Gloria's gone." He sounded like he'd lost his best friend.

I knew what that felt like. I'd lost two.

"Gone where?"

He exhaled, picked up the bottle, pressed it to his lips, and then burped. That was rude. But there were moments when I was in jail that I wished I could do that from guzzling champagne. All my life I'd taken my freedom for granted. Not anymore.

He scratched the nape of his neck. "She left me for her son's father."

My jaw dropped, right along with my empathy. "Are you saying?"

He nodded. "Yep. That bitch—"

"Wait a minute." I held up my hand. "Stop right there."

Raynard was a well-known gynecologist; yet he didn't know, or was it that he didn't want to believe that his son wasn't his?

"I'm not going to listen to you call her that. You were the one who was so thrilled to have the former Miss Houston as your wife that you paraded her at Raynell's first birthday party. How do you think I felt watching her cling to you with her nine-month, naked, stretch marks–free stomach shining in my face like it had LED lights! You thought that shit was okay? Well, be okay with the fact that you were a fool."

Like all the rest of those men with trophy wives and runway bitches whom they once had, ran around with, and were then fucked over by,

Raynard got exactly what he deserved. Now he was trying to be my savior. I didn't need no man to rescue me. The Lord was my savior.

"You're right. And I apologize. I can't believe Gloria had me take care of a kid who was for another man, and she knew it."

"Mommy, you okay?" Raynell asked.

Normally, she would've run to Raynard and jumped in his arms. She stood on the bottom step of the stairway.

"Say hello to your daddy," I told her.

"Hi, Daddy. Mommy, you okay?"

"Hey, baby. Can I get a hug? Look what I brought you."

Raynell took a step backward.

"I'm fine, princess. Go back upstairs. I'll come up when I'm done talking to your dad."

"Okay," she said, skipping up the steps.

"Damn, like that? Is she mine?" he asked, staring at me.

"Don't go there. I'm not Gloria. I don't know what you allowed her to do to our daughter while you had your dick stuck in your ear and your balls in your eyes, but you are going to have to earn Raynell's trust again," I said, picking up the bottle. I poured, but only drops fell into my glass. It wasn't enough for me to sip. I plopped the bottle down.

"Sorry about that," he said.

"About what? Drinking up all of the champagne or letting Gloria act a fool?"

"Loretta, I know I messed up. Let me earn back your trust too."

I laughed. "I'll let you do that. But we can never be together."

"Loretta, I want us to be a family." Leaning in for a kiss, he asked, "Can you let me do that?"

"Raynard, I think I'm a lesbian."

He reared back. "Dang, prison turned you out like that."

"No, prison didn't turn me out. You didn't turn me off. Granville didn't make me hate all men. Chicago didn't break my heart." Well, actually, he did. "And Chaz didn't ruin it for the next guy. I've struggled with this for a long time and . . . I think it's the reason why I hate Madison so much. I'm in love with her."

CHAPTER 40

Madison

Two months to go before my due date:

A lot of situations have changed since Granville's sentencing. The judge gave him fifty years. Add that to the forty-five he'd lived and Granville would be ninety-five years old before he was released. His brother had liquidated his assets, and his mother was dead. I had mailed anonymous letters to inmates in state pen, hoping they'd believe he was a rapist. From what I'd heard, Granville had been somebody's bitch every day.

A girl can dream, can't I?

Being seven months pregnant, I had no empathy for that idiot. Had no love for Loretta. I'd truly forgiven my mother for not sharing our family history of breast cancer. I was healing well; and according to my doctors, I was still cancer free. If my status was the same after I had my baby, I'd refuse chemo and radiation treatment and get my implants right away.

I hadn't spoken much to Tisha since the hearing, but we were still close through texting. She was dealing with Darryl's relentless begging for her to take him back. He was a homeless dog with no rich bitch to bone. Tisha wasn't listening to him relive the past. Good for her.

My cell rang. I checked the ID. I didn't recognize the number but answered, "Hello." Sindy would contact me eventually; I refused to miss that call.

"This is Beaux. Granville asked me to call and see how you and his baby are doing?"

"Tell your criminal brother to stay the fuck away from me and my baby, and don't you ever call me again," I said, ending the call. Hearing Beaux's voice, I feared the next call would come from Granville.

Everywhere I went, I expected Granville to show up. I hadn't seen him since court. Guess I'd gotten comfortable too soon. If that nincompoop started stalking me, he'd ruin all chances I had to reunite with my husband.

I wasn't a beggar; but for the first time in my life, I was genuinely jealous. Pleading with Roosevelt to take me back wouldn't be smart. I'd come up with something before it's too late.

This new woman Roosevelt was seeing, Sindy Singleton, was making and keeping my husband happy. She was two years younger than Roosevelt. I was five years older than her, but her youthfulness made me feel a decade her senior. The fact that I was healthy shouldn't have made me blue. But it did. Roosevelt didn't have a reason to feel sorry for me.

My cell rang again. I answered, "Yes, Papa."

"Good morning, sweetheart. Are you coming to the office to review our financials? This new accounting system Chaz installed is confusing me."

"I'll come by tomorrow. I've got business of my own to handle today."

"All right. See you then," he said. "Bye."

Roosevelt's generosity should've made my dad happy. Papa's pride was dwindling. His frats knew he wasn't "the man" of Tyler Construction. Papa was the face of the company, but that wasn't enough. He was old. He didn't understand new technology. He didn't want to learn. He simply preferred things go back to the way they were.

Getting out of bed, I removed my pink lace nightie, then stood in front of the mirror. Tears streamed down my cheeks. From my neck down to my stomach, I really did resemble my mom. How did she deal without having her twins in place most of her life? I fell to my knees, crying.

It's temporary, Madison. I gave myself a pep talk. *After you have the baby, you'll get your implants, and you can have boobs the size of Wendy Williams's, if you want, girl.*

Chuckling at the thought of having football-size breasts, while my baby was learning how to walk without falling down, I'd have to learn too. I got up. Looked at my stomach in the mirror and said aloud, "Madison, you're a complete woman."

My belly resembled a basketball. Daily workouts kept my weight gain under control. Being pregnant was no excuse to overeat. I was determined to return to my original size soon after I gave birth.

Men will fall at my feet once more. There was no need to shed tears about the truth. I was beautiful. More men had hit on me since I was showing than before.

I showered, put on my red yoga pants and an off-the-shoulder sweatshirt. Sitting behind the wheel of my Bentley, I cried again. It was easy to detest someone who treated you like shit. Roosevelt got me a new car and he'd gotten my house back. Why was he so damn nice? He let me keep the keys to his house; but the two times I went there, he was on the road. After the trial he didn't want to be near me.

Entering the gym at Roosevelt's condo building, I headed for the treadmill and walked briskly for five miles. Then I did three miles on the bike. Ten laps in the pool, then relaxed in the Jacuzzi. Lounging on a chair, I rubbed tanning oil all over my body. Soon I wouldn't be able to reach my toes.

This was my daily routine at my gym, but for some reason I came here today. Part of me wanted to run into Sindy. I decided to head up to Roosevelt's place and freshen up. Standing outside his door, I thought, *What if she's in there?*

I quietly slid my key in the lock, entered, and then closed the door. My heart started pounding hard. I softly said, "Roosevelt, sweetheart."

This was crazy, like the day Granville had trespassed on my property and I found him naked in my Jacuzzi. I should leave.

Opening the refrigerator, I reached for the orange juice. It was Simply Apple juice. We never drank apple juice. I put it back and went to his bedroom. One bottle of Clive Christian perfume was there, next to a framed photo of Sindy.

I flashed back to when the cameras showed her in the background, parading inside Roosevelt's suite on game days. He'd revoked my reserved parking pass at the stadium and had denied my access into his suite for the entire season. My husband didn't want to see me, but he never told me to stop coming to his condo.

A woman cocking her leg up and pissing to mark her territory was desperate. I flushed the toilet. Roosevelt's mother, Helen, despised me the most. The DuBois men—Martin, Chaz, and Wally—weren't fond of me either. They were all waiting at a distance for me to have this baby. I was ready too. Turning sideways, I rubbed my stomach.

The bathroom vanity had a Clarisonic skin-cleansing brush. For a moment I thought about putting something on it that would peel the flesh from her flawless face the second she used it. See how much Roosevelt liked her then. Then I remembered the check Roosevelt had given my father to bail out our family's business. I recalled Loretta being handcuffed.

I decided to shower. That way, Sindy would know that I was the wife with a key. The few pieces of clothing I'd left had been removed from the closet and placed in a bottom drawer. I slipped on a dress, got a pair of low heels. How dare she touch my belongings! I went to the kitchen, got a thirteen-gallon plastic bag, and tossed her stuff from the vanity and top of the dresser inside. Marching to the trash, I dumped it in his can, then left.

Make someone happy, I told myself, choosing Papa. I was getting hungry. I started to call and invite him to lunch, but I decided to surprise my dad, instead. We could go over the financials after we'd finished eating.

The office was quiet. Monica, the receptionist, wasn't at her desk. Opening the door to the office that was once mine, but now my dad's, I gasped.

"If you don't get my daddy's dick out of your mouth . . . !" Thank God, it wasn't Monica. I had never seen this girl before. "Get out!"

The girl sprang from her knees, then wiped her face. She put on her clothes.

Papa pulled up his pants. "Madison, you should've called first, sweetheart."

"I said, 'Get out'!"

Pausing between steps, she took her time leaving. "I'm not on your payroll," she said, standing in the doorway. "Call me later, Big Willy." She blew me a kiss.

That lil girl had no idea who she was playing with; and if my dad was paying her, she was on *my* payroll, but not any longer. "You're lucky I'm pregnant or I'd hurry your ass up out of here. And don't come back!"

I pushed her, slammed the door, and then stared at my father. All my life I thought my dad was *so* in love with my mother and faithful to her. "How long have you been cheating?"

"Please don't tell your mother," Papa begged, buckling his belt. "It won't happen again."

"I don't have to tell her. Now I see where I get my indiscretions."

Children could grow up either to be exactly like their parents or the complete opposite. Women who stayed with unfaithful husbands usually already knew. Wish I'd valued the man I had and never sexed Granville. I left the office, got back into my car, and drove to the stadium. I owed Roosevelt a real apology.

I parked in the general lot, closest to his office, and took the elevator to the second floor. The receptionist buzzed me into the secured area. His secretary wasn't at her desk. Although I hadn't seen my husband face-to-face since Granville's release, I was certain I wouldn't see a repeat of what my dad had done. I opened the door to Roosevelt's office.

He was seated behind his desk. The photo he had of me had been replaced on his credenza with one of Sindy.

"What brings you here?" he asked, walking toward me.

He stood in front of me as though I was an unwelcome guest. I stepped back. A guy I didn't know was seated at Roosevelt's conference table. He stepped in front of my husband.

"It's okay," Roosevelt told him. "Look out the window. Scan the lot for suspicious cars and Granville."

"Roosevelt, it's not like that, and you know it. I apologize." Tears flowed. "Please stop distancing yourself from me. He's not going to hurt you again."

Chaz appeared from the adjoining office, shook his head, and fanned his hand at me. "Put her ass out, Chicago. We have no idea where that crazy guy is. He probably followed her here." Chaz disappeared back where he'd come from.

"Apology accepted. He almost killed me because of you, Madison.

That man is more in love with you than I'm willing to compete with. Now he's a free man. Listen, this isn't a good time to talk. You have no idea what it feels like to look over your shoulder everywhere you go or to have a twenty-four-hour bodyguard. Don't come here again. I'll call you later," Roosevelt said, escorting me to the door.

The guy who was staring out the window stepped between us.

I wanted to sit, stay, scream, cry, and explain my side, until my husband understood I was truly sorry for the pain I'd caused him. "Regardless of what you think about me, I'm still legally your wife."

Chaz stuck his head out of his office. He said, "Not for long," then disappeared.

Speaking to the guy's back, Roosevelt said, "Madison, don't go there. You have nothing to gain. Please leave."

Sitting in my car, I let the tears flow. My chest tightened. How did I get here?

A white Bentley parked next to my car. I dried my eyes and saw why this was bad timing.

I got out of my car as she got out of hers. "Excuse me, Sindy. I need to have a word with you," I said, sniffling as I approached her. "Roosevelt is a married man. You need to stay away from my husband."

A security guard in a jeep slowly drove by. She waved. "Hey, Terrence. Good job!"

His lips curved so high, they damn near touched his eyes. "Yes, ma'am. Thank you, Miss Singleton."

Okay, so if we got into a physical confrontation, it was obvious whose side he'd be on. I glanced up at Roosevelt's window, expecting to see that bodyguard. He wasn't there.

Sindy stood inches from me. "Your husband won't be yours much longer, and you have no one to blame but yourself."

That wasn't true. She didn't know me or my situation.

"Make this your last time confronting me. Do it again and that baby inside you will be mine too. That is, if it's Roosevelt's."

My legs and hands trembled. She called him by his first name. I thought I was the only one who'd done that. Even Roosevelt's mother called him "Chicago."

"Roosevelt doesn't know it, but I've had my attention on him the second he became GM. I'm not in love with that billionaire guy my dad wants me to marry." She waved her hand in front of her vagina like it was a magic wand. "I'm saving myself for my honeymoon with your soon-to-be ex."

"Please, it ain't hardly pure," I said.

"How would a tramp know what's pure, when she can't recognize what's sacred? You did me a favor. Well, let's just say, Loretta did me a favor."

What? Loretta? Okay, Madison. Chill out. You've done it enough to know how females play the mind game when they want your man.

Frowning, I was convinced that Loretta would forever haunt me. My chest rose and fell rapidly. I had trouble breathing. I couldn't risk subjecting myself to a fight. I was Roosevelt's wife and had to make sure it stayed that way.

"What type of woman are you?" I asked her.

The bodyguard was quickly approaching us.

"Just be thankful I'm not the woman I used to be," she said, flinging her long cinnamon hair over her shoulder.

Getting into my car, I started the engine, pulled out of the parking lot, and turned left onto Kirby. Entering the freeway, I closed my eyes, then plunged my accelerator. I didn't want to kill anyone; but if God ended it all for me right now, He'd make someone happy.

Opening my eyes, I slammed on my brakes. I stopped inches from the car in front of me. I couldn't let Sindy get into my head.

CHAPTER 41

Chicago

Soon as Madison got out of her car and confronted Sindy, my bodyguard said, "Let me see what's happening to Sindy. Stay away from the window. In fact, go into Chaz's office."

Staring up at my monitor, I watched Madison. She recklessly sped out of the lot. I didn't care about the Bentley. It could be replaced with the swipe of a card Madison didn't know I owned, a black card.

Chaz called out, "See how unstable she is!"

What he'd done to get rid of Loretta was dehumanizing. Why did women let men misuse them? I'd never dogged a woman out. Maybe I was too nice. I ignored him.

I never tried to buy a woman's affection. My grandfather was wealthy. He told us, "Men who spend to impress, work for others, ain't used to having anything, and they end up broke. Men who let their money work for them, labor because they want to, not because they have to." My mother never had a nine-to-five. Growing up, my brother and I were privileged to choose any career. I loved managing our football team. This year was Houston's turn to win the championship.

I prayed, *God, please keep her safe.*

How does a man reason with his heart? That was the woman I'd fallen in love with. The woman I was falling for was waiting for me in my reception area. Was I wrong for trying to move forward?

I couldn't lie. I was scared. But knowing another man loved my wife enough to kill me, I had to let Madison go. I wasn't hard to find. Granville could try again.

God had sent someone new, but Sindy was not a replacement. There was only one Madison Tyler.

I walked into Chaz's office.

"She finally got the balls to come here. Get a protective order against her," Chaz said, staring at the flat screen. He was reviewing footage for our upcoming game.

Shaking my head, I answered, "She's pregnant. She's sick. She's still my wife. And she might be carrying my baby. I won't do that to her."

"Changing the subject—Mom is having the family lawyer prepare your divorce papers."

"But she can't make me sign them. Mom has too much idle time. First she wants to run the company, now this. Why can't you guys stay out of it? I'm the one who married Madison. I'll take care of it when I'm ready!" I snatched the screen from the wall, then slammed it to the floor.

"You keep doing things like this and Blue Waters will have your job. We can't keep playing Humpty Dumpty, man," my brother said, hugging me. "Pretty soon I'm not going to be able to cover you. We're going to the championship."

I leaned on my brother's shoulder and cried.

"It's okay, man. Let it out. We need you."

"Knock, knock. I hear you guys. I need you too, Roosevelt."

I recognized that sweet voice, but why was Sindy in my office?

Chaz whispered into my ear, "Stay in here. Get yourself together. Take as much time as you need. I'll deal with Sindy until you come out."

"Thanks."

He closed the door. I sat in his chair. Maybe I should get a gun; my bodyguard might not be enough.

I picked up the TV screen, placed it on Chaz's desk, then texted the contractor: The screen fell again. Send a replacement now.

This was the last time I was taking out my frustrations on objects. The dreams of drowning in blood still haunted me. When I closed my eyes at night, I struggled to breathe, fought to wake up. No more sleeping at my brother's condo, fearing Granville would show up at my place. Hopefully, the nightmares would end soon.

I wasn't going to lose my mind, but at times it felt like it. I took a few deep breaths, then opened the door. Seeing Sindy calmed me. This woman was amazingly gorgeous.

"Hey, you," she said, giving me a hug. She always greeted me with open arms. I liked that.

"What were you and Madison talking about in the lot?"

Sindy gave me a kiss. "Nothing that matters. You ready?"

Chaz said, "Let me grab my iPad and I'm ready. Numbiya is going to meet us after she finishes with her client."

"Why don't we go solo tonight," I told Chaz. "You can meet your girl and I'll take Sindy out."

"You sure?"

"Positive."

"Cool. No problem," Chaz said. "I'll see you tonight."

"I'll see you tomorrow." I looked at my bodyguard and said, "I'll see you tomorrow too."

I had Sindy follow me to my place, park her car, and get into mine. Brennan's on Smith was an excellent choice. I valet parked. The host right away seated us upstairs. We sat at a table in the corner of the wine room.

"I've got it," I said, pulling out Sindy's chair. Her back was to the door. Mine was against the wine rack glass-enclosed wall.

"Thanks." She reached for my hand, then softly asked, "Roosevelt, how are you?"

I wasn't sure how much she'd seen or heard earlier. She was here with me. That was all that mattered. "I'm good."

Squeezing my hand, she said, "It's time for you to be honest with yourself. You're a good man. You deserve a good woman. But you are not good."

"I'll be your waiter for this evening. Would you like to start by sampling one of our finest wines?"

"Yes, anything red, please," Sindy said.

The waiter left. She gazed into my eyes. "I'm in charge. No questions asked. And I'm staying at your place tonight."

Suddenly I remembered I'd never gotten my key from Madison. I'd placed Madison's clothes in a drawer to avoid seeing them in the closet. The Clarisonic on the vanity was my mom's. She carried those things in her purse all the time and left them like they were disposable. The framed picture of Sindy on my dresser, next to her favorite perfume, would seem strange if she saw it, since she hadn't given them to me.

"Sindy, I like you. A lot. I don't want the start of our relationship to be entangled in what's happening in my personal life."

"Then what do you want from me?" she asked.

"Right now, I need a friend. One I can trust. One who won't judge me. I understand if what I require is more than what you have to offer. But friendship is all I can give you or any woman at this moment."

I had no desire to practice abstinence forever. My dick would happily screw Sindy. I'm sure her pussy was plush, hot, juicy, pretty—all of that and more. Some women were worth the wait. Busting a nut too soon crushed potentially good relationships. There was no recovery from fucking first, if you fucked up shortly thereafter.

The waiter returned. Sindy sampled three wines; then she said, "We'll have a bottle of the Pinot Noir. We'll order an appetizer momentarily."

He nodded. "Of course."

There were a few couples dining across the quaint room. "Tell me about your ex."

She shook her head. "You know all you need to know. My father wants me to wed an obnoxious billionaire. I won't. I'm interested in you."

"You can have any man you want. Why me?" I asked.

I was worthy of a woman of Sindy's caliber. When a woman is dropped in a man's lap, and her beauty exceeds all he'd imagined, he has to question it if she doesn't get up.

The waiter poured Sindy's wine first, then mine.

"Thanks," she told him. Lifting her glass, she said, "Cheers."

Tipping my glass to hers, I said, "Cheers."

"Roosevelt."

I loved the way she said my name. Light. Seductive.

"When a woman chooses the man, check. When a man recognizes

he has a real woman, and he chooses that woman, checkmate." She tapped her glass to mine.

I scanned the menu. "So you play chess?"

"Roosevelt."

Looking up, I answered, "Yes."

"The key to winning at the game of love is when the king respects the fact that the queen holds more power."

When I equated her analogy to life, she made me think how the queen moves freely and the king takes one step at a time. Her point was definitely debatable.

Curious, I said, "Go on."

Sindy stuck out her tongue, pressed the tip to her glass, and then sipped. "Most men believe they're a knight in shining armor, but they'll forever remain a rookie. They pick the wrong woman because they're not willing to give up their pawns in order to capture a queen."

I told her, "I like that."

"Are you hoping the baby is yours?"

Whoa! After all she'd just said, her question was bigger than whatever answer I would give her. I opened my mouth, then closed it.

Sindy smiled, and then she said, "Roosevelt Chicago DuBois, I like you. You are a man worth waiting for. Promise me that if you don't believe I'm the one, you'll be honest with me."

She was definitely a queen. Not a pawn.

I quietly exhaled. I didn't want what Madison and I had to end. Despite all she'd done, I couldn't explain why I was still in-love with her. Before viewing the video in court, yes, I prayed I was the father. Seeing my wife screw another man in front of everyone in the courtroom, I did not want Madison's child to be mine.

Why did Sindy make me comfortable, yet uncomfortable? I told her, "You deserve that much."

Pushing away from the table, she said, "When you're over her, and when you're done patronizing me, let me know. Maybe I'll still be available." Sindy left me sitting alone.

What did I say to deserve that?

CHAPTER 42

Granville

Speed dating? What's that?

Beaux had stopped by unannounced, again. This time he had on a suit and tie. A shoe box, with a gold bow, was in his hand. "Happy birthday, bro."

It wasn't my forty-sixth yet. With my new bod, I was getting younger by the day. Prison had taken ten years off me. Guess for me, my stay at FDC was a workout minivacation.

Women introduced themselves, asking, "Are you available?" If I stopped on my way home to get something to eat, they asked, "Mind if I join you?" Where were these females before I fell in love? I had sex with a few of them, but none more than once. Didn't want them getting attached.

"Thanks for trying. You can stay, but I'm not going out," I said.

I was lounging in boxers, letting my balls swing freely. I went from being an inmate to a visitor. I hadn't forgotten about No Chainz. G-double-A proved himself the man. I asked him why his last words about me were "He'll be back."

"You needed a reality dose. And you damn sure didn't need both of us telling you the same thing. I knew you were going to walk," he said. From misdemeanors to felonies, he was making a lot more money in the pen helping guys who were representing themselves.

None had won their cases. Guess I was the lucky one. Since I was acquitted, I didn't have a record. I'd gotten another construction job, making six figures for real. This time I wasn't lying. Every week for No Chainz, I padded his books with a C-note, and I accepted collect calls from both of them. No Chainz would be out in a month, in time to celebrate his twenty-first birthday. I was getting his ass lit all day. The only thing I wouldn't do was the request from G-double-A to sneak him ten cell phones. Why would he ask me to do that?

"What the hell?" Beaux said, staring at the wrapped boxes in my living room. He placed the shoe box on my coffee table. "It's not Christmas yet, bro. What's all of this shit? Damn, it's not even Halloween. And I know no one sent you gifts."

He was right. No birthday, Halloween, or Christmas gifts were in those packages. Spending my cash on clubs and women wasn't happening either. In between screwing strangers, Precious came over to empty my sacs when they got too heavy, but I didn't do anything special for her. She could stop doing me whenever she got tired. It didn't matter. She didn't matter.

I splurged a little on myself. I loved, and was not giving up, my brew. I enjoyed a few beers every night and a few extra on weekends. That was it.

Inside the three boxes were a playpen, a car seat, and a stroller. It was close to that time. Madison probably wanted to pick out the crib, but next week I was getting her a walker and some other stuff. She didn't need a baby shower. She had me to make it rain on her and the baby.

Picking at the paper, Beaux asked, "What is it?"

"Don't touch that!" I wished he wouldn't be nosy. "It's some things for Mom," I lied.

Our mother was struggling to survive. Her health was going down quickly, but she refused to move to Houston and live with Beaux or me. She wanted to spend her last days in the house our dad had died in, in Port Arthur. Her sister—the mean one who hadn't spoken to our mother in years—was at the house taking care of Mom. She probably wanted to be the first to get whatever she wanted out of the home. The doctor had given Mom two weeks, so we were going to see her this weekend. We'd planned a huge barbeque and seafood boil. All of Port Arthur was invited.

"Liar," Beaux said.

I'd saved six grand for my kid and Madison. I didn't have as much as the dudes she'd dated, but I was working on it. Child support wasn't going to be necessary. When we brought the baby home, we'd make space at my one-bedroom penthouse apartment, or I'd move-in with Madison.

Her photos were on my nightstand. Madison's sweet, creamy praline face was the first one I saw in the morning, and the last one I kissed at night. I'd found this place online where they could take any pictures and make wallpaper. Six rolls with Madison on them were in the back of my closet. Since I wasn't sure where I was going to live, once my baby arrived, I'd wait to decorate.

"Put on one of those suits, your favorite cowboy boots and hat, bro. We have cause to celebrate. You have to get out of the house. Madison is not your woman, and she's never going to be yours. She's not pregnant with your baby. Move on with your life before you end up—"

"Shut up!" I curled my fingers tightly.

That wasn't true. The baby was *mine.* My dick was so big and long—my sperm didn't have to swim far to penetrate her egg. I thought about how tight Madison was. Her pussy had snatched off my condom. It was destiny. We were meant to be.

"If I go to this thing, I just want to meet a girl and fuck. No headaches. Just head banging. Mine inside of her. Hers against the headboard. I want to come and go," I said. "Let's hit the strip joints. Or get tickets to the football game tomorrow."

"No!" Beaux jumped up. "You trying to get locked up before we go see Mom." He hit me in the jaw and pinned me to the floor. "You cannot go to a football game while Chicago is GM. Where's your gun?"

I pushed him in the air, rolled from under him, then stood. "I don't have a gun," I lied.

Beaux shook his head, then straightened his shirt. "You're lying. If your dumb ass goes back to prison, I'm disowning you."

He didn't own me. He said some dumb stuff, but he wasn't stupid. I'd gotten a lot stronger than him. That would probably be the last fight he'd start.

What if Chicago wanted revenge? He was the one running around with a personal bodyguard. I wasn't going to do anything to him. He had his new woman and I had mine back.

"Speed dating is where we're going. I'm getting you fucked up and laid. Wash your ass and get dressed."

Beaux grabbed a cold beer from my refrigerator, picked up the remote, and then sat on my sofa. I was not excited. Staying at home kept me out of trouble.

"What's in the shoe box?" I asked.

"If I can't touch your shit, don't touch mine."

"All right." I went to my bathroom.

I shaved my head and my mustache; then I got in the shower, which was over the small tub. There wasn't enough space for me to bathe. I recalled soaking in Madison's Jacuzzi. Yeah, I'd have to move into her place, but I was paying the mortgage.

Lathering up, I thought my new bod was irresistible. A thousand sit-ups and push-ups every day were still the norm. I never wanted to lose my sexy. Not feeling lucky today, I didn't put on the power suit Beaux got me for my verdict day. I was saving that super one for my wedding, or maybe for Mom's funeral. I let the shower wash away my tears.

No way I was wasting dollars on a big ceremony or funeral. A plain burial for Mom, and a nice, short honeymoon to Lake Charles with Madison would be romantic. We'd have to take the baby, of course. I looked at my jeans.

"Suit and boots," Beaux shouted from the living room.

"Fine!"

Buttoning up a black shirt, I put on the gray slacks and jacket with my black gators and grabbed my hat. "Almost forgot." I sat my hat on the bed, poured cologne in my hands, and then slapped my face and head.

When I stepped into the living room, Beaux had dozed off. I could go in my bedroom, throw all of this on the floor, and go to sleep too. I reached for his shoe box.

He sprang into a sitting position. "What did I say?" He picked up the box. Opened it.

My jaw dropped. "Is that what I think it is?" I asked, staring at the gun.

He nodded.

I kept staring at this gun inside a plastic bag inside a box. "How? How do you know for sure?"

"Don't worry about that. When Mom dies, we're putting this gun in the bottom of her casket and burying it with her. She wouldn't have it any other way."

"Mom knows?"

"Of course not. She still thinks you're innocent, and that's how we're going to let her leave here."

My brother had done this for me. Rubbing my head, I said, "You do know I can't be retried for the same charges. You might be setting yourself up if we get caught. You've got to tell me how you got this gun."

Beaux stared at me.

"Never mind," I said. If I had to testify on his behalf, I didn't want to lie on the witness stand and end up behind bars like Loretta.

Beaux clapped his hands once, then said, "Let's rock and roll." He stood tall. "You look like money, bro. The women are going to be all over you."

CHAPTER 43

Loretta

Lesbian? Me?

The restaurant in Sugar Land was filled with men and women. I'd come here after work with the intention of escaping my part of town, having a few drinks, and opening myself up to meeting a female. Waiting for the Long Island ice tea to give me the courage to move from this table to the bar, I sat alone.

A tall, thin woman, with short, dark hair, came over. She was attractive, but I couldn't see myself in a relationship with her. She wasn't my waitress. Certainly wasn't dressed as though she worked here. Since she approached me, I decided to let her initiate the conversation.

"Would you like to sign up?" she asked.

"For what?"

Placing an iPad on the table, she asked, "What's your age?"

"Thirty-five," I said, glancing around the room. People seemed very friendly with one another, as though they were already familiar. "Is there a private party going on?"

"Not at all. Great!" she chirped. "The age range tonight is thirty-five to forty-five. We're having a singles mixer. Ever done speed dating?" she asked.

I'd heard about it. Saw posts on Facebook for events in Houston. To me, these gatherings were just another word for "booty call." I could open myself to having sex with a stranger. Why not? The Lord knew my needs.

"No, but what the hell. I've heard about it. Sign me up." Maybe I'd meet a man I liked so I could dismiss these weird feelings I have for Madison.

"We'll start in fifteen minutes. What's your name?"

"Loretta." Soon as I'd given her my real name, I wished I'd lied and told her, "Brenda" or "Carmen."

"Great, Loretta. You stay here. The men will come to you. You have ten minutes to ask and answer questions. If you meet a man you like, you'll have more time to mingle with him after the speed-dating part is over. Cheers!" she said, whisking away.

My cell rang. I looked at the screen, debating on whether I should answer. Before it went to voice mail, I said, "Hey, Tisha."

"Hi, Loretta. Look, I can't take a friendship feud among Madison, you, and me. Madison already agreed. I'm inviting you to my house tonight so we can talk this out."

My heart raced. I could use the opportunity to come out to them. Or I could stay here. "What time? I'm in Sugar Land."

"Whenever you get here is okay. What time is good for you?"

The event was starting. Speaking into my Bluetooth, I looked at my phone. "I'll be there in two." I paused. There was a pair of cowboy boots firmly planted to the floor. A man with a cowboy hat sat at my table, with his head down. He smelled good. My pussy puckered. "Make that three hours."

He got up and walked away as Tisha said, "See you then," ending our call.

I exhaled, sat up straight, and then glanced around the room. He was standing, facing the bar. Hopefully, he'd make it back to me before the event was over.

Placing a sign with the number 11 on the edge of my table, the waitress asked, "Another ice tea?"

I nodded. I'd better slow down and make this next drink last. I'd have a couple of hours for the alcohol to wear off before driving.

The tall woman announced, "Gentlemen, find your match. Whatever number I've given you, that's the person you'll meet first. When I tell you to start, you have exactly ten minutes. When I say 'stop,' you get up and move to the next number in numerical order. Do not skip. Do not linger. No backtracking, or you'll be excused from speed dating."

Dang, why so many rules?

A guy about my height, five-nine, sat in front of me. The waitress removed my drink from her tray, placed it on the table, and then went to the next table.

"Start."

This guy did nothing for me. I smiled. "Hi, I'm Loretta, and you are?"

"Donald. You're pretty. Here are my three questions—Where're you from? What do you like to do for fun? And what would you do for a living if money didn't matter?"

His questions were decent. I answered, "I'm from Houston. Born and raised."

Lord, please don't let him be from Port Arthur.

"For fun, I take my daughter to the park."

His brows stretched toward his hairline.

"And if money didn't matter, I'd be a concert pianist." As a young girl I loved the piano. Sister Odom, the church pianist, could make it sing like a bird or holler the same as the preacher.

"Okay, my turn. One, are you truly single? Two, did you come here looking for a woman to date or a one-night stand? And three, have you ever done time in jail?"

He looked at his watch. I couldn't remember the last time I'd seen anyone use a watch for time.

Donald said, "I've never been to jail. I have had several one-night stands, but that's not why I'm here. And yes, I am totally detached. I'm looking for the right woman. How about you?"

I chuckled. "You could say that. Maybe."

"Stop."

Donald extended his hand. "We might have something in common. Nice meeting you, Loretta. Hope to see you after this is over. Just in case, here's my card. Call me." He didn't wait for a response. Guess he didn't want to get eliminated for lingering.

The next three guys who sat at my table were well-dressed. Though I wasn't interested in any of them, they all seemed nice enough for someone else. The fourth man was more feminine than I was. Down South, that didn't mean he was gay, but he could be bisexual. It didn't matter. I wasn't remotely interested.

Finally the man with the cowboy hat and boots had come back to me. He eased into the seat. His cologne greeted me.

"Start."

He tilted his hat away from his face. "Hello, dear."

I picked up my purse and tossed thirty dollars on the table for my two drinks. Didn't need any problems.

Granville said, "Tell Madison I hope she likes the baby gifts I sent her for our child."

CHAPTER 44

Tisha

Friends should forgive.

That was easier when we were kids. An argument here, a fight there—a week later we were playing together. We held no grudges. We could talk about one another, but no one else had better mess with one of us or they had to deal with all three. Back then, we had loving hearts that didn't hold hatred. Even when we were mad, deep inside we cherished our friendships.

Despite all that had happened, what Madison, Loretta, and I had was worth holding on to. Once again, I had to initiate our meeting face-to-face. Hopefully, in five or ten years, we'd forget the horrible events of the trial. Maybe we'd joke and laugh about it. There were less than four months left, but I couldn't wait for this year to end.

Lining my coffee table with a yellow cloth, I placed six small, heart-shaped silver trays for the hors d'oeuvres in a circle. The tips touched at the center. A beautiful unbroken heart was formed, symbolizing what I hoped we'd have today.

I was serving bacon-wrapped scallops, beef skewers, popcorn shrimp, chicken fingers, raw vegetables, toffee-covered peanuts I'd bought from the Girl Scouts, and dipping sauces; and, of course, bottles of champagne were in the refrigerator. The food would take minutes to prepare once Madison and Loretta arrived.

I wasn't sure what made Loretta call me back an hour later to say she was on her way, but I was glad we didn't have to wait three hours. Candles, bath fizz balls, scented soap bars, lavender lingerie packs, eye masks, cotton spa gloves and socks to make hands and feet extra soft, facial masks, and lip plumper were inside all three gift bags in the living room. I had to treat myself too.

Madison probably had everything in the bag and more; but with one month to go, she could use it after she had her baby. Loretta more than likely didn't have any of what I was giving her, but learning to relax between all that praying, which wasn't working, might help her to become a better person.

The doorbell sounded. I cheerfully called out from the kitchen, "Come in." Hopefully, whichever one it was had heard me. If not, Madison or Loretta would eventually realize the door was unlocked. There was something that made friends and family feel entitled to enter the home of loved ones, making them turn the knob.

"Tisha, we need to talk."

I took off my apron and placed it on the chair. Walking toward Darryl, I said, "Get the hell out of my house."

Instead of turning around, he stood still. His nose almost touched mine. I was not backing away.

He said, "Our house. And I'm not leaving. I live here too." Spit flew from his mouth and landed on my lips.

I wiped it off. "Not anymore you don't. Wherever you been laying up for the last year, go back." I wanted to wipe his spit on him, but that would be too intimate.

Darryl's jaws dropped. His clothes were too big; his tennis shoes were dirty; a beard had grown in. He had that sour gym stench. "Where's my boys?"

I laughed. "Darryl, please. Stop yelling. Your breath stinks. Get out before I call the police. I'm serious."

"I stored my things in my mom's garage and someone stole all of it—TV, clothes, video games, everything. I'm sorry, Tisha. Give me one more chance."

All the nice items I'd bought for him were stolen? Right. "You want another chance? To do what? Keep lying to me. Stay out all night. Treat your boys. Spend my money on your bitches."

"I don't want those women, Tisha. I want my wife. My car needs a tune-up and I do too. Look at me."

"You're not man enough to get your shit from your girlfriend's house. You can't even tell me the truth about that. You moved your stuff into her place, but she put your ass out, and then kept your things. I don't blame her. Every woman isn't going to put up with your lying and cheating."

"Ti—"

"You don't owe me an explanation. When you should've given me one, you didn't give a damn! Thought you were the man. Never believed I'd put you out. Huh?"

"That's besides the point. You're my soul mate. My high-school—"

"If you need a place to stay, I can help you." I picked up my cell phone and dialed Madison. "I'd like to report a home invasion."

"Darryl?"

"Yes." I recited my home address, then said, "I know the intruder. His name is—"

Darryl threw up his hands. "Be like that," he said, then left.

"I'm on my way over," Madison said. "Don't hang up until I get there."

Standing in the doorway, I watched Darryl drive off in the car I'd bought him. Nothing about him was attractive. The man I once loved—vowed for better or worse—I couldn't imagine any part of his body touching mine. I didn't hate him. I was done with him. I scrubbed my hand to wash off his saliva.

Loretta parked in her driveway and walked over with Madison. After they were in the house, I locked the door, then gave each of them a hug.

"Have a seat wherever you'd like. I'm going to put the appetizers in the oven and grab the champagne. Madison, do you prefer juice or water?"

"Not today. I'm having what you guys are drinking," she said.

"Okay. One glass won't hurt, but I'm not serving you two."

Surprisingly, no one had an attitude, but I sensed underlying tension. Madison was lounging on the chaise; Loretta was seated on the sofa. I filled our glasses, placed the bottle in the ice bucket, and then sat in the chair. In case I had to get up quickly, I didn't recline.

"Since I asked you ladies to come over, I'll start. First I want to say, I miss you both. I'm not perfect. I'm not pointing any fingers or taking sides. Whatever I say is how I feel. Madison, you look beautiful pregnant."

I had to remember to take pictures before they left. We hadn't done that in a while, and I had no pics of Madison pregnant. I did have three photo albums with identical layouts beside my seat. I'd put together one for each of us. All of our graduations from kindergarten through college were in chronological order. Birthday parties. Outings at the theme park we used to have in Houston. The front cover was a collage of our baby pictures. On the back was a picture we had taken at the Policemen's Gala. We were all smiling and happy. That was right before Loretta had met Granville.

I told Madison, "Thank you for not judging me for having an abortion, and thanks for being there for me." Tears clouded my eyes. "I don't have regrets, but I do have remorse."

Loretta gulped her champagne, then burped. No "excuse me"?

"You need to repent," Loretta said.

"Loretta, the older we get, the less I understand you. I'm not going to bring up anything that you've done or didn't do. You can tell us why if you'd like. Just know that I love you."

Loretta didn't say anything. She sat there, staring at Madison.

Madison said, "Tisha, if not for you, we would've stopped being friends after college. For real. Although you and I don't go to church every Sunday, *you* are the most spiritual and forgiving person I know. Loretta, I don't understand you, honey, and probably never will. But what I want is for you to tell me why you hate me so much. What have I ever done to you to make you feel that way?"

Madison started rubbing her stomach. She hadn't touched her drink. Maybe she just wanted it to sit there so she'd feel like one of the girls.

Loretta exhaled. "I still don't condone abortions. Tisha, if you believe I wronged you, God will judge us individually. What's done is done. God don't like ugly."

Madison and I stared at Loretta. She still didn't get the purpose of our getting together.

"You can lead a horse to water, but I didn't make Madison have sex with Granville. But at least you kept the baby," Loretta said, staring at me.

I wanted to put Loretta's ass out of my house, but that would . . .

"I'll be right back. I forgot about the food in the oven." From the kitchen I yelled, "Madison didn't say anything about Granville. She asked why you hate her so much. Answer that question please. I want to know too."

I raked the scallops on one plate, the baked chicken fingers on another, and did the same with the other food. I placed the baking pan on the stove, refilled Loretta's and my glasses, then put an assortment on three small plates.

"Thank you," Madison said, taking her plate.

I handed one to Loretta. "Thanks, Tisha."

Leaning back in my chair, I crossed my legs. "Loretta, why are you jealous of Madison?"

She hunched her shoulders, nodded, and then raised her brows. Shaking her leg, she said, "I'm not."

"I might not have breasts at this moment, but I do have a heart. Loretta, you need a heart transplant."

I didn't want to change the subject. I told Loretta, "Yes, you are jealous."

I was glad Madison had spoken up. Loretta must've thought cancer was going to destroy Madison. It hadn't altered Madison's attitude. She was still confident.

"You're sitting there, using the Lord's name in vain. Tell us what you told the Lord when you came to the hospital and punched me in my face. I bet you won't try that after I have my husband's baby."

Loretta's leg started shaking faster. She knew better than to act a fool in my house, because I would kick her ass.

"We're waiting for you to answer, Loretta."

"Okay, then why did you make the bet?" Madison asked. "Tell us that."

Loretta stared at Madison. "You're not innocent. You don't love Chicago. You left him for dead. I nursed him back to health. You should thank me. I'm indirectly responsible for saving your company, your house, and I'm the reason you got that new car. I—"

"Bitch, that's my husband. Mine! Not—"

"Not for long," Loretta interrupted.

Madison looked toward me and started eating.

I told her, "Don't give Loretta the satisfaction."

"You still think this was a good idea?" Madison asked.

The tone had to shift if we were going to get through the night without fighting. I picked up the albums. Handing Madison and Loretta theirs, I placed mine on my lap. "Let's remember the good times."

Madison laughed. "I didn't know I had a bad hair day in my life. Where'd you get this picture?"

"Your mom gave me a copy. My mom didn't have any before we were all five years old. I got a few from your mom too, Loretta."

Loretta slowly turned the pages.

Madison laughed again. Louder this time. "Me in a playpen! No wonder I'm crying. Oh, Tisha, I forgot to tell you. I got a playpen, a car seat, and one of those luxury strollers today, but I have no idea who sent it. Did you?"

I shook my head.

Loretta finished her champagne and hurled her book. Pages scattered. The book hit the wall behind Madison. "Bitch!"

"Not in my house." She could've hurt Madison again.

Madison sipped her champagne for the first time. "Why am I not surprised? Go home and pray and stay the hell away from me."

Loretta stood. "Your real future baby's daddy sent all of that."

"You wish!" Madison sat her flute on the table, then scooted to the edge of the chaise.

Friend or not, before Madison's feet touched the floor, I got up and put Loretta's ass out of my house.

CHAPTER 45

Granville

"Wake up. I have a driver waiting for you downstairs."

I sprang to a sitting position, smacked myself in the face, and then started swinging. The stranger standing at the foot of my bed pointed a gun at me.

"Who are you? I'm not letting you rob me, man. You'll have to shoot me first."

"Get up, get dressed, and get your ass downstairs. You've got fifteen minutes. If you're not downstairs by then, the driver will be gone, and you can let the police give you a ride. You'll be going back to prison—this time to stay. And your brother will be joining you."

Police? I knew Beaux shouldn't have messed with that gun. I went to my closet. Looking at the top shelf, I saw the shoe box was gone, yelled, "Fuck!" Then I remembered I'd moved it. I checked under my bed. It was there.

Stumbling into the shower, I took three minutes. I skipped shaving and put on my jeans. I didn't care much for the tennis shoes I'd put on. My feet looked like hammertoed claws from wearing cowboy and work boots all the time. Sometimes I wore open-toed sandals. A man was supposed to have rough dogs.

The lock on my door was clean picked. No sign of forced entry. That was probably why I didn't hear anything. When I got back, I was getting an alarm system. I had to rethink that. If I moved in with

Madison, an alarm would be a waste of money that I could spend on the baby.

I left my second-floor penthouse. I trotted down to the black car, with the tinted windows. A man dressed all in black, with a chauffeur hat, got out and opened the door. I didn't know why he had those dark sunglasses on. The sun hadn't come up yet.

Standing by the opened door, I asked, "Who are you, dude? Where are you taking me?"

He didn't say a word. I should've gotten my other gun, but I wasn't trying to go back to jail. I wasn't sure if it was there. I turned around. I'd take my chances at home. Two steps toward my penthouse, I heard a click. Stopped. Turned.

Aiming at my head, this dude still didn't say anything. Maybe he couldn't talk? Perhaps he got shot in the neck like I had. If I was about to die, I might as well find out why. I got into the Town Car. He closed the door. The guy who had been in my house wasn't in the car. The driver drove for about twenty-five to thirty minutes.

Fuck! I forgot my cell.

I could barely see the huge black iron gates parting. Maybe they weren't black. It was too dark to tell when they closed behind us. I couldn't lie. I was scared, but I kept my cool. Massaging my knuckles and loosening up my shoulders, I regretted not putting up a fight before getting into the car. Probably could've taken his gun and beaten him with it.

The car door opened. "Get out," he said.

Well, at least he could talk.

"Hey, buddy, what's this all about?" I asked, standing in front of a place so big there was no way all of this was somebody's house.

"Follow me. And don't try anything stupid. This place is surrounded by security."

Did he mean security cameras or were there really people hiding out? The wooden floor was shiny, but it wasn't slick. Maybe that was 'cause I had on my rubber-soled tennis shoes. The chandelier was round, and had hundreds of crystals. If I lay on the floor and spread my arms and legs like a bear, if that thing fell, it would bury me alive. Two staircases? Show-off. Who needed two? They both went to the next floor.

I walked behind this guy until we arrived in a room with the longest dinner table ever. Two, four, six . . . eighteen, and with the two chairs, one at each end, twenty people could eat here. The room was halfway lit. A high-back chair at the end of the table faced the wall.

"Sit here," the driver said.

"Glad you could make it."

"Who said that?" It came from that chair facing the wall.

"You don't need to know who I am. What's important is I know who you are," he said.

I should punch him hard on the side of his neck and burst his jugular vein.

The man in the chair said, "You're going to do an important job for me."

"I don't even know you, and you got your back to me, and you want me to do you a favor?" I asked. A light shined in my face. He was in the dark.

"Two million dollars," he said.

Two what? For me? Is he serious? I began listening closely. He didn't say anything.

I questioned, "You gon' give me two million dollars?" I had to be sure I wasn't jumping the gun.

"Yes. One now. I need you to kill someone. After the job is done, you'll get the other."

"Whoa, buddy. I'm no killer. Are you trying to set me up? Are you working for Chicago? Y'all trying to send me back to the pen? I didn't do it, dude."

G-double-A said I wasn't that smart. If I got locked up again, he'd be right.

"You didn't kill him? Or you didn't shoot him? Don't answer that. Both of us know what happened. If you don't want to do the job—"

"You keep saying 'job,' like it's a nine-to-five. You—"

"Will not interrupt me again. Do the job or go back to prison. And your brother will join you. State, this time. Your mother will die before either one of you gets out. I've got the gun."

What gun? Was he bluffing? Now I wished I'd questioned my brother.

Confidently I replied, "I was acquitted."

I was too black to be blackmailed. No one pushed me around. I decided to take the Fifth and not say anything else.

"Your package is in the car."

Okay, I had to ask, "What package?"

"Everything is there. The cash."

Cash? I'd never get away with depositing that much money. Uncle Sam would audit me immediately. I couldn't keep it in my house. Who was this guy?

"The weapon you'll use to complete the job."

There was that word again. "Dude."

"Shut up!"

I wasn't his damn child but I was in his house. What if he killed me, then lied and said, "He broke into my house." I got quiet.

After a few moments of silence, he continued, "The phone you'll use is preprogrammed with your Facebook and Twitter accounts. Don't change the profile pictures. And definitely don't add new accounts."

I'd never used social media. The closest I came was installing GPS on Madison's phone to track her. Beaux had Facebook and Twitter. Women were always putting pictures of themselves and what they had to eat on his page. That was boring.

"Using your phone, you will track the person you must kill. You are already friends with the person too. Don't change any of the settings, especially places and locations. Everywhere this person goes, you'll know."

Whoa, that means if Madison has one of those accounts, I could follow her? A smile grew on my face. I couldn't change his phone, but I could do what I wanted with mine. My smile disappeared. Would she know it was me if I used my phone?

"Okay, all this talk about what? Tell me who."

"Roosevelt 'Chicago' DuBois. Do this after he gets a divorce and before he marries my daughter."

My heart felt like it stopped beating. When I wasn't in my right mind, I almost killed Chicago. Now that he was alive and I was free, I didn't want to pull the trigger again.

"There's a billionaire who has handsomely paid for my daughter's hand in marriage. She's in love with Chicago and insists on becoming his wife."

What good would $2 million do if I ended up in jail? His daughter marrying Chicago was doing me a favor. "Sounds like your head is on a chopping block. No can do, bro. Hire a professional hit man for 'the job.' "

"I'm not asking. If my virgin daughter marries Chicago . . . You understand why you will do this."

"So Sindy Singleton is *your* daughter?"

Sindy was advising G-double-A. She was at the trial not to support me but because she's dating Chicago. Now her dad wants me to do his dirty work. Why?

"You're free to go. I'll be in touch."

I'd never had a virgin. Considering the size of my dick, that was a good thing. We'd both get hurt. I wasn't in prison long enough to become institutionalized. This guy had gotten himself into a pickle and he wanted me to get him out.

There were times when I wanted to say something, but I had been quiet.

This was the first time I was speechless.

CHAPTER 46

Chicago

Today's game was different.

My suite was full. Mom. Dad. Grandpa. Chaz. Numbiya. A great time was being had by all, except for me. We were ahead by fourteen. My heart was empty. Four games into the regular season and we were off to an undefeated start. Preseason was a sweep. I'd hoped that Sindy would've called since she'd walked out on me at Brennan's. She hadn't, and my ego wasn't begging for another chance. She had a suite ticket to the game, but she hadn't shown her face.

Chaz patted me on the back. "Cheer up, man. Another mermaid will wash ashore soon. Trust me."

"You know, it's close to Madison having the baby. I've been thinking about having her come stay with me until the delivery."

"No," my brother said. "She's got Loretta and Tisha next door. That's what friends are for."

Mom wedged herself between us. "You are not moving that girl into your place. Let her in before she has that baby, and whether it's yours or not, you'll have a hard time moving her out."

What difference did that make if I loved Madison? Sindy could've convinced me not to move Madison in. My mother could not.

"She's my wife, Mom. I know how you feel. Let it go."

My mother asked, "Have you told Johnny yet?"

The main reason I hadn't fired Johnny Tyler was Madison. I didn't want to upset her. For $250,000 a year, he was doing a lousy job of operating the company. Tyler Construction had the potential to go global, but not with Johnny in the CEO position. We'd already begun interviewing for his replacement.

"Mom, we agreed. After the delivery."

"Why does everything center around that baby? I didn't agree to that," she said. "He's fortunate to own forty-nine percent of the company. He doesn't deserve a salary too. I raised you better. Fire him, Chicago." My mother walked to my dad.

That's what I wanted—a marriage that would last despite the ups and downs.

I turned to Chaz. "I'm tired of her telling me whom to love. What to do. When to do it. I did not get this job because of her, or you, or Dad. I am an honorable, respectable man who is in love . . ."

"You need to lower your voice," he said.

"You need to chill out." I'd spoken my last words, and turned my back to him.

Chaz tapped me on the shoulder.

"What!" I yelled, facing him . . . then turned away.

There she was. Sindy. High heels. Sleeveless maxidress. Diamond and pearls.

I couldn't breathe.

She opened her arms. I stepped into her embrace. Those fingernails scraped my spine as her palm slid up and down my back. I was glad the three words I was going to speak a few minutes ago—"with my wife"—never escaped my lips.

Why was romance so complicated?

"Thought you could use some cheering up," Chaz said, leaving to join Numbiya at the wet bar.

Sindy reminded me so much of Madison, it was eerie. I exhaled my feelings for my wife. I could not risk having Sindy read me the way she'd done the last time we were together.

"Good to see you," I said, embracing her.

Mom nodded at me. I knew she preferred Sindy over Madison. All of my family did.

"Likewise. I see you're winning," she whispered, then kissed me on my ear.

I whispered back, "Am I really?"

"Yes. I miss you, Roosevelt."

"I'm ready to listen to you. Ask whatever you'd like, but promise you won't walk out on me again. Will you come to my condo after the game?"

"Yes."

CHAPTER 47

Madison

"This way. Put the crib in here."

"Are you sure we can keep the queen bedroom set?" the worker asked.

"Positive. Don't put the crib against the wall. Move it to the center of the floor. I need to have access to my baby from all sides."

"Yes, ma'am," he said, repositioning the baby's bed.

I felt like the guy on the Geico insurance commercial who was directing traffic, but I wasn't standing in the middle of the street in my underwear. The workers I'd hired completely set up the all-white crib for my baby. Linens, sheets, pillows, lining, and the canopy were all white. The carousel had many of the Disney characters.

I was due any day now, and I couldn't take another day of not having everything in place. Breast-feeding wasn't an option, so I had formula stacked in the cabinets. The baby's bed was in its room. A bassinet was next to my bed.

Motioning for one of the guys to follow me, I instructed, "I want the playpen over here, the stroller right there, walker in the corner, and crawling mat set up near the playpen."

I glanced around to see if there were any additional items I could give the guys. My cell rang.

"Hi, Papa, I'm busy preparing for the baby."

"Sweetheart, I need you to come over. Helen called, and said, 'Don't get comfortable, Johnny Tyler. Your replacement will be on board in three months.' You're the only one hundred percent owner. We have to discuss how to stop this from happening."

"We don't have to discuss it now, Papa. She said 'three months.' "

He'd gotten himself into this situation. After walking in on him having that young girl suck his dick, I agreed with Helen.

"You know how ruthless that woman is, sweetheart. Three months could be seventy-two hours. It's okay. She leaves me no choice. I've got my own plan. You'll thank me later, sweetheart."

"Bye, Papa. I love you." I ended the call and refocused my attention on what was important to me.

Whoever had sent all of these things—and they were all new—I was not letting them go to waste. I believed it was Roosevelt.

The wallpaper border, with angels and white horses, was plastered along the middle of the wall. I'd added a beautiful white crown molding at the top of the wall and changed the baseboards to white too. Glow-in-the-dark galaxies were painted on the ceiling. The baby monitor was on the baby's white dresser.

"Scatter the balloons throughout the house. Place the diaper bag here. Baby blankets tied with ribbon go on the sofa. Stuffed animals, spread them everywhere."

When I came home from the hospital, I wanted the house to feel like I was bringing my baby to a wonderland. I didn't want fashionable domes with cameras inside in the rooms. I had the cameras concealed in the crown molding throughout the house. I'd downloaded the apps so I could view everything happening from wherever I was. I'd heard about too many strange abductions of kids from their own homes. I couldn't put anything past Granville.

Tisha called my cell. I answered, "Hey, what's up?"

"You still want to go to Rice to grocery shop."

"Girl, I'd forgotten all about food. I'm busy. I'll have a personal shopper do that."

She asked, "Your hospital bag packed?"

"I have two. One at the house. Another in my car." After I had this child, I had everything required to look better than Sindy. I'd even scheduled my implant procedure for three months after delivery. I was going from having double D's to triple D's. Why not? Sindy Singleton was not taking my husband from me.

"I'm on standby. Call me when it's time."

Tisha and I had grown closer since the last time Loretta acted crazy. Granville deserved her. They should get back together. Thankfully, I hadn't heard from him or Beaux.

"Will do. Bye." Admiring the breathtaking ambiance my baby would come home to, I smiled.

Roosevelt was at the game and I was at his condo. The decorating was done; the workers were leaving; I was exhausted and going to sleep in his bed.

CHAPTER 48

Chicago

"Thanks for having dinner with me."

When a woman gave a man a second chance to get it right, saying less wasn't always better. I am the youngest GM/VP in the league. I'm accustomed to making tough calls. I determined the salaries for all the players, coaches, and staff. Being in the presence of this gorgeous woman, I could barely think straight.

To start over, I wanted to pick up where we'd left off. I'd taken Sindy to Brennan's again. We sat at the same table, on the second floor, in the corner.

The waiter brought the wine list and handed it to Sindy.

"Xavier Monnot," she said this time, without looking at the selections.

"That's an excellent Pinot Noir," I said, then added, "We'll have the fried green tomato and blue crab, oysters Rockefeller, and braised oxtail and dumplings. Bring them out in that order, one at a time."

Sindy smiled. "Okay. I like that. Roosevelt, I'm not a complicated woman. I—"

"Hold that thought. Excuse me for a moment," I said, leaving the table. I didn't want to text in front of Sindy. I sent my chef a message: Can you make me one of your especially creamy cheesecakes with the gingersnap crust with mint leaves and take it to my place? And leave some of your fresh, thick whipped cream in the fridge.

If he was able to accommodate, that would become our special dessert.

It was too early in getting to know Sindy to do the "she loves me; she loves me not." I was just trying to settle into the phase of "she likes me." I'd use the whipped cream to draw a heart in the middle; then I'd hand the decorating wand to her.

Returning, I saw the fried green tomato and blue crab were on the table. I apologized for walking away.

"I'd love to turn my phone off, but with my job an emergency could come up." That, and Madison could go into labor. Just in case the baby was mine, I was definitely going to be at the delivery.

Damn, what if that fucked-up dude, Granville, shows up too? I'd have to address that with Madison tomorrow.

I held up my glass. "A toast to a beautiful and amazing woman."

She smiled. "Thanks. You're amazing yourself. Roosevelt, when we're together, I need you to stay in this zone."

Raising my brows, I nodded, and then I shook my head. Was this woman clairvoyant? I diced the tomato into small pieces and fed her first. Sindy leaned forward. She opened her mouth. I wanted to dive in and trade places with that crab.

"Umm, this is so good," she said, moaning. Sliding the appetizer onto her fork, she said, "Open your mouth and close your eyes."

I did. The tomato touched my tongue; then I felt her fingers in my mouth. I gently held her hand in place as I sucked, probably longer than I should have. The erection inside my pants grew fast.

Opening my eyes, I told her, "That was tasty. Thanks." I eased my hand under the table and squeezed my dick.

Sindy nodded and sipped her wine. "You've got nice skills. I can tell you're a very good kisser. Can't wait for our first."

Sindy was a tease. I liked that. Had to make sure I did not give her a reason to leave before having her tongue in my mouth tonight. I looked into her eyes. "Tell me about yourself," I said. Other than she was thirty years old, had a wealthy family, and was an only child, like Madison was, I didn't know much.

"I don't rest on my father's accomplishments. I own a nonprofit organization, I'm Not Locked Up."

Ah. I smiled. For the first time I pieced together Chaz's computer gig with her organization and their meeting. It didn't matter how they connected, I was one happy man.

Sindy continued, "We help children whose parents are incarcerated. A lot of these kids are too young to understand what's happening. But the preteens and teens need the most assistance. We work hard to make sure they don't end up behind bars too."

I wondered if Granville's father was a criminal. Shifting my focus back to Sindy, I said, "That's admirable. Tell me more."

"We pay for counseling for the children and for the nonincarcerated parent. When there is a loss of income, we pay their rent and living expenses for a minimum of six months. If the nonincarcerated parents are unemployed, we find them jobs they're good at so they'll be successful. We make sure the kids are either enrolled in sports or volunteer for community service. If the teenagers are old enough and prefer to work, we find them a part-time weekend job so it won't interfere with them going to school. I have a great staff and we do a lot. I love what I do. I also know how to shut it down when I'm sharing quality time with a man I like."

Okay. I hesitated for a minute. I understood her point. I decided not to respond to it. I wasn't turning off my cell.

Wow. I nodded. "Looking at you, I would've never guessed. If you'd like, I'd love to have our football team partner with your organization. I'm sure there's something we can sponsor."

Tipping her glass to mine, she said, "I'd like that."

"Let's talk business at a later date."

"Now you're reading my mind," Sindy said.

"My place?"

"I'd like that, Roosevelt."

The waiter arrived with the oysters Rockefeller.

Sindy touched his hand. "Cancel this. Package the braised oxtail and dumplings to go, and bring the check."

"Certainly, ma'am. Anything else for you?" he asked, looking at Sindy first, then at me.

I said, "That'll be all. Thanks."

I had Sindy follow me to my condo. The valet parked our cars. Sweeping her off her feet and carrying her across the threshold would be a bit much for the first date. What if she stayed and discovered my night sweats and nightmare? Exhaling, I unlocked the door, opened it, and waited for her to enter first.

My chin damn near hit the floor. "What the hell!" My condo had been turned into a nursery.

Sindy stared at me. We were both speechless.

Madison came out of my bedroom. There was a dessert plate in her hand. "Hi, honey. . . . Oh, hey, Sindy. This cheesecake is amazing, Roosevelt." She seductively slipped a forkful into her mouth. "Thanks for having it delivered. You guys have to taste this," Madison said. Shoveling another forkful, she offered it to Sindy.

The door was still open. I expected her to walk out on me again—this time for reasons I understood.

Sindy looked directly into my eyes. "Roosevelt, you need to decide. Right here. Right now."

CHAPTER 49

Madison

"Roosevelt, honey. Wake up."

A puddle of fluid was beneath my butt. A few days had passed since Sindy had gotten the surprise of her future. If Roosevelt wasn't at the office, I made sure he was by my side, not hers.

I shook him hard. He didn't move. "Baby, it's time."

"What? It's time," he mumbled. "Oh, damn! It's time!"

Scrambling from underneath the covers, he looked at me; then he put his hand on my stomach. I smiled at the angel God had sent me; I was eternally grateful that that Sindy woman was gone from our lives forever. Love filled my heart. If the child inside me wasn't for my husband, I was blessed for all he'd done, and had to find a way to make my marriage work.

Adoption was an option. I could sign my parental rights to Granville. That way, he wouldn't have a reason to contact me.

This man in bed with me had loved me through my double mastectomy. I didn't care that I wasn't able to breast-feed our child. I was extremely excited knowing that shortly after giving birth, I'd start the process for treatment and reconstructive surgery. Would they feel real? Would my nipples have sensitivity? I sure hoped so.

Roosevelt scrambled for his cell, reminding me to get mine. "Yes, I'd like my car, please. It's an emergency."

It was bold of me to rearrange his condo without his permission. A real woman knew it was always best to ask for forgiveness, when she knew she'd never get permission. I slipped my dress over my head. He quickly put on his pants and shirt, then grabbed my bag. We walked to Chaz's condo. Roosevelt knocked on the door.

Chaz opened it. "Man . . . is it—"

"Yes. Tell Mom, Dad, and Grandpa to meet us at the hospital."

Touching my stomach, I winked at Chaz. He hated me, but he loved his brother.

"Ow!" I faked a contraction to annoy him.

Roosevelt placed his arm around my lower back. "Baby, let's go."

Glancing at Chaz, I placed my hand above my butt and pushed my stomach forward. I wobbled to the elevator. Roosevelt's car was parked out front. He opened the door for me. The valet opened the door for him.

Roosevelt became silent. I called my mom. "I'm in labor. Meet me at the hospital." I had no idea what my dad was up to but he'd been too quiet since Helen told him he had three months. Hopefully, Papa would show up.

I phoned Tisha with the same message, and then added, "Don't tell Loretta." After hurling that photo album at me, Loretta had better not come near me or my baby.

Roosevelt parked outside emergency and escorted me in. Everyone knew who we were, but my husband gave the requested information for me.

"I'm going to move my car and I'll be right up. Don't push until I get there," he said, running out the door.

Someone rolled me in a wheelchair to delivery. Handed me off to staff. They whisked me into a birthing room. "Where's my doctor?"

"We've notified your doctor. She's on her way."

I was nervous. What was taking Roosevelt so long?

A doctor came into the room, but he wasn't mine. "I'm going to check you," he said. Probing my uterus, he said, "You've dilated six centimeters. Hopefully, your doctor will make it here before you're ready. If not, I'll have to do it."

"No. I want my doctor!" I cried out as my stomach contracted.

Roosevelt entered the room and stood by my side. "Sin . . . I mean Madison. Sorry about that," he said.

Was that what took him so long? He'd been talking to her? I was not happy that at our special moment he was obviously thinking about her.

"Our families are outside waiting to come in. You ready?" he asked.

No, I wasn't. I'd never be comfortable with his people standing around, staring at my vagina, watching the birth of our baby. This time they'd see the real thing up close. I'd had my last Brazilian a week ago so Aphrodite was prepped for the doctor. I couldn't remember the last time Roosevelt called my kitty by her nickname, Aphrodite, or the last time I'd called his dick, Tiger. All I envisioned was those who were in the courtroom flashing back to the video of me with Granville.

God knew I didn't want to say, "Sure, they can come in."

When Roosevelt opened the door and offered a come-hither motion, they scurried in, in a single-file line, like the baby's head had already popped out. My mom stood on the opposite side of the bed from Roosevelt. Behind the faces that I recognized came a group that I didn't want to see. Camera crews and reporters rushed in. Lights flashed so fast—they blinded me.

"Where is security? How did all of the people get access to my room?"

A reporter shoved a microphone in my face. "Mrs. DuBois, or should I say Ms. Tyler, do you know who the father of your baby is?"

Before I answered, a different reporter asked, "Where is the guy who shot Chicago? Is he the father? How did Granville Washington get off? Did you help him?"

The newscaster who announced our pregnancy on television squeezed her mic in. "Madison," she said, acting as though we were on a first-name basis, "do you have any regrets?"

Where was Roosevelt? Where was my mom? I couldn't see through the media crowd.

I screamed, "Get rid of them! Get out! All of you!"

One by one, the crowd thinned. Roosevelt was back at my side. "I'm sorry. I'm not sure who called them, but they are all over the place. I asked the police to remove them."

If the policemen were the same as the ones who were here when I signed the papers to take my husband off the respirator, those reporters weren't going anywhere.

Helen lifted the sheet, tilted her head, and stared between my legs. "I sure hope this baby isn't one of ours."

My mom reappeared, stood by my side, and held my hand. I pulled away—not because I didn't want my mother to touch me. The IV in the back of my hand was uncomfortable. Mom went to the foot of the bed by Dad.

When the door opened, I heard the commotion outside the room. The doctor had returned.

"I guess this is what goes along with being a celebrity couple," the doctor said. "Relax, I'm going to check on your progress."

I wanted my mom. As his hand slid into my uterus, and he pressed on my stomach, I cried.

This is what happens when reporters are bored and desperate to deliver the breaking news, even if it tears people apart or kills them. Their coming into my birthing room made me angry. I should press charges. The police should handcuff all of them, put them in a paddy wagon, haul them to the precinct, lock them up, and then swallow the key. There should be consequences for those ruthless reporters.

"Ow!" I yelled. Struggling to breathe, I squeezed Roosevelt's hand. "Your mom," I said, pleading with my eyes. I wanted her out of the room! "Get her from between my legs!"

Yelling made my stomach hurt more.

Roosevelt kissed my forehead. "Don't worry about my mom. She just wants to see the baby. Breathe," he said.

Helen stood beside the doctor like she was his assistant. She insisted on being one of the first to see "the child," as she'd called it.

Of all the times he'd shown up, I didn't want my father here. Chaz was next to his mom. Roosevelt's father, Martin, and his grandfather Wally were in the waiting room lineup too. They stood in a huddle, looking like it was fourth and goal for the win.

"It's about that time," the doctor said.

This was all wrong. Where was my doctor? Where was Tisha?

The door opened. "Who is that?" I couldn't see around Roosevelt.

"On the count of three, Madison, I want you to push," the doctor said.

Roosevelt placed his hand between my shoulder blades and held it there. I sucked in as much oxygen as I could. My stomach tightened.

The doctor counted, "One. Two. Three."

I pushed hard.

Why was I sweating in a cold room?

"It's me, honey," Tisha said. She stood on the opposite side of the bed and held my hand.

Tisha whispered in my ear, "He's here." She stared into my eyes. "He's outside, and he's talking to the media. I thought you should know. Sindy is here too."

Karma was all mine.

The room suddenly got colder, as though someone had locked me, alone, in a morgue with the Grim Reaper. The chill penetrated me so deep that I froze from the inside out. Reminded me again of the trip I'd taken to New York City to celebrate New Year's Eve. Except this time, I was scared.

I didn't wait for the doctor to tell me again. Out of frustration I pushed as hard as I could.

"Oh, my!" Helen's voice escalated. "I can see the head." Abruptly she became silent.

Tisha moved closer to the foot of the bed. Chaz stood beside her, videotaping with his phone.

I screamed. Not because of the pain. I was annoyed with Helen. If Roosevelt hadn't insisted they be there, I'd ask them to leave. If the baby hadn't just slipped into the doctor's hands, I'd get up and go. Not sure if Granville was outside the hospital or outside my room, I wanted to hold everyone captive until they cleared the crowd.

Roosevelt kissed me. "We did it, baby."

Helen joyfully said, "Oh, my God. He's so beautiful."

"He." I exhaled. My doctor had said it was a boy, but I waited until we were sure because some doctors have been wrong.

Roosevelt let go of my hand and I felt alone. In a room full of people, I felt like I was by myself.

The doctor handed Roosevelt the scissors. "You want to do the honor?"

"Mom, why don't you do it," Roosevelt said.

What? I couldn't believe what I'd heard. Why shouldn't my mother be asked to do it? I kept quiet. I motioned for Tisha to come closer; then I whispered, "Go get rid of him. I don't care how you do it, but he can't be out there when Roosevelt and his family leave."

"What about Loretta?" Tisha asked.

I frowned; then I whispered in her ear, "I thought I heard you say 'Sindy.' "

"Her too."

Damn. "Get rid of all of them."

"Consider it done. Congratulations, Mama."

"Oh, baby." Helen's voice was full of pride. "My first grandchild."

"Hurry up and cut the cord, Mama, so I can hold him for a few seconds," Roosevelt said.

It was like I was invisible. I said, "I want to hold my baby." The room got quiet.

Roosevelt placed him on my chest. There was no doubt he was a DuBois. I was relieved.

The door opened.

Helen gasped. "What on earth?"

Roosevelt looked over his shoulder. Froze. Sindy opened her arms. Like a magnet to steel, he was drawn to her. They embraced. She cut her eyes toward me. My mouth opened, but nothing came out.

Sindy walked toward the doctor and glanced at my baby. She didn't say a word. Roosevelt didn't ask her to leave.

The nurse said, "It's time to get this handsome fella cleaned up. I'll bring him back to you later." She left with our baby.

I started crying.

My mom seemed sadder than I was. She said, "We'll be in the waiting area until they clean up the baby."

Roosevelt leaned over and hugged me.

"Congratulations, Mama," Tisha said, reentering the room. "It's done."

I nodded and darted my eyes in Sindy's direction.

"Oh . . . I wondered where she'd gone."

As quietly as Sindy had come, she turned and left.

Things were happening so fast. Where was security or Roosevelt's bodyguard? Were they plotting against me? This was supposed to be my day.

"What are we going to name him?" Helen asked.

I take it she wasn't talking to me.

Chaz said, "Let's go watch the video. We'll come up with something."

Roosevelt looked at his brother and said, "I can't believe how light he is. I want to name him Chaz. That way, I'll have two."

"Naw, man. I'm flattered," Chaz said, "but don't do that. Name him Zach."

I was relieved. I did not want my son to be named after Roosevelt's brother. I repeated the name. " 'Zach.' I like that."

Loretta entered the room. I looked at Tisha. She hunched her shoulders.

"What the hell is this—a revolving-door delivery? Tisha, get her out of here."

"Good going, Madison. I saw your son on the video Chaz posted," Loretta said.

What the hell? He did what? Without my permission.

Bitch! Her ass was determined to start shit every fucking chance she got.

Helen came back into the room, then said, "Chicago, that crazy man is here, demanding a paternity test. Have your paternity test done today."

CHAPTER 50

Granville

"Can she do that, Beaux? Can she?"

"I keep telling you, bro. I don't know."

Madison had refused to let me take a paternity test yesterday. Why would she do that? After all the gifts I'd sent for my son, I had to wait for her to tell the reporters the truth. Zach's last name is Washington, not DuBois.

While I was at the hospital, the reporters treated me like a celebrity. The newscaster who had Madison and Chicago on her show—when Madison told all of Houston, "We're pregnant"—gave me her card. The other half of that "we" should've been me. The reporter told me to call her first if the baby was mine.

Wasn't anybody listening to me? I told her on camera yesterday, "That's my baby."

That guy who'd given me that money and a gun was still in a pickle. I had the briefcase in my Super Duty truck outside, but I hadn't opened it. For all I know, there could be bricks or a bomb in that thing. If he was telling the truth, I didn't want to leave $1 million lying around my place. What if they came back to take it all back while I wasn't there, then accused me of stealing?

"I guess she wants to do process of elimination. You made the right decision coming here today," Beaux said.

My brother had another seafood boil for our mom and invited the neighborhood yesterday. That would be the last one for Mom. She hadn't gotten out of bed in a week. She couldn't control her bodily functions. Her caregivers did a good job of keeping Mama clean. The people Mom did know—my brother said she didn't know they were here yesterday. A few of her friends dropped by this morning to say their good-byes.

Looking at Beaux, I wanted to ask him if that was really the gun in the shoe box that was now inside our mama's closet. Sadly, this wasn't a good time for that conversation. There was only one weapon used at the scene, but there were two possible guns? Maybe Sindy's dad meant he had some other gun. We still planned to bury with Mama the one Beaux had found.

I wanted to be here yesterday, but I didn't want to miss the birth of my baby. Loretta was the only one who was nice to me when she saw me. Chaz acted like I'd shot him. His eyeing me didn't scare me. Bet if none of those cameras were there, he wouldn't have disrespected me. Loretta showed me how to download the YouTube app. Then she showed me how I could see the video online on my iPhone.

The nurse stood in the living-room doorway. "Excuse me, gentlemen. It's that time again."

"I'm going to check on Mom," Beaux said, leaving the living room.

Sitting in my dad's old recliner, I didn't move. I didn't want to watch her give Mom another dose of morphine. I'd seen her do that every hour since I'd been here. The baby had to be mine. Mama had to hold on to see him. I felt like if I went to her bedroom . . .

Tears rolled down my face. No sense in drying them. I wasn't finished crying.

Holding my phone in my hand, I clicked on the link Loretta had given me over the phone. Guess she didn't want to text it. I understood. The last fifty views were mostly mine. Madison pushed and the head popped out. If I had been in the room, I would've put all of Chicago's family out. They were rude, standing in front of my future mother- and father-in-law. But if Chaz hadn't stood close enough to record, I wouldn't have proof.

Madison pushed really hard. This time my son slipped out like he'd stepped on a banana peel. I knew he was mine. All that light skin didn't mean nothing. Beaux agreed. If Mama was aware, she'd say the same.

Zach's dick and balls were big and black. From the neck down, his baby picture looked just like mine.

I didn't care that my mother was not in her right state. I wanted my mom to hold her grandson before she died. Madison and I should've made plans for that before the baby was born. Mom might not hang on too much longer. I think the only reason she was still here was because of Zach.

"Granville," the nurse said. "It's that time. She's struggling through her last breaths. Please come. Your brother needs you."

This time my eyes burned with tears. I wanted to move, but I couldn't. I sat in Dad's chair like the nurse was talking to someone else. No, my mama was not going to die!

A horrid sound. The cross between an eighteen-wheeler's horn, a whistling kettle, and music from a horror movie traveled throughout the house.

Beaux yelled, "*Noooooo,* Mama, please!"

I picked up the recliner as though it was my wrestling opponent, then slammed it to the floor. If the baby wasn't mine, I had no reason to live—and no reason not to kill Chicago.

CHAPTER 51

Chicago

"Why did you come here? My baby and I are fine. You're free to be with her."

Madison probably thought I was upset from all that had happened a few days ago. I wasn't. She was beautiful. After hours of labor and sweating, Madison had looked amazing. She and the baby were leaving the hospital tomorrow. Every man would want this woman—if they knew not the drama she towed.

My voice trembled. "Madison, I love you. I'm so excited—"

She interrupted, "What's the 'but,' Roosevelt?" Her tone was flat. Unemotional.

She knew me well. "It can wait until you get home."

" 'Home'? I haven't seen you in three days. Are you referring to my place or yours?" she asked. "I'm okay, either way."

"I have a driver picking you up in the morning. Madison, let's just wait—"

"Roosevelt, please. Our son is born. He's healthy. He needs his father. There's nothing we can't work out."

"You're right about some of that." I reached into my back pocket.

My wife stared at the television, picked up the remote, then increased the volume. It didn't matter if she screamed or cried. I expected her to perform. Nothing she'd do would change my mind.

No one knew what was about to take place. I hadn't told Chaz, my grandfather, my dad, or my mom. I removed three sets of legal documents; then I handed the first set to Madison.

She glanced up at me. She slowly unfolded the papers. Her eyes scanned left to right, again and again. I kept quiet.

After ten minutes of shared silence, I handed her a pen. "I know you're good at signing. You can do this." I pointed to where I needed her signature.

"One day you love me, and now you want a divorce? You brought these papers here, to the hospital! That's inhumane."

"I don't need to tell you what's *inhumane,* Madison. I loved you like—"

" 'Loved'?"

I hesitated for a moment. "Okay, I love you. But I'm finally over you. I'm not in love with you anymore."

"Since when? Is it Sindy? You let her come in the birthing room and didn't ask her to leave. That was wrong, Roosevelt!"

I could've said, "I didn't know Sindy was coming, and I didn't know what to say to her. But the second I saw her, I knew I wanted to be with her."

I could've asked Madison, "Why was the dude who tried to kill me standing outside the nursery, pacing back and forth?" Loretta had come and warned me of all the things Madison wouldn't. If I stayed with Madison, Granville was going to kill me. Well, he could have Madison.

"What about you getting my house back? Buying me a car? Saving my family's company? You took care of all of my medical expenses for my breast surgeries. You made sure I had the best health care. You let me come home before I had the baby. Now that our son is here, you want to divide our family? I can't sign this."

Sindy had warned me this would happen. Good ole Madison Tyler. Always expected things to be right, even when she knew she was wrong.

"You can. And you will. Madison, you married a man. A real man. Money don't make me. I make money. I have no regrets for anything I've done for you. And I'm keeping my commitment to pay for your implants. You deserve the best. You just don't deserve me as your husband. No matter how generous I am, I'm nobody's fool. You didn't have a problem leaving me for dead. Don't have a problem letting me go. Sign the damn papers."

Madison nodded. "Yeah, that's Sindy, all right. You don't even sound like Roosevelt. If this is what you really want, be sure. Once I'm gone, I'm not coming back."

"I'm sure" was all I said. This wasn't as easy as it may have appeared. I loved this woman.

Tears streamed down her cheeks as she scribbled her name in several places. "What about our son? What about Zach?"

When we heard, "Breaking news," we glanced up at the television.

"A child is listed in critical condition this morning," the reporter said.

My heart pounded against my chest like a bass drummer beating with all his strength.

The reporter continued, "It happened at the pool area of the famous hotel—"

I gasped. That was where Madison and I had our reception. That five-star hotel didn't deserve bad publicity again.

"The two six-year-olds were playing, when one child reportedly found a gun. It's believed that the little boy didn't know it was loaded. He pointed it at his twin sister's head, then pulled the trigger."

Madison buried her face in the pillow and screamed, "That could've been our child!"

Fast-forward six years, and she was right. But right now, she was desperately trying to hold on to our marriage.

That was the type of hotel where we'd take our child for the experience. Backtrack seven months, that could be the . . .

The reporter said, "Investigators believe that could be the same gun used to shoot Roosevelt Chicago DuBois. If it is, the judge who acquitted Granville Washington could be in very hot water for overruling the jury's decision to give Granville Washington two possible life sentences. Keep it here. We'll keep you posted."

I took the signed divorce papers from Madison, then handed her another set. "Sign this one too. I'm selling Tyler Construction, and it's not open for discussion."

"What about my dad?" she asked.

"Don't. You know we were firing him. He can take his money and start all over, or keep spending it on sexing young girls. Either way, my family wants no part of it."

"I am your family," she said.

I waved the divorce papers in her face.

Quietly she scribbled. I looked to make sure it was her real signature.

My eyes watered for those children. When I leave here, I'd stop by the hospital and offer support to their family.

"Here's the paternity test results," I said, dropping the papers onto her lap. "And I have one more set of documents for you. You'll get those later."

It hurt me to admit that Loretta was right. I had to end everything with Madison.

Zach was mine, and I was filing for sole custody.

. . . To Be Continued

A READING GROUP GUIDE

I'D RATHER BE WITH YOU

Mary B. Morrison

ABOUT THIS GUIDE

The suggested questions that follow are included to enhance your group's reading of this book.

Discussion Questions

1. What do you believe is Madison's motivation for taking Roosevelt off the respirator? Under her circumstances, what would you have done? Why?

2. Give an example where a character feels another character is wrong, but the character who is pissed off has done the same exact thing to someone else in the story. Do you know people who have done this as well?

3. Does Tisha have an obligation to tell her husband that she is pregnant? Under the circumstances, should Darryl (or any man) have any control over whether or not a woman has an abortion?

4. Do you believe Loretta is a lesbian? Is she in love with Madison or just jealous of Madison?

5. Do you feel Chicago unconditionally loves Madison? Is Madison in love with Chicago? Should they stay together? Or should Chicago leave?

6. Is Sindy Singleton the woman for Chicago? Or does she have a motive?

7. What's the deal with Raynard? Why did he wait so long to turn over the videotape of the shooting? Why didn't the tape help convict Granville? Should Raynard and Loretta reunite?

8. Who is ultimately responsible for Chicago being shot?

9. Do you feel Rosalee knows her husband is a cheater? Assuming she does, why is she still married to him? Is infidelity a justification for divorce? Would you vote in favor of divorce becoming illegal?

10. Based on testimonies from Loretta, Madison, Chicago, and Chaz, do you believe the judge made the right decision in declaring a mistrial? Why?

11. If you saw a man with an amazing body, would you think he's an ex-con? Do you believe women fall for attractive men and seldom question their backgrounds? Would you marry an excon if you were friends with him/her before he/she was convicted? Why?

12. How many happily married couples do you know? What do you believe makes their marriage successful?

13. Are you happy that Madison's baby was fathered by Chicago? Or would you have preferred Granville as the father? Do you think Granville would've been a good dad? Would you have his baby? Why?

The IF I CAN'T HAVE YOU series continues with

If You Don't Know Me

In stores April 2014

CHAPTER 1

Sindy

"When he walks in, you'll walk out."

"Are you sure?" Nyle Carter asked me as the prison guard closed the door to our private glass-enclosed room.

I didn't blink as I said, "Help me get Granville back behind bars and you'll be discharged the same day he's booked. The remaining two and a half years of your three-year sentence will vanish. You'll be on a one-year probation with an officer I know personally. It's all taken care of."

Trust your instincts. That was how I lived. My word was a firm commitment. Since I was a little girl, if Sindy Singleton made a promise, I kept it.

This morning I'd coiled my long, straight, cinnamon-colored hair into a donut-size bun, which sat at the nape of my neck. My cream-colored pants, which I only wore when I visited the federal detention center, were loosely fitted. A simple short-sleeved white blouse draped to my hips. Soft leather flats clung to my feet. No lipstick. No perfume. No jewelry. My purse was in the trunk of my Bentley. My keys were in one of the small lockers in the lobby. My Texas driver's license was left with the guard at the security entrance.

Sitting in a room reserved for attorney/client face-to-face privileges, I was the attorney. Nyle Carter was not. I needed this inmate's help, the same as he desired mine.

"Let me get this straight. I have to find a way to bring Granville back to prison before you'll get me out of here?" he asked.

Scanning the visitors' room, there was a handful of folks who had come to see what I called "the sick and locked up." I'd bet all of them were guilty, but each had pleaded innocent.

Nyle was known to those on the inside as "G-double-A." Some youngster by the name of No Chainz had given Nyle the name, saying it meant, "Got all the answers." I wished that were true.

Nyle was handsome, above average. Put a suit on this man—the way he used to sport one every day—and no one would believe he waited until he was forty years old to get himself arrested. Not that there was a better time, but there were some people you never envisioned behind bars. With others, you know it wasn't *if* they're going to do time, but when and for how long?

"You were supposed to make sure he never got out. I paid you twenty thousand to give Granville advice that would get him convicted, and make sure he got two consecutive life sentences."

I was a woman in love with a man who was another woman's husband. Whatever, and whomever I wanted, was mine. I was thirty. Ready to walk down the aisle. Tired of Madison Tyler-DuBois interfering with my getting to know her husband. I added her to Sindy's shit list.

Marriages weren't roped and bound by a license, but our country's values were still divided. Infidelity was seemingly contagious.

In the South, during slavery, the slaves had ownership papers. If they were fortunate, they lived to see the day the master signed over their freedom. Even when they were freed, they didn't know where to go or what to do. Some migrated to Chicago, New York, or California to begin a new life. But marriage for a lot of couples, especially those below the Mason-Dixon, was the same. Ownership, control, and, if necessary, abuse blanketed the household. It was better to take the beating and stay than to get a divorce and leave.

This was the case for Madison. She'd almost gotten her husband killed; then she'd taken him off the respirator to watch him die. God had a different plan. Her husband survived. And rather than her letting him love me, she'd prefer to keep him and kill his happiness. Having his baby was the lucky charm that I was about to snatch from her.

He had no idea what to do with Madison. Men generally embraced the "Do as I say" philosophy. The women, "Do as I do." Neither gave a damn about how the other felt, as long as the women obeyed. Madison wasn't that type. Neither was I. I was a true Southern belle, born and wrapped in a cloak of confidence.

I was soft, only on the outside.

When I saw on the news that Roosevelt "Chicago" DuBois had been shot three times, I had to get involved. Right now, I had to get more involved with every aspect. If Roosevelt was going to propose to me, I couldn't give a damn about his trifling wife. She wasn't nearly as smart as she believed. I had to stop that idiot, Granville Washington, from trying again to kill my future fiancé.

Nyle sat across from me. "He's not so dumb. He's actually smart. Tell me what I need to do to walk out of here. I'll make sure it's done."

Nyle's son was in my I'm Not Locked Up nonprofit program for kids with parents in jail. His son was an amazingly brilliant child. Landry was so impressive that six months ago I accompanied him on a visit to the federal detention center to meet his father.

What kind of man could have single-parented such a child and then ended up behind bars? I had to know. I'd learned that Nyle had an office downtown. He represented hundreds of clients for a decade. Problem was, he'd never passed the bar. How could people retain a lawyer without certifying if the attorney was legit?

I nodded. "Granville is the smartest, dumbest person I've seen as well. Do you know how many inmates represent themselves and get off? Almost none. Hearing Granville question Chaz, watching him get Loretta arrested, seeing him present that sex tape of Madison, made me realize we cannot underestimate this guy. When he degraded Roosevelt on the stand and made a mockery of my man, that was it. We've got to get him to state, and I'm not talking about a high-school championship. Prison is where Granville belongs."

Plan A had failed. The two consecutive life sentences he should be serving right now didn't happen.

Plan B—I had to stop my dad from executing a hit on Roosevelt. My father should've never accepted the billionaire's money. Now he was indebted because I was not marrying that guy. My dad was ruthless, greedy for money and power, and he was also brilliant. He was getting older, but I was getting wiser. I knew never to go against him.

If Plan B didn't work, then Plan C—I was putting a hit out on Granville. Only his younger brother, Beaux, would miss him. Their mother had recently died. Their father was already dead.

"What do I need to do?" Nyle asked.

"I want you to tell the guard to inform the warden that Granville Washington is attempting to kill Roosevelt again. Lie and say Granville told you this in confidence after his release. Then you must insist that they issue a search warrant for all of his property—his apartment, his car, his mama's house, and her grave. Trust me, they'll find the gun somewhere because the gun Granville's brother had, I planted it and I gave him that lead on where to find it."

Leaning back, Nyle said, "Her what?"

"You heard me right. Her grave. If they don't find what they need at any of the first locations, tell them to dig her up, search the soil and her coffin. Roosevelt's life is dependent on you."

Roosevelt was a good man. He was the youngest vice president/general manager in the league, and we were blessed to have him for our football team. After all the wrong his wife had done him, he did all the right things for her. A man that wonderful deserved a wife like me.

I didn't disclose to Nyle the details of what the authorities would find. What my father had done, I was about to undo.

CHAPTER 2

Granville

There had to be a mistake.

My son was a week old. My son. You hear me! I said *my* son!

People stood at the altar, saying their final words. My mind was on the living. What those people had to say about my family was for them, not for me. There was nothing anyone had said that could bring my mama back.

I didn't care about my woman texting me a copy of the results showing her husband was 99.99 percent the biological father. That meant there was almost a .01 percent chance the baby could be mine.

People with money think they can buy whatever and whomever they wanted. Well, almost. I might look dumb, but I'm not. All that money Chicago had didn't keep me behind bars for shooting him. Didn't matter how much Loretta hated me, I was responsible for making her do thirty days at the federal detention center.

How do I know Madison didn't pay someone at the lab to alter the results? I had to either find a way to do my own paternity test, or pay a detective to investigate who's the real daddy.

Madison wouldn't let me near my baby. Maybe if I showed up at her house tonight, she'd let me in. Or . . . I laughed out loud. Loretta hated me, but she hated Madison more. Maybe I could convince Loretta to help me with my own test.

But first, my brother and I had to bury my mom.

Other than getting a glimpse of baby Zach through the nursery window at the hospital the day he was born, I hadn't seen him in person. I'd watched the video of his birth two hundred times before someone took it off YouTube.

"Man, it's time," Beaux whispered in my ear. "We've got to hide this gun in Mom's casket before they close it for the last time."

We sat in the front pew. Beaux was still claiming the gun he had was the snub-nosed I'd used to shoot Chicago three times. How could that be if the man who'd hired me to kill Chicago—for $2 million—said he had the gun? Then there was a third gun that these kids found at the scene of the crime. A news reporter alleged that was the gun used to shoot Chicago.

I didn't know, as Mama used to say, "Who's lying and who's telling the truth?" I hoped the gun found by those kids at the hotel wasn't it. What made that six-year-old boy shoot his twin sister in the head was probably his mama's fault for letting him play violent video games.

My son was going to be raised the way my mama raised me and my brother. "Y'all go outside and play," she'd tell us.

I whispered back to Beaux, "All right. When you say your last goodbyes, fall into the casket and cry like a baby. I'll cover you. Slip the gun under the lining. When you're done, look at me. I'll hug you then and help you sit on the pew, until it's time for us to carry her out."

We'd given some thought to how we were going to do this. Had gone over it many times. But now that the moment was here, could my brother follow through with his plan?

I hadn't gone through with mine. I still hadn't opened the briefcase, more like a suitcase, that the man gave me. Inside was supposed to be $1 million in cash, a gun, and an iPhone. There was a Facebook account for me, but it wasn't under my real name. The e-mail and password weren't linked to me either. Under this account, Chicago was my friend and I could track his every move as long as his locations were on. I didn't want to go back to jail for shooting that man again. Might not be so lucky this time if I represented myself again for attempted murder or worse, murder.

The pastor started closing the service by reading my mom's eulogy.

"Sarah Lee Washington was a woman of God. She had a full and fruitful life. This here is a celebration of her life. She moved her family out of the projects of Port Arthur and into a great neighborhood near the tracks."

The pastor wiped his face with his cloth, then continued speaking. "Sarah Lee moved, but she never stopped being neighborly. Whatever she could do to help others, or help out here at the church, she did it until her health wouldn't allow her to do it no mo'," he said.

This man didn't know my mother. The preacher who knew Mom best had gone to glory years ago. He'd died of cancer too. Mama was with Daddy now. He'd died of cancer too. Seemed like everyone who lived close to the refineries in our town, all their lives, got some kind of cancer.

I nudged Beaux in his side with my elbow. If we were carrying out our plan, now was the time.

"We're going to miss Sarah Lee just as much as her family. Sarah Lee was family. She leaves with us her two sons, Granville and Beaux Washington, and her sister, Wilma Sims," the pastor said.

Beaux stood. I stood too. Side by side we walked up to Mama's casket. Forcing himself to cry, my brother fell over Mama's dead body. When he reached into his jacket, I leaned closer.

"Hurry up, bro," I said as I felt a heavy hand on my shoulder. I faked the kind of cry that was more sound than tears.

"It's going to be okay," someone said. "Your mother is no longer suffering."

Aunt Wilma came up, just as Beaux finished covering up the gun. "Okay, boys. Sarah don' gone home. I'm here for you now," she said. "You know my sister don't want y'all doing this. Get yourselves together."

My aunt was there to take charge, all right. She was being nice—that is, until she'd receive the long list of things she wanted out of Mama's house. Then things would return to normal and we wouldn't see her for years.

Mama had on a beautiful, long white lace dress that Aunt Wilma had picked out from Mama's closet. She wanted to put jewelry on Mama, but Beaux and I didn't want to give anyone a reason to dig up Mama's body, so we insisted no jewelry. Mama's hands were folded at her waist; her Bible lay on her stomach, right underneath her palms.

Standing, Beaux and I tucked the white satin liner deep into the casket. The guys from the funeral home rushed over. "We'll do this. That's our job."

"We want to do it," Beaux said.

When I slammed the top, the coffin slid. People in the church gasped; then somebody laughed.

What's funny?

Beaux caught Mama's casket before it hit the floor. "Bro, you still clumsy," Beaux said, laughing too. "Mama probably got a kick out of that."

I should kick him. What if the gun was on top of Mama's Bible? It was a good thing we didn't have to open the casket again. I locked it.

It was time to go to the cemetery. Beaux got into my Super Duty truck. We didn't want no fancy limo driver. We followed the hearse.

"What's in the suitcase?" Beaux asked.

I said, "A million dollars."

Beaux laughed. "Yeah, right."

While he was busy laughing, I'd just come up with another brilliant idea.

CHAPTER 3

Madison

"Hush, little baby, don't you cry. Daddy is gonna buy you whatever you want."

I whispered to Zach, "Your daddy will be here soon. His football game is over."

I'd watched from kickoff until the last second of the fourth quarter. Houston won by ten, but I felt as though I was losing. When the cameras flashed to Roosevelt's suite, Sindy was there. She tucked her long cinnamon hair behind her ear. The diamonds were more brilliant than the lights in the background. Her teeth were perfectly straight and superwhite. The harder I tried to find a flaw, I noticed this woman appeared ideal for Roosevelt. Plus, there was another thing—she seemed to have a glow of happiness that I didn't.

I was home with Roosevelt's baby, and Sindy was on national television with my husband. The holidays were starting next month. Thanksgiving. Soon would come Christmas. Roosevelt and his family would want to share these joyous occasions with my baby and his mistress. Where would I be? None of them liked me.

I had all intentions of dragging out our divorce long enough for Roosevelt to change his mind. Signing the papers didn't make it final. We still had to go to court. I had my plastic surgeon on standby for breast implants.

"Shhh. Hush, baby," I said, rocking in the chair I could never nurse him in.

My lawyer had been prepped. When Roosevelt's attorney set a court date, I'd set my surgery for the same day. The day of the hearing, we'd let Roosevelt show up; then my guy would request a continuance. That should work two or three times, granting me ninety to one hundred eighty days. Add another three months from surgery to recovery, and I could stall for almost a year. If that failed, I had a trump card or two.

I kissed Zach's feet and wiggled his soft toes. Fingering his full head of dark, wavy hair, I loved my baby's pecan tone. Zach's skin was a combination of Roosevelt's tan and my nearly white complexion.

I was fortunate not to have a whining child. Whenever our baby fussed, something was wrong. I'd just finished feeding him. Peeling back the tape from his diaper, I saw it was wet. I'd learned in a bad way not to stick my finger inside his diaper if I wasn't sure what was in it.

Laying him on the changing table, I opened his diaper. His penis and balls were growing faster than the rest of his body. Maybe that was my imagination. The darkness of his genitals wasn't fading. The only thing that reassured me Granville wasn't the father was the paternity results Roosevelt and I had taken. That, and Zach's silky hair. Granville's head was bald, but he had pubic hairs that could be plucked and used as a scouring pad.

"Thank You, Jesus." God had granted me the one thing I'd prayed for: the right father.

My doorbell rang. Tisha was on the monitor. I taped a fresh Pampers diaper to Zach's bottom, snapped his onesie, and then we headed downstairs.

After I opened the door, Tisha instantly took her future godson out of my arms and lovingly placed him in hers. I handed her his receiving blanket.

"This has got to be the most attractive baby. Madison, you should get him an agent and put him in commercials," Tisha said, hugging Zach to her shoulder.

We sat in the living room. The doorbell rang again.

"I got it." Tisha handed me the baby and the blanket, then opened the door. A florist handed her a bouquet of long-stemmed white roses. Before signing, Tisha sniffed them. "Oh, wow! These are nicely scented."

"Who are they from?" I asked.

Signing, she closed the door. "Smell."

I shook my head. She placed them in the center of my coffee table. Tisha took Zach. I read the card: *White represents purity (for Zach) and new beginnings (for us). Please forgive me. I love you.—Loretta*

I ripped the card into as many pieces as I could.

"Dang, Madison. You don't have to make confetti. She's trying to apologize. She wants to see the baby."

"I don't want her around my child or me. In fact, I don't want to live next door to her. Just in case Roosevelt is serious about leaving me for Sindy, I'm going to buy a condo where he lives. That way, I won't need his permission to get access into the building."

Tisha shook her head. "That could backfire. What if he remarries and you have to see his new wife all the time?"

"I'll make her wish she hadn't. I have his firstborn son."

My doorbell rang again. I glanced at my monitor.

"I got it," Tisha said, handing me Zach.

When she opened the door, my dad walked in. "Madison, sweetheart. You've got to stop him. Roosevelt gave me notice. He's stealing my company."

"Papa, don't be rude," I said, tilting my head toward Tisha. "Here, hold Zach." I wasn't looking for his response. I placed the blanket and his grandson in his hands. "Hold his head."

Papa sat on the sofa, placing Zach on his lap. "Hi, Tisha. How're the boys and your mom?"

"Everybody is fine, Mr. Tyler. I'll tell my mother that you said hello. Madison"—Tisha held her hand to her ear—"call me later so we can continue. Take care of my baby."

I was glad Tisha had left. I needed to speak with my dad in private. "Papa, he's not stealing Tyler Construction. He's putting it under new management, pending our divorce being final. He can't sell without my consent."

Zach spit up on Papa's suit jacket. My dad kept the blanket; then he handed the baby to me. "What am I supposed to do? Sit around the house all day with your mother? If I'm forced to do that, we'll be next to get a divorce."

"You worried about not having a twentysomething suck your dick? Or are you seriously concerned about the company?"

I didn't ask about Mom. Papa wasn't going anywhere. After I walked in on my father having sex with what he called his "personal assistant," who was on payroll, I was in favor of his replacement.

Papa paced the full length of my ten-foot area rug. Back and forth he marched, as though whatever he came up with would work. "You can't stop him."

Women were much smarter than men. Roosevelt visited me in the hospital seventy-two hours after my double mastectomy surgery. But I was months ahead of him. The second I saw Sindy on his arm, I had to make certain every decision he made was in my favor.

"Papa, would you agree that women are more intelligent than men?"

He frowned. Stared at me. Nodded. "Most, not all."

"Do you believe I can outthink you?"

I wasn't challenging my dad. He didn't come from money. He grew up in Port Arthur. His parents were poor. But I can proudly say my papa had a field full of dreams and a heart filled with love.

The harder Papa tried to get one of those "good jobs" at one of the three refineries in town, the more they gave him the run around. "Come back tomorrow," or "We're not hiring right now." They lied to his face and hired workers the same day. Workers from Houston, Lake Charles, and even New Orleans were given a golden opportunity to earn a decent salary.

The people those toxic fumes were killing slowly couldn't get employed by those companies and provide health care for their families. When I turned five, Papa decided to move Mama and me to Houston and start his own company. That was almost thirty-one years ago.

"Sweetheart, my ego says 'no.' My head knows better."

"You think you owe me an apology for leveraging my house, selling my car, and pawning my eight engagement rings?"

"You know I did those things to save our company. Tyler Construction would've gone bankrupt if I hadn't taken charge."

I only had one Papa. No amount of money could make me disown him, no matter how ruthless he was at times. That didn't mean I agreed with what he'd done. If it weren't for Roosevelt, our baby and I would be living at home with my parents.

Papa sat on the sofa beside me and patted Zach on the back. My dad shook his head and stared at the floor. "I'm sorry, sweetheart. But—"

"No, 'but.' "

"Let me finish—"

"It's not necessary. I spoke with my attorney. I've got a plan to change Roosevelt's mind."

"But—"

Interrupting him again, I said, "I signed those papers under duress. He was stupid to come to the hospital and force his wife to sign over her company and grant him a divorce. I—and you're really going to like this—requested pain meds every four hours so there would be a record, but I wasn't taking them."

I wasn't sure how far my husband would go, but I knew he'd come while I was in the hospital. "Couple that with all of what Roosevelt had done, and consider Sindy's alienation of affection. You know I can sue her for that. And I'd recently had Roosevelt's baby—"

Papa smiled. "I guess you are smarter."

I kissed my son's stomach. " 'Guess'?"

My dad had a strange look on his face.

"What now?" I asked, praying he hadn't done something again.

"Sweetheart, there's something I've been meaning to tell you about the baby."